RIDER OUTLAW TRAIL

Slowly, the outlaw called Nightshade rode closer. Jim could see the man's eyes, which seemed to blaze with unholy fire. There was no mistaking the threat of the uptilted gun barrel that, in a mere flicker of time, could spurt flame and leaden death.

"You're an intelligent young man," said Nightshade suddenly. "Pass over the pouch, please."

Jim fumbled clumsily with the mail pouch, trying to lift it from the pommel of the saddle. Suddenly a shout ripped from Jim's throat that surprised him as much as Nightshade. Holding tightly to the pouch, he lashed out with it, catching the wrist of the outlaw's gun hand. The Colt cracked and Jim yelled again in a mixture of terror and rage.

For a second, earth and sky seemed to trade places as he tumbled through the air. Then everything straightened out and Jim crashed to the ground. The hooded outlaw now stood over him, the barrel of his gun only inches from the young man's face.

"You're not so smart after all, I see," said Nightshade.

FOR THE BEST OF THE WEST–
DAN PARKINSON

A MAN CALLED WOLF (2794, $3.95)
Somewhere in the scorched southwestern frontier where civilization was just a step away from the dark ages, an army of hired guns was restoring the blood cult of an ancient empire. Only one man could stop them: John Thomas Wolf.

THE WAY TO WYOMING (2411, $3.95)
Matt Hazlewood and Big Jim Tyson had fought side by side wearing the gray ten years before. Now, with a bloody range war closing in fast behind and killers up ahead, they'd join up to ride and fight again in an untamed land where there was just the plains, the dust, and the heat–and the law of the gun!

GUNPOWDER WIND (2456, $3.95)
by Dan Parkinson and David Hicks
War was brewing between the Anglo homesteaders and the town's loco Mexican commander Colonel Piedras. Figuring to keep the settlers occupied with a little Indian trouble, Piedras had Cherokee warrior Utsada gunned down in cold blood. Now it was up to young Cooper Willoughby to find him before the Cherokees hit the warpath!

THE WESTERING (2559, $3.95)
There were laws against settin' a blood bounty on an innocent man, but Frank Kingston did it anyway, and Zack Frost found himself hightailin' it out of Indiana with a price on his head and a pack of bloodthirsty bounty hunters hot on his trail!

HELL-FOR-LEATHER RIDER

JAKE FOSTER

ZEBRA BOOKS
KENSINGTON PUBLISHING CORP.

ZEBRA BOOKS

are published by

Kensington Publishing Corp.
475 Park Avenue South
New York, NY 10016

First printing: July, 1991
Printed in the United States of America

ONE

Flat Rock was howling.

The little settlement was packed, seemingly from one end to the other, with cowboys, miners, bullwhackers, fur trappers, and prospectors, along with the slick-haired and slicker-fingered gentlemen of chance and the garishly painted, strangely sad, soiled doves who preyed on them. The cowboys were dashing figures in bullhide chaps and high-crowned hats; many were quite young, full of bad whiskey and the immortality of youth. The miners in work shoes and slouch hats were a different breed, as were the long-bearded bullwhackers and the buckskin-clad fur trappers with the madness of lonely places lurking behind their eyes. The prospectors were the oldest—gnarled desert rats who had spent their lives chasing dreams which seldom if ever came true.

But all of them had at least a little money to spend, from one source or another, and the gamblers and the bartenders and the saloon girls were all too glad to take it, the transfer of funds often accompanied by great hilarity. This was Flat Rock's night to howl, all right, and nowhere was the tumult any greater than in the Ace High Saloon, with its gaudy false front that was the pride of the town.

Along the boardwalk in front of the Ace High came a shuffling figure, at first little more than a shadow close to the wall. But as the form neared the light that spilled from the windows and the bat-winged entrance of the saloon, it was revealed to be a young man, slender and perhaps a couple of inches below medium height. The youngster was hatless, clad in a shirt that had once been white and a pair of pants worn almost through at the knees and seat. His shoes had seen much hard wear, too, and he walked gingerly. Earlier in the day, he had foolishly decided to walk over to Flat Rock from one of the neighboring towns. He was young and strong, he had thought, and Flat Rock was only ten miles from the settlement where he had been staying.

Ten miles in this country, however, was not like ten miles over smooth sidewalks and gentle roads back East. This was a rugged land, full of sand and rocks and hills and gullies. The holes in the soles of his shoes had caused blisters to rise. Once he had covered more than half the distance, though, it made no sense to turn back. He had plunged ahead, if not fearlessly then stubbornly, and now he had reached Flat Rock . . . with less than a dollar in his pocket, no hat, no horse, no gun, no prospects.

His name was James Patrick McReady, although he had taken to calling himself Jim since he had come West, and at times like this, he almost wished he had stayed in the reform school back East. There was a bench on the sidewalk in front of the saloon, and he sank gratefully onto it to catch his breath and rest his sore feet.

He had been there less than a minute when the glass behind and above him suddenly shattered, showering him with hundreds of tiny slivers and shards, and a great weight crashed against his head and shoulders, sending him spilling onto the rough planks of the sidewalk. The impact rolled him off, and he fell the twelve inches or so from the raised sidewalk into the dust of Flat Rock's only street.

The weight that had knocked him off the bench was now sprawled across his lower body. Jim lifted himself on his elbows and saw that a man wearing buckskins was lying on his legs. Summoning some strength that he had not known still remained in him, he pulled himself out from under the burden of the unconscious man.

"What's the matter, sonny? Get in the way of Rusty

when he came flyin' out that window?"

The questions came from a man who slapped aside the batwings and stepped through the saloon entrance onto the sidewalk. This individual also wore buckskins, and had a scraggly black beard. His battered hat was shoved to the back of his head. He gave Jim a gap-toothed smile and continued, "You got to learn to watch out for trouble in these parts, little fella. Never know where it might be comin' from."

Jim hoisted himself onto his feet and shook his head fiercely in an attempt to dislodge the slivers of glass that dotted his thatch of slightly curly brown hair. Anger flared up inside him, and he snapped, "That bastard could've killed me, falling on me like that."

The eyes of the man he addressed began to narrow. "You got no call to talk like that," said the trapper. "Hell, I didn't know you was sittin' out here when I hit Rusty."

"You're the one who knocked him through the window?"

The buckskin-clad man shrugged. "If a man can't wallop his own partner in a friendly lil' disagreement, who can?"

Jim was starting to realize that the man was probably quite drunk. He stood steadily enough upon the sidewalk without swaying back and forth, but there was a certain slurred thickness to his speech which betrayed his condition. Jim's eyes dropped to the cartridge belt draped around the man's waist. A holster was suspended from it, and Jim could see the walnut butt of a large revolver protruding from the top of the holster. Instantly, his anger dissipated and was replaced by a nervous fear.

He held up his hands, palm out, and said, "Sorry. I didn't mean any offense."

"None taken," said the trapper after a moment. "Just be careful who you go mouthin' off to in the future, sonny. Ain't everybody who's as tolerant as me."

Having said that, he stepped down off the porch and went over to his fallen comrade. Hooking a booted toe under Rusty's shoulder, the man rolled him over. Rusty's arms flopped loosely to either side; he was still unconscious.

Jim backed slowly away, studying the situation. The one called Rusty was considerably larger than his companion.

How could the second man have hit him hard enough not only to send him flying through the saloon window but also to render him senseless? It had been Jim's experience that the biggest man in a fight always won.

The trapper removed his hat, went to a nearby horse trough, and filled the hat with water. He dashed it in Rusty's face. Spluttering and cursing, Rusty came back to consciousness. His partner bent and helped him to his feet, then slapped Rusty's brawny back and said, "Let's go inside and drink some more, old son."

Rusty rumbled his agreement, and the two of them disappeared into the saloon, arm in arm.

Watching them enter the building, Jim sighed and shook his head. As long as he lived, he thought, he would never understand the rough camaraderie of men like these. They could be fighting tooth and nail against each other at one moment, and then, in the twinkling of an eye, be back to back, each protecting the other with his very life. Jim had never had such a friend, and he doubted he ever would again.

The raucous celebration inside the Ace High seemed not to have been disturbed in the slightest by the crash of window glass. It was going on at the same level as when Jim first came walking painfully along the sidewalk. He looked wistfully at the bench where he had been sitting, covered now with shards of glass. He would have to move along and find some other place to rest.

Maybe there would be a livery stable down the street. Most liverymen were willing to trade a night's rest on some straw in a vacant stall for a day's work around their place, Jim had found during his wanderings.

His strength began to ebb as he walked along, until he almost staggered from weariness. The journey to Flat Rock had taken more out of him than he had realized, until now. His brown eyes squinted as he peered through the darkness at the buildings he passed. Finally, he came to a big, barnlike structure with high double doors at its center. One of the doors was open, and the warm yellow glow of a lantern was visible inside. Jim headed for it, drawn to the flame like a moth.

As he stepped into the stable, a man emerged from one of the stalls that lined the long central corridor. He carried a bucket in one hand, and he stopped in his tracks as he saw Jim. "Here, now!" he said sharply. "What do you want, tramp?"

Jim pulled himself up to his full height. "I'm not a tramp," he said, putting more strength into his voice than he actually felt.

"Well, you look like one to me," said the liveryman. "And I've seen more than my share of tramps, let me tell you. Reckon you're lookin' for a place to bunk for the night, eh?"

Jim nodded. "That's right. I . . . I'll work for you all day tomorrow, doing whatever chores you like, if you'll give me a place to sleep tonight."

"Oh, you want your pay first, is that it?" The liveryman shook his white-whiskered head. "Not likely."

"But it's night," said Jim, as he blinked in confusion. "How could I work now?"

The liveryman pointed with his free hand, a callused finger indicating the lantern that hung from a peg on the wall. "Plenty of light for muckin' out stalls. There's a shovel and a rake, leanin' there on the wall behind you, and fresh straw aplenty in the loft up there. I got six stalls vacant, and all of 'em need cleaning. Best get at it, if you're of a mind to sleep here tonight."

A shudder ran through Jim's shoulders as he considered the prospect. The old man's proposal was brutal and unfair, he thought, and for a moment, Jim thought about turning with a sneer and marching out of the place. He could find somewhere else to sleep, he thought.

But there was always the possibility he might not be successful in his search, and despite the heat of the days, the nights in this territory were usually cold. His tired bones would not be able to stand the chill of a night spent out in the open. Not with him as weak as he already was.

He turned and saw the shovel and rake the liveryman had indicated. Hobbling over to them, he picked up the implements and then faced the old-timer again.

"Show me the stalls you want cleaned," he said.

"You can find 'em," said the liveryman, stumping past Jim and heading toward the small office in the front corner of the barn. "They're the ones with no horses in 'em," he added dryly.

For a moment, as the old man presented Jim with his back, the youngster's hands tightened on the handle of the shovel. How simple it would be to lift the tool and whip it around in a deadly blow that would crush the liveryman's skull! Surely there was money in the stable's office, money that could buy Jim a real bed in a hotel room and even some hot food in the morning. It was doubtful that anyone had seen him come in here; there had been no one on the street when he entered, as far as he could remember. Everyone was either in a saloon or at home. He could get away with it if he struck now. . . .

Jim's grip loosened, and he sighed. If the old man had any inkling of the danger he had briefly been in, he did not show it as he proceeded into the office and shut the door behind him.

He had never been a criminal, Jim told himself. Even when everyone else had been convinced that he was no good, a thief who would even steal from a church, he had known differently. A coward, yes, there was no denying that. A fool, even.

But not a thief. And certainly not a murderer.

Leaning on the shovel and the rake almost as if they were crutches, Jim walked along the corridor until he came to an empty stall. The reek of manure assaulted his nostrils. Jim had always liked horses, even back in the city, where the only ones he had seen were pulling delivery wagons. However, the animals did have their disadvantages, and cleaning up after them was one of those disadvantages.

His feet throbbing, his shoulders aching, his arms as heavy as lead, Jim somehow forced his muscles to obey him and got to work.

He raked the soiled straw out of the vacant stalls, making a pile of it in the center aisle. Then, catching it between the shovel and the rake, he picked up as much as he could carry at one time and took it to the back of the barn. A rear door led out to a walkway between two large corrals. Jim stumbled along that lane, his steps guided by the light from the moon and stars, until he came to its end and found a shallow gully. He pitched the straw in the gully and went back for another load.

More than a dozen trips were required before he finally deposited the last of the filthy stuff in the gully. He was unsure if this was how the liveryman had intended for him to dispose of it, but if the old-timer had wanted the job done differently, he should have said so, Jim thought. With this part of the chore finished, he went back into the barn to bring down fresh straw from the loft to replace what he had cleaned out.

By this time his body had gone beyond pain. He had no idea how long he had been working here in the stable, but it seemed like hours at the very least. His feet were numb; the intolerable ache in his shoulders had vanished, as well. His head felt strangely light, as if it would float away from his body were it not attached. He knew from experience that he had surpassed exhaustion. A few times in his life, he had been forced to work this hard. Soon, if he did not stop and rest, he would collapse.

At the moment, that would have been welcome. To be surrounded by black nothingness might be a relief.

He climbed into the loft; the part of his brain that was still functioning properly warned him to be careful. Considering the shape he was in, a fall from high on the narrow ladder might finish him. When he reached the platform, he found a huge pile of straw and a pitchfork. His hands were blistered now, just like his feet, and he winced as he grasped the handle. As fast as he could, he shoved what he thought would be a suitable amount of straw over the edge of the loft, letting it fall into the aisle below. Then he returned to the ladder and descended slowly. His whole body was beginning to quiver from exertion, and it seemed as if he would never reach the ground again.

When he did, he grabbed up the rake and began spreading the straw in the vacant stalls. That enfolding darkness was closer now, drawing ever nearer, and something inside him wanted to finish this job before he passed out. He had left too many things unfinished in his life. Perhaps this was a chance to atone for them in some small way.

Or maybe he was just a damned stubborn bastard, Jim thought with a weak smile. That had always been his problem—too afraid to go ahead, too stubborn to turn back.

Suddenly, when he had not even realized that he was so close to the end of his task, he was done. The job was completed, and he could rest now. First, however, he replaced the shovel and rake against the wall, and walked over to the stable door to peer outside. He would not have been surprised to see the sun rising, but it was not morning yet. Indeed, judging by the few stars he could see, he had been working in the livery for only a little over an hour. It had just seemed much longer.

Jim lifted both hands and wiped them over his face, trying to ease his weariness and hold the stygian depths away from his mind for a few moments more. He turned and stumbled back to the first of the vacant stalls. The old man had not reappeared since going into the office, and Jim did not summon him now to inspect the work. He blew out the lantern and went into the stall, stretching out full length on the clean straw. The scent emanating from it blended with the smells of horses and old leather, combining to create an aroma that Jim knew very well. He'd slept in a great many stables since coming West.

His feet hurt, but he did not take his shoes off. If he did, he knew, his feet would probably swell so during the night that he would not be able to get them on again the next morning. That would be disastrous.

He rolled onto his side, burrowing into the straw for warmth. As his eyes closed, all the aches and pains he had suffered earlier came back double and triple. He had not eaten since the middle of the day, either, and that lack was beginning to make itself felt. Forcing himself to ignore the pain, Jim kept his eyes shut tight and waited for sleep to claim him. As usual, it did not take long. Within minutes his breathing was deep and regular, making a soft, rhythmic sound as it flowed in and out of his body.

Sometime during the night—Jim never knew exactly when—someone covered him with a horse blanket.

TWO

The dreams that came to young Jim McReady on most nights were not the usual formless jumble of images that mark the slumber of most people. Many times they were crystal clear, as if he had actually been transported back across the miles and years to a childhood of grinding poverty in one of the big cities of the East. His parents had tried their best, but there were always too many mouths to feed, not enough money, too much competition for too few jobs. As a young boy, Jim had been possessed of a quick, intelligent mind, but no matter how sharp witted a lad was, it was incredibly difficult to climb out of the great pit of despair that had been formed by the endless infusion of immigrants into the cities. Only the very lucky had a chance to escape from the short, grueling, unhappy life that awaited most of Jim's generation.

And good luck had never been something that followed Jim McReady around like a puppy trailing its master.

As he grew older, after having been forced to leave school and take a succession of jobs in a variety of tenement sweatshops, he began to realize that nothing would ever change as long as he remained in the city. The circumstances of his poverty might differ slightly from time to time, but there was no real escape for him there.

When he was of an age to make it feasible, he struck out on his own, leaving behind an abundance of brothers and sisters and two parents glad for even the slightest lessening of their burden. Jim moved in with a couple of friends, young men in similar situations who craved a change.

What Jim did not know was that they planned to accomplish their ends by thievery.

He discovered that fact soon after, however, when one of them invited him along on one of their expeditions. They were planning to rob a storekeeper who was rumored to keep a great deal of money in his establishment. Not wanting to seem the innocent he actually was, Jim covered up his shock at the suggestion and turned down the invitation, evading the questions of his companions when they wanted to know why he was refusing this opportunity.

If the truth had been told, Jim was tempted for a moment. He himself could not have said if his refusal was prompted by some sort of moral consideration—or by fear. Something could go wrong, he reasoned, and then he would be in real trouble.

He was unaware of it, but he was already on that path.

The robbery was successful, although the loot his friends garnered was considerably less than they had expected. Flushed with success, they became more daring, and still Jim continued to refuse to join them. Finally, one night, Jim entered the tiny, cramped room to find that his friends were not there. A few minutes later, however, he heard rapid footsteps on the tenement stairs.

The door was jerked open, and one of his friends rushed in, carrying a canvas bag. Without a word of explanation, he shoved the bag under one of the narrow bunks and then ran to the room's single smoke-grimed window. As he thrust up the glass, he said hurriedly, "Better make yourself scarce, McReady!" Then he was gone, clattering away on the rickety fire ladder.

Jim sat on his bunk for a moment, baffled and confused by what had just occurred. He swung his feet off the thin mattress, stood up, and crossed to the other boy's bed. Kneeling there, he reached under it for the canvas bag. He felt the weight of whatever was inside it and heard a muffled clinking as he withdrew the bag.

Abruptly, there were more footsteps outside the door. Angry voices shouted questions. His instincts screaming a warning at him, Jim was about to shove the bag back under the bunk when the door was suddenly flung open again. A burly, blue-coated officer stood there, a murderous glare on his red face as he shouted, "Here's one of 'em now! And he's still got the loot with him!"

Jim's denials went unheard as more policemen poured into the room. Two of them took hold of his arms and jerked him to his feet while another picked up the canvas bag and upended it onto the bunk. Several golden candlesticks tumbled out. He looked up at Jim, who was quivering in the grip of the other policemen, and said, "And for that ye killed a priest!"

Jim felt every square inch of his insides turn cold as ice.

Luckily, the priest in question, who had been clouted over the head when he interrupted several young men robbing his church, didn't die. Since there was no proof Jim was the one who had actually struck the blow, the only charge against him when he came to trial was that of robbery. He maintained his innocence, but no one believed him, even when he gave the authorities the names of the boys who had really committed the robbery. The judge refused to accept the possibility that Jim might not be one of the gang of youths that had been terrorizing the neighborhood. He was found guilty in a trial remarkable only for the speed with which it was conducted.

None of the real thieves were ever apprehended. They had vanished somewhere into the maw of the city.

Although Jim was considered an adult in most circles, in the eyes of the law he was still a boy, and so he went to reform school instead of prison. There was little difference. Both were filled with harsh conditions and hardened, embittered inmates; the ones in the reform school were a little younger, that was all. And Jim knew that if he stayed there for the full term of his sentence, he would emerge the same way, little more than an animal, fit only to commit more crimes until once again he was caught and put back behind bars. There seemed to be no way to escape that fate.

One prison, after all, was much like another, whether it was tenement, reform school, or penitentiary.

* * *

Jim was thrashing around in the straw, his mind back there in the old building with the high, thick gray walls, when he suddenly came awake and found the blanket twisted around his legs. He sat up and gave his head a shake, unable for a moment to remember where he was or what he was doing there. But every movement sent pain screaming through his muscles, and that was ample reminder of the work he had done earlier, not to mention the arduous walk to Flat Rock in the first place.

He reached down and touched the blanket, lifted a corner to his face, smelled it. The blanket bore the unmistakable scent of horses, but at least it was warm. Actually, he thought as he reclined again, pulling the blanket tighter around him and settling his shoulders in the mound of straw, this was about as warm as he had been at night in the recent past. He lay there for a moment, listening to the sounds of the night, the shuffle of the horses in adjacent stalls, the rhythm of the animals' breathing. He heard a faint snore coming from somewhere in the barn and reasoned that the source of the sound must be the owner of the place, who perhaps bunked in the office. The stable was in darkness, and Jim had no idea what the hour was. Sometime near morning, he would have guessed. Dawn had to be close.

Had the old man draped the blanket over him? That seemed to be the only logical answer. Jim supposed he must have done a good enough job on the stalls, then; otherwise the crusty old-timer would have been in here kicking him back to his feet and telling him to do it over again. Jim had no doubt of it.

He dozed again, and it seemed as if his eyes had just closed when a foot was indeed prodding at him. Jim blinked and moaned, and then his nose caught a whiff of two things he had not smelled in too long a time—bacon frying and coffee brewing.

"Get up and get to work," said the stable owner, "if you want to earn your keep. No breakfast until the horses are grained and watered."

Jim rolled over and tried to pretend he had not heard the

summons, but the old man was insistent: "I'll get that pitchfork down here after you if you don't rattle your hocks!" he threatened. "You got your night's sleep, tramp. We're square now. You want anything else, you got to work for it, like everybody else."

At that moment, as Jim's eyes finally opened and he stared up at the seamed, whiskery face, he hated as he had never hated before. This old man had no idea of the depth of his weariness.

"This ain't a hotel where you can lay around until noon," continued the stablekeeper. "Now, are you gettin' up, or do I go get that pitchfork?"

"I'm getting up," Jim replied hoarsely. "But someday, somebody's going to teach you a lesson or two, old man."

A snort of contempt issued from the liveryman. "If someone does, it won't be the likes of you, sonny." He turned and strode away as Jim climbed slowly and painfully to his feet.

A gasp of pain took Jim's breath away. His feet hurt even worse this morning. His bladder was uncomfortably full, and the prospect of hobbling all the way to the gully at the back of the property was not an appealing one. Better to get it over with, he decided. Taking one short, pained step after another, he went out the rear door of the barn and started between the corrals.

He was about halfway to the gully when a whickering sound made him look to his left. A horse stood there at the corral fence on that side of the lane, its nose thrust between the top two rails as it watched him. It made the same noise again, and in an annoyed tone, Jim demanded, "What the hell are you laughing at?"

The horse didn't reply, of course. It was an ugly, jugheaded creature, Jim saw, a roan of a rather unappealing shade, with a stocky body and legs that seemed a little too short. Jim glowered at it for a few seconds more, then moved on, wondering why he had wasted valuable time getting angry at a dumb animal.

When he finally got back into the barn, the old man was waiting for him. "Well, I was about to decide you'd done run off, boy . . . though I reckon you couldn't run very far on them feet. You're goin' to have to take them shoes off sooner or later, you know. Sooner the better, else you might wind up havin' to cut 'em off."

"My feet?" asked Jim.

"The shoes. Although the feet might have to go, too, if they're in bad enough shape." The old-timer hesitated, then said, "Tell you what we'll do. I'll help you with the horses, then we'll get some hot grub and coffee inside you. Once that's done, we'll tend to your feet."

Jim could hardly believe that he was hearing an offer of assistance from this whiskered devil. He was not going to turn down any help he could get, however. He said, "Let's get busy."

The old man pointed to a bin that sat against one wall. "Grain's over there. I'll fetch the water. By the way, my name's Deakins."

"I'm called Jim," said the youngster, after a moment's hesitation. There was no real need to conceal his identity, since it was highly unlikely any lawmen from back East would be looking for him out here on the frontier, but caution was a matter of habit with him.

"Glad to meet you, Jim," said Deakins with a chuckle. "Gladder, I'll wager, than you are to meet me."

Jim did not reply as he headed for the grain bin. He was anxious to finish these morning chores, so that he could get some of that bacon and coffee. Then he would find out just how badly hurt his feet actually were.

Limping painfully, he used the bucket he found inside the bin to carry the grain, which he emptied into the troughs in each stall. At the same time, Deakins brought in water from the pump out back. The old man whistled cheerfully through a gap in his teeth as he worked. Jim could have strangled him without the least hesitation.

When they were finished tending to the animals, the old man summoned Jim into the office, which was furnished with a rough-hewn table that served as a desk, a cook stove, a broken-down sofa, and several ladderback chairs. Deakins indicated with a wave of his hand that Jim should take a seat at the table. As Jim sank gratefully onto the chair, Deakins went to the stove to fetch the coffeepot and the frying pan with its strips of crisp, almost blackened bacon. When he had placed those items on the table, he lifted another pan from the interior of the stove, this one loaded with biscuits. Jim could hardly restrain himself as he eyed the food, but he forced himself to wait while Deakins brought out cups and plates and a jar of wild honey. When everything was on the table, the old man nodded and said, "Dig in."

Jim complied with a vengeance.

The coffee was a black, thick, vile brew, and Jim drank three cups of it, shuddering as he swallowed but feeling strength beginning to seep back into him. The bacon was burned, but he ate strip after strip of it. The biscuits, on the other hand, were somewhat undercooked and doughy, but when he dipped them into the honey and stuffed them into his mouth, he had never tasted anything better. Deakins ate rather sparingly; that was a good thing, because it left more for Jim. When the young man was finally finished with the meal, he poured himself another half-cup of the strong coffee and leaned back in his chair to sip it.

"You look mighty satisfied with yourself," grumbled Deakins. "Don't know what you got to be proud of. All you proved is that you can eat as much as three normal men."

"It's been a while since I've sat down to a spread as fancy as this," admitted Jim.

"Well, if you consider this fancy, you must've been livin' pretty poorly, boy. Let's see them feet."

Jim frowned. The satisfaction of having a full belly for a change had made him forget momentarily about his other problems. But Deakins was right, and Jim knew it. He had been a fool to treat his feet so badly, and a bigger fool to ignore them once they were injured. Yet he had had no choice. The old man was the one who had forced him to work for his bed.

Jim propped his right foot on another chair as Deakins moved his own seat around to face him. Deakins frowned darkly as he undid the laces of the worn shoe. Jim grimaced and drew his breath in sharply between his teeth. Even the slight movement caused by unlacing the shoe had been enough to send daggers of pain shooting through his flesh.

"How far'd you walk in these shoes yesterday?" asked Deakins as he looked at the holes in the sole.

"About ten miles," replied Jim. He did not want to tell Deakins exactly where he had come from. The habit of secrecy was still ingrained in him.

"Then you got to expect your feet to hurt," said Deakins. "Well, there's nothin' for it. That shoe's got to come off." He gripped the leather and pulled.

Jim almost screamed and then almost fainted, the pain was so great. A foul smell came to his nostrils, and he gasped, "Is . . . is it . . . gangrene?"

"Nope, the foot ain't mortified on you, not yet. It don't look any too good, though."

Jim peered down at the swollen thing at the end of his leg. Portions of it were an angry red color, while other areas seemed as white as a slug's belly. Even the touch of air against the tender flesh seemed to hurt.

"Get the other foot up here," commanded Deakins. Grimly, Jim complied.

If anything, this one was even worse than the first. The shoe would not come off until Deakins had worked the blade of his jackknife down beside the foot and sliced through the stubborn leather. Jim lowered his hands to the seat of the chair and gripped it firmly, pressing his lips together to keep from crying out. Deakins could not have helped but notice the pain he was in, but the old man offered not one word of sympathy. Finally, when he was done and the second foot was freed, Jim asked, "What will I do for shoes, now that you've cut that one up?"

"You wouldn't have wanted these back anyway," said Deakins with a shake of head. "I've got an old pair of boots around here somewhere that ought to fit you. I'll sell them to you. Good pair of boots beats shoes all to hell and gone, once your feet get used to them."

Jim doubted that his feet would ever return to their normal state, but he kept that pessimistic opinion to himself. Besides, he had an idea that the payment Deakins would demand for the boots would be more work around the stable. Maybe

Deakins intended to keep him here indefinitely, doing small favors for him and then insisting that he pay them back by way of chores. Cheap help, that was what he represented to the old man, Jim thought.

"Best soak them feet," went on Deakins. "I'll get a bucket of hot water and some epsom salts. You sit still."

The liveryman heated water on the stove, then poured it into a bucket and added the salts to it. When Jim lowered his feet into the bucket, he almost shrieked as the hot water touched his tortured flesh. Holding tightly to his chair again, he forced himself to leave his feet in the bucket until some of the pain had eased. To take his mind off the ordeal he was enduring, he asked, "You . . . you live here in the stable, do you?"

"Why not?" responded Deakins. "Got everything I need right here. Stove for my grub, bunk on that old sofa. I ain't one for havin' a lot of things around me. Don't need 'em. I live a simple, uncluttered life, boy, and I aim to keep it that way."

Jim could see the advantages of a life such as the old man described, and yet within him was a desire for more. Even though he had never possessed fine things, he felt a longing for them. Delicate china for his meals, thick carpet underneath his feet, exquisite paintings and tapestries to sooth his eyes, a soft pillow on which to lay his head at night. . . . All this and more, Jim McReady wanted, although he kept those yearnings bottled up deep inside him most of the time, unwilling to admit them even to himself. These dreams were the stuff of fairy tales, and so unlikely ever to come true that to allow them even the slightest existence would only increase his misery. He shook his head now as the thoughts threatened to spill out of his brain.

"How's them feet doin'?"

Deakins' question brought Jim back to reality. He frowned down at his feet, still reposing in the bucket of salts-laced water, and had to admit, "They feel better."

Deakins nodded. "Let 'em soak a good long while. We won't try the boots on you today. You'll have to make do with some thick socks until the swellin' goes down in a day or two."

The old man put his hands on his knees and pushed himself up into a standing position. "Customers'll be here soon. I'll handle 'em for the time bein'. You just take it easy this mornin'."

As Deakins started toward the door of the office, Jim stopped him by asking the question that had begun to plague his mind. It would probably be better to let it remain unanswered, Jim thought, but he had never been one to leave something alone once it began to chafe at him.

"Deakins," he said, "why are you doing this for me? Why are you helping a . . . a tramp?"

The stablekeeper looked back at him for a long moment, squinting so that even more lines joined the network of cracks and seams at the corners of his old eyes. Finally, Deakins said, "Damned if I know, boy. Damned if I know. But it seems like there ought to be a good reason, if I look long and hard enough."

THREE

Jim had no real plans, of course; he had been drifting for so many months that the very concept of sitting down and figuring out what to do next was foreign to him. When he had come West in the first place, the only thing that had concerned him was freedom. He had that now, certainly, but little else.

However, as he sat there in the stable office that morning, soaking his feet and sipping the cold coffee in his cup, he found himself considering his future. He was on his own in a rugged land, a coward, a greenhorn, a man with no real skills. He could ride a horse, but the work of a cowboy was beyond him. He lacked the strength to work in the mines, and his physique was not the sort which could ever adapt itself to such labor. Was he really any better off now, he asked himself, than when he had been back East?

But then he remembered seeing the sun rise over the mountains. He remembered sitting on a rock in the foothills and watching in awe as the purple clouds of a thunderstorm rolled across the desert and then burst in tremendous explosions of lightning against the heights. He remembered sunlit fields of wildflowers waving gently in a breeze.

His existence might be a miserable one most of the time, but it did have its moments, Jim realized. Whatever happened, he could never return to the East, and he reached that decision not only because the law might still be seeking him.

Through the open door of the office, he could hear Deakins dealing with the customers who came to the livery

stable. Some came to rent horses, others to inquire about leasing stall space. It all seemed rather straightforward to Jim. Maybe he would stay here and help Deakins, he thought. Maybe someday he could even have his own stable. There were worse ways to make a living. And Flat Rock, although it was still in a wild, booming phase of growth, might someday turn out to be a pretty nice community, a good place for a young man to make a life for himself.

Maybe the best thing he had ever done, sore feet or not, was to make that painful hike of the previous day.

Later in the morning, Jim dried his feet and slid them carefully into a pair of socks Deakins had brought him. He winced a little as he stood up and walked out into the stable, but after the morning of inactivity, it felt good to be moving around again. His muscles had stiffened some, but they loosened up quickly as he took the rake and began raking the dirt in the center aisle.

Deakins watched him for a few moments, then said, "Look, boy, you got to know somethin'. You don't have to pay me back. Hell, I'd doctor any wild animal that came in hurtin'. You're free to go, any time you want."

"I'm not a wild animal," Jim replied, without looking up from his work.

"Oh, you're not? Could've fooled me. I could tell last night when you thought about usin' that shovel on me."

Jim's face turned hot with shame. Deakins' scornful words cut deep into the center of him. The old man had known perfectly well what was going on—and still he had helped Jim.

"I pay my debts," said Jim, his voice surly, as he continued to rake. "I'll help out around here until I've repaid you for what you've done . . . and for those boots."

"Fine. Just don't go makin' out like I'm some sort of slave driver. Hell, I'd *give* you the boots 'fore I'd let you go around tellin' tales like that."

"I don't plan on telling anybody any tales," ground out Jim. "I just want to do my work."

"Well, then, shut up and do it." Deakins went into the office and shut the door firmly.

The cantankerous old coot! Jim thought. Deakins had realized he was actually attempting to be nice to someone, and that idea had been more than he could stand. After all, he had his reputation as town curmudgeon to uphold. And to think, Jim told himself with a shake of his head, he had actually considered staying around here permanently.

When noontime arrived, they shared beans and cornbread and more coffee, in silence. This was the first day Jim had had two solid meals in more weeks than he liked to remember. Afterward, in a small room at the rear of the barn, he found some harness that needed mending. He took it on himself to do it, not wanting to ask the irascible old man to assign him some chore. When he was finished with that, he walked around from stall to stall, familiarizing himself with the horses. They were all fine animals. Most of them belonged to other people and were only being kept here because their owners had no barns of their own. Deakins kept his own plugs in the corrals in back, bringing them in only when bad weather threatened. As Jim stood in the rear door and looked out at the corrals, he saw the same ugly roan he had noticed that morning. The horse was standing by itself in one corner of the pen, and whenever any of the other horses wandered too close, the roan nipped at them, not in a playful manner but rather as an old cat will whenever a kitten foolishly disrupts its sleep.

"Don't look like much, does he?"

The question came from behind Jim and made him start. Deakins could move quietly when he wanted to. Jim glanced around at him. The old man had not had much to say to him ever since their exchange that morning, but now Deakins was looking past him toward the corral with a bemused expression on his bearded face.

"You mean that roan?" asked Jim. "He looks like a grouchy sort. Other than that, he's not very impressive."

"Maybe not, but he can run all day, when he's of a mind to. Ain't seen many that could beat him over the long haul."

"What's his name?"

"Name?" repeated Deakins. "He ain't got a name. He's a horse. Oh, I know some people give names to their horses and their dogs and such, but it's always seemed like foolishness to me. You wouldn't give a name to a shovel or an ax, would you? Horse is a tool, just like them."

Jim felt a smile tugging at the corners of his mouth. "I don't know," he said slowly. "If I had a horse or a dog, I think I'd give them names."

Deakins snorted. "Reckon *you* would."

"In fact, I think I'll give that horse a name." Casting back through his memory to find a name that would match the roan, Jim suddenly remembered the fur trapper who had come crashing through the window of the Ace High Saloon, knocking him into the street. "Rusty! That fits his color, don't you think? I'll call him Rusty."

Deakins' only reply was another disgusted grunt and a shake of his head as he turned and walked away. Jim thought he should be ashamed of himself. He had only persisted in the conversation to annoy the old man, and he knew it. But as he glanced again at the roan, he realized that the name he had given it was very appropriate. "So long, Rusty," called Jim, just before he turned and went back into the barn.

He would have sworn that the horse lifted its head, just a little.

Jim slept in the same empty stall that night after soaking his feet again, and this time his sleep was deep and dreamless. He was tired, but it was not the sick weariness of the night before. This was a healthier tiredness, even though he did not sense it as such.

The next morning, he found that the swelling in his feet had gone down to a surprising degree. Evidently old Deakins had known what he was talking about when he'd prescribed the treatment. After breakfast, the stable owner rooted around in a bin full of odds and ends for a few moments, then brought out a pair of black boots. The leather was scuffed and wrinkled with age, and Jim frowned as he took them. "These won't last very long," he said. "They're nearly worn out."

"Better'n nothin'. Besides, they might surprise you."

Jim shrugged, pulled on the socks, then prepared to slide

his feet into the boots. His frown deepened as he easily slipped them on and stood up. Within a matter of seconds, the ancient leather seemed to mold itself to the contours of his feet.

"Pretty comfortable," he admitted.

"Thought they might be," said Deakins. "I could tell by lookin' that they was your size."

Jim tucked the legs of his pants into the tops of the boots and then walked around the barn. His feet were still sore, but they felt much better than they had when he'd first arrived in Flat Rock.

"You folks open for business this morning?"

The voice came from the front doors, both of which had been pushed back to let the sunlight into the barn. The stable faced east, so the early morning glare was behind the man who had spoken, rendering him nothing but a featureless black shape in a high-crowned hat as Jim and Deakins turned to face him. The man was leading a horse, and from the way the animal's head drooped forward, it had been running for a long time and was exhausted.

"Yeah, we're open," said Deakins. "What can we do for you, mister?"

The man came further into the barn, tugging the tired horse with him. Jim got a better look at him now. The man's face was all hard planes and angles, the lower half of it covered with several days' worth of dark stubble. His mouth was a thin, taut line, and his eyes were deep-set. He wore the clothes of a range rider, including the kind of six-gun that most cowboys carried. The walnut grips of such weapons were usually not so well polished from use, however, as his.

Still, there was nothing particularly threatening in his stance or his voice as he said mildly, "My horse is about worn out. I'd like to buy another one, and whatever you could give me in trade on this old fella would be appreciated. He's a good horse when he hasn't been ridden into the ground by some damn fool."

Deakins moved forward, his eyes narrowing as he studied the animal. He said, "Uh-huh, I can see that. You must've been in a powerful hurry, mister. Been ridin' all night, have you?"

The man shrugged and said, "That's my business, old-timer. Now, how about selling me another mount?"

The stranger's voice was still mild, but there was something in it that made an icy tingle run along Jim's spine, and the comment had not even been directed toward him. In fact, the man was paying no attention to him at all. Well, that was only to be expected, wasn't it? A man like this, on some sort of important errand, would have no time for a young drifter like Jim McReady.

"Sure, I'll sell you a horse," replied Deakins. "Reckon this black over here in this stall would do you just fine. Got plenty of sand and speed to burn."

A grim smile twitched the corners of the stranger's mouth upward for a brief second. "That's what I need," he declared.

Jim felt a surge of relief. For a moment, he had been afraid Deakins would try to get the man to buy Rusty. Jim could not have said why such a prospect bothered him, but it did.

Deakins and the stranger quickly concluded their deal. The black horse was led out of the stall by Jim, but the stranger himself transferred his own saddle from his old mount to his new one. He paused long enough to pat the tired bay on its flank, then glanced over at Jim and said, "Rub her down and take good care of her, you hear, son?"

Jim's head bobbed up and down. "I sure will, mister." The gentleness he had heard in the stranger's command seemed at odds with his hard appearance, but Jim's time in the West had already taught him that things often seemed that way.

The man swung up into the saddle, urged the black into a trot, and rode out of the stable. Jim and Deakins stayed where they were, but both of them could tell from the sound of the hoofbeats that the stranger was galloping before he reached the edge of town.

"Outlaw," said Deakins.

Jim blinked and looked over at the old man. "What?"

"Said that fella was an outlaw. Can't miss that type. I'd wager that 'fore the day's over, there'll be a lawman ride into Flat Rock lookin' for him. Why else do you think he'd've ridden all night like that and let his horse get so wore out? He didn't have no choice. It was that or a noose, more'n likely."

Going by the stranger's appearance, Jim had thought at first that the man might be some sort of owlhoot, but that impression had faded somewhat after listening to him speak. Jim said, "He didn't talk like an outlaw. He talked like a regular man."

Deakins chuckled, but there was not much humor in the sound. "Just because a man rides on the wrong side of the law don't mean he can't talk like anybody else. A lot of outlaws got more schoolin' than the lawmen who're after 'em. Hell, some of 'em got homes and families, and they go to dances and ice-cream socials when they ain't out robbin' and killin'. You just can't never tell about a man like that." The old man spat into the dust of the aisle. "He was headin' west when he rode out, toward the Prophet Mountains. He'd best shy away from 'em if he knows what's good for him."

"Why's that?" asked Jim. He had never been any farther west in his wanderings than Flat Rock, and he was unfamiliar with the territory Deakins had just mentioned.

"Why?" The old man sounded surprised as he echoed Jim's question. "Because if he goes into them mountains, Nightshade'll get him, that's why. Outlaw or star packer, it don't matter. That's Nightshade's country up there."

And that was the first Jim heard of the man called Nightshade.

Deakins would say no more on the subject. "There's work to do, and we ain't got time to stand around here gossipin' like old women," insisted the liveryman. He and Jim resumed their chores, but the young man could not get the image of the outlaw's face out of his mind.

Little conversation passed between the two of them until the middle of that afternoon, when Deakins suddenly asked, "Well, you made up your mind yet? Are you stayin' around here or not?"

The abruptness of the question made Jim hesitate. How had Deakins known that he was considering staying on at the livery stable? Jim's thoughts had been bouncing back and forth erratically since the day before as he tried to come to a decision. At times, continuing to work with the crochety old stableman seemed to be the last thing he would ever want to do; at other times, that course of action seemed to be the most logical one. Certainly, he could not commit himself to stay forever, but it made sense to stay on for a while. Deakins would have to pay him some sort of wage, and perhaps he could save a little money, maybe even enough for a ticket on the stage line that ran through this territory. Maybe he could go all the way to California—!

He realized that Deakins was staring at him, waiting for an answer. He swallowed and said, "I . . . I haven't decided yet. I've got to stay here long enough to pay you back for these boots—"

"I told you, I don't care about the boots."

"Well, *I* do. I may be a tramp, Mr. Deakins, but I like to think I'm an honest tramp."

The words sounded a bit hollow even to Jim. Deakins listened to the declaration, then snorted and turned away.

Half an hour later, Jim was carrying in a bucket of water from the back when he saw a man ride into the stable. Deakins emerged from the office, looked up at the newcomer, and said, "Howdy. Somethin' I can do for you?"

The sun was coming through the back door now, and its rays struck the chest of the stranger, bouncing back in a bright reflection from the star pinned to his coat. He said, "I'm looking for a young fella who might've come through here. He's on the dodge."

Jim dropped the bucket.

His eyes had fastened on the stranger's badge as soon as he saw it, and the man's words to Deakins stabbed into him. Water splashed over Jim's boots as the bucket overturned and the liquid began to pool around his feet. The stranger turned his head slightly, seeking the source of the noise, and a gaze that missed nothing swept over Jim.

Swept over him, and moved on. A young stablehand held no interest for him.

"On the dodge, eh?" repeated Deakins, looking up at the

lawman. "What makes you think he came here?"

"He was heading in this direction, and his horse should've been played out by the time he got here. This is the only livery stable in town, isn't it?"

"Yep, reckon it is."

"Don't try to lie to me, old man," grated the marshal in a hard voice. "I'll just look through your stalls and see if the horse he was riding is here. He's bound to have let you have it in trade when he bought another mount."

"I ain't tryin' to lie to nobody," said Deakins, his whiskery jaw tightening. "The man you're lookin' for was here, all right, first thing this mornin'. He's got a long lead on you, mister; you ain't likely to catch him."

"Oh, I'll catch him, all right. I'll stay on his trail until I come up to him, however long it takes." The lawman rested his hands on the pommel of his saddle and leaned forward, glaring at Deakins. "Why'd you sell him a horse if you knew he was an outlaw?"

"Well, what was I supposed to do? Let him steal one? I don't ask a man's business, long as he deals honest with me. I ain't just about to try to do your job for you, Marshal."

"Proddy old goat, aren't you?" The lawman grinned down at Deakins, but it was an ugly expression. "Which way did he go when he lit out? And I'll say it again: Don't lie to me."

"Fella headed west, toward the Prophets." Deakins gave a short bark of laughter. "You go right ahead and chase him into those mountains, mister. Won't neither one of you come out alive."

"We'll see about that." The marshal wheeled his horse and rode out of the stable, leaving an unpleasant tension in the air behind him, even when he was gone.

Finally, Deakins dragged a deep breath into his body and turned to look at Jim, who was still standing there in the puddle of water which was rapidly soaking into the dirt floor. Deakins came over to him, moving slowly and deliberately, and stopped in front of Jim, regarding him with narrowed eyes.

"For a second there," said Deakins, "when that badge-toter rode in, *you thought he'd come for you,* boy. Reckon it's time you did some explainin'."

"Yes," said Jim, barely recognizing his own voice. "I suppose it is."

The story tumbled rapidly from his lips, once he was seated at the table in the office, across from Deakins. The old man listened intently as Jim told him about the robberies committed by the young men with whom he had lived. Not a flicker of expression crossed Deakins' leathery features when Jim's story reached the robbery of the church and the assault on the priest. Jim watched the liveryman closely while he swore that he was innocent of any wrongdoing, but he could not tell if Deakins believed him or not.

"They called the place they sent me a reform school," said Jim. "It might as well have been a prison. The only learning that went on was from the other boys who were there, and all they taught was how to be a better criminal. I wasn't interested in that."

Still Deakins' face remained a mask. Jim took a deep breath and went on, "A few of the others decided to leave. They planned to jump one of the guards and knock him out. I . . . I was asked to join the scheme, but I refused. Don't get the wrong idea; I wanted out of there. But I didn't think this was the way."

"You were afraid," said Deakins, speaking up for the first time since Jim had begun his story.

The young man dropped his head. "I was afraid," he admitted. "I knew that if we got caught, it would mean longer terms for all of us, perhaps even a transfer to a real prison. I didn't think I could stand that." He grimaced and shook his head. "But as it turned out, I didn't have any choice. The escape attempt came when several of us were in the yard of the school. The guards carried clubs but not guns; after all, we were only children, not hardened criminals. But that didn't stop them from swarming over the poor man, taking his club away from him, and breaking open his head with it. Still, some other guards heard the commotion and came to see what was wrong. They laid into all of us with their clubs, the ones who had not been involved with the escape attempt at all as well as the ones who had. I tried to get back into the building, but one of the guards grabbed my arm and wouldn't let me go. He hit me across the back with his club three or four times and I couldn't stand it. I tackled him. That's when I felt the gun under his coat, tucked into the waistband of his pants. He had forgotten to take it out and leave it in the building before he ran out. I wasn't even thinking. I just got my hand under his coat and took the gun."

Jim paused in his recitation and lifted a hand to his face; the fingers trembled slightly from the strain of the memories that were coursing through his mind. "I never fired it," he insisted. "I just waved it around, and everyone must have thought from the look on my face that I'd lost my mind. The guards all got out of the way, and the other boys ran for the gate. They had the key, taken off the body of the guard they had killed. I . . . I went with them. I knew that if I stayed, no one would believe that I had wanted no part in what had happened. I tossed the gun away as soon as I was out of the reform school, and then I started running. I ran and ran . . . and then there was a trainyard.

"I've learned since then how hard it is to slip past the yard bulls, but I must've had blind luck on my side that day, because I got into a freight car and rode it out of the city. How long I stayed on that train, I don't know. Finally the bulls found me and threw me off, but I caught another ride a couple of days later. I stayed with it until the railroads ran out. Since then, I've been hitching rides with freighters or immigrants, working at odds jobs here and there, walking when I had to—like the other day when I came to Flat Rock. All I cared about was that I kept going west."

Jim's voice trailed off, and his eyes were still downcast. He was afraid to look up at Deakins. Now that the old man knew what sort he was, he would surely want nothing more to do with Jim. Deakins would probably regret the assistance he had already given him, would perhaps even demand that Jim return the boots and then leave the stable for good.

For a long moment, not a sound was uttered by the liveryman. Then, abruptly, he blew out his breath between his lips with a sound of disgust. "Let me see if I got this straight," he said. "You didn't do nothin'. You got stuck for this robbery when you didn't have anything to do with it. You escaped from reform school even though you didn't want to. The world's got you treed, and you don't have no choice but to go along with whatever happens to you." Deakins' tone was filled with scorn.

"If you want me out of here, I'll go," said Jim. "I can understand why you don't want a criminal—"

"Criminal?" uttered Deakins in astonishment. "You ain't a criminal, boy. Even that takes some backbone. You ain't much of nothin'."

The weight of the old man's contempt was heavy. Jim wanted to be angry; who was Deakins, after all, to be passing judgment on him? But he could not manage it. Every statement Deakins had uttered was correct, and Jim could come up with no argument to refute his accusations.

Without a word, Jim pushed himself to his feet and turned toward the doorway. Ever since he had come here, his emotions had been leaping wildly back and forth. One moment, he wanted to stay, to work and earn the old man's trust, perhaps even his friendship; the next, he wanted nothing more than to put this stable and the entire town of Flat Rock behind him, most especially Deakins' sour, bearded visage. For his own peace of mind, he had to do *something*, and leaving seemed to be the most logical choice.

The sound of hammering made him pause before he reached the door of the office.

Deakins lifted himself from his chair. "What the devil?" muttered the old man. "Who's that out there bangin' on my walls?"

He stepped past Jim and strode out of the office. Jim hesitated only an instant, then followed, curiosity getting the better of him. Deakins walked rapidly to the open double doors and stepped into the fading sunlight.

"Here now! What're you tackin' up, mister?"

"Hello!" came a bluff, hearty voice. "Sorry I didn't ask permission first, but I didn't think you'd mind, sir. Especially in view of the fact that I have a business proposition to make you."

Jim walked out through the doors and saw that a buggy drawn by a fine-looking chestnut horse had pulled up in front of the livery. A man in a dusty eastern suit and a hat that looked like a cut-off stovepipe was using a small hammer to finish tacking a poster to the front wall of the stable. He had side whiskers, sweeping moustaches, and a cheery smile that he turned toward Deakins and Jim.

"You see," went on the stranger, "I represent the firm of Russell, Majors, and Waddell, founders of the greatest venture in the field of transcontinental communication that this country has ever seen!" He waved a pudgy hand toward the poster. "Gentlemen, I give you the Pony Express!"

FOUR

Jim turned to study the poster indicated by the well-dressed stranger, and as he saw the picture adorning the upper half of the advertisement and the words beneath, their impact burst upon him with stunning force. It was as if Fate itself had driven into Flat Rock in that buggy, searching for him and him alone.

The poster was beautiful. Even though the sunlight was fading, its colors were bright and garish. It depicted a slight young fellow, not unlike himself, sitting atop an astonishingly fast steed. The horse's neck was stretched out, mane flying, and all four hooves were off the ground. Looking at the picture, Jim could almost feel the wind of the rider's passage whipping against his face and blowing his hair.

Beneath the compelling picture, words in garish red print read:

> WANTED, YOUNG SKINNY WIRY FELLOWS, NOT OVER EIGHTEEN, MUST BE EXPERT RIDERS WILLING TO RISK DEATH DAILY. ORPHANS PREFERRED. WAGES $25 PER WEEK. APPLY CENTRAL OVERLANDS EXPRESS.

Slowly, Jim became aware that Deakins was speaking. " 'Central Overlands Express'," read the old man. "What the deuce is that? Never heard of it."

"I'll be setting up an office of the express company here in Flat Rock," said the stranger. "We'll be buying horses as well as hiring riders, arranging for relay stations, and the like. It's my responsibility to set up the route between Elk Horn and Moss City, on the other side of the mountains." He extended his hand. "Leland Grayson is my name, sir. And you are . . . ?"

"Deakins," grunted the old man. He hesitated, then took Grayson's hand and shook it briefly. "I've heard a little about this here Pony Express. Didn't know you planned on runnin' it through Flat Rock."

"Oh, yes, indeed. Your fair city is right on our main route."

"And you're headin' on through the Prophets?" Deakins squinted in disbelief.

"Absolutely. The mountains are rugged, I'll grant you, but our maps tell us there are sufficient passes for the riders to get through. This range won't be nearly as difficult as the Sierras, say."

Deakins still appeared to be dubious, and Jim knew what was on the old man's mind: Nightshade. Whoever—or whatever—that was.

Jim forced his mind off that mysterious personage and returned his attention to the poster. He certainly fit the description of the type of lad sought by this Pony Express, except for a couple of things. He was skinny and wiry enough, and the proper age. Actually, now that he thought about it, he might as well be an orphan. He had not seen his parents for over a year, and he doubted he would ever see them again. Given the harsh conditions under which they lived, it was even possible he might *be* an orphan by now. The only sticking point was the requirement concerning riding ability.

No one would ever call him an expert rider, not by any stretch of the imagination. He could stay in a saddle . . . as long as the mount was not too frisky and he was not required to ride at too fast a pace.

From the looks of the illustration on the poster, speed was of the essence in the Pony Express. If he tried to ride as fast as the young horseman in the picture, he would no doubt go flying off his mount and smash his brains out against the ground.

Still, he was curious, and he surprised himself by asking, "Mr. Grayson, sir? What exactly *is* the Pony Express?"

The Easterner glanced at him in surprise. "Where have you been, my boy?" inquired Grayson. "The Pony Express has been on the front page of practically every newspaper in the land!"

"Well, I . . . I don't see many newspapers," mumbled Jim. He told the truth. Only rarely did he encounter a sheet of newsprint, and when he did, he generally used it as cover to keep out the night chill, rather than as reading matter.

Despite Jim's ignorance, Grayson seemed happy to answer his question. "The Pony Express is primarily a mail delivery service, son. When it gets under way, a person will be able to mail a letter in Saint Joe and have it arrive in San Francisco a mere ten days later! Can you imagine? And you're probably wondering how we will achieve this remarkable feat, aren't you?" Grayson was warming to his subject now, and without waiting for Jim to reply, he went on, "We're going to use relay riders, each man carrying the mail pouch a specified distance, then handing it over to the next man along the route. That way our horses and riders will always be fresh and at top efficiency. It's a remarkable idea, don't you think?"

For a moment, Jim pondered what the man had said, then pointed to the poster. "That's a Pony Express rider, then?"

"That's right."

"And you've come to hire them for this stretch of the route?"

"Right again, lad." A grin spread over Grayson's face. "Giving it some thought, are you?"

"No, sir," said Jim with a shake of his head. And the next words out of his mouth were as much a surprise to him as they were to Deakins, who glanced at him in astonishment and disbelief as he went on, "I don't have to think about it . . . sign me up."

Grayson's smile widened. "That's what I like to hear !" he exclaimed. "Enthusiasm! That's what will make the Pony Express a success, my boy, just you wait and see. Ah, however, I cannot just sign you up, as you put it. We want only the best riders, so the job is open to all. I intend to spread the word around this vicinity, and then, a week from now, I shall select six young men from all of those who make application. The six best suited for the job, needless to say."

"Oh." Jim did not try to hide his disappointment. If he was put in competition with the other lads from these parts, there was little doubt who would win the coveted spots as Pony Express riders. Most of the boys around here could ride before they could walk, or so Jim had heard. They'd spent their childhood in the saddle, riding the range and working cattle. Grayson's problem would not be finding six youths who fit the bill; his difficulty would lie in narrowing the field down to that few.

Not knowing that he was speaking to an Eastern boy who had spent only a matter of hours on horseback in his lifetime, Grayson said, "Just come on down to the office one week from today, son. You'll be welcome to try out with all the other boys who are interested in the job."

"You claimed you had a business proposition for me," said Deakins. "Seein' as how I'm a mite old to be one of your riders, I reckon you're lookin' to buy some livestock off me."

"That is correct, Mr. Deakins," responded Grayson. "I'm visiting all the livery stables and ranchers in the area, seeking to buy only the best horseflesh available. No nags for the Pony Express, no, sir! We need our mounts to be fast, with plenty of stamina."

"Expectin' trouble, are you?"

Grayson shrugged. "There are savages to consider, as well as highwaymen. Even though our riders will be carrying only mail pouches, some desperadoes might get the idea it would be worth their while to hold up our riders and steal whatever they can."

"Ever hear of Nightshade?" grunted Deakins.

"The outlaw?" Grayson laughed and did not seem troubled by the mention of the name. "The mythical outlaw, I should say. The closer I get to the mountains, the more I hear about this Nightshade fellow. Well, I'm here to tell you, Mr. Deakins, I haven't seen the slightest shred of proof that he exists! Everyone who speaks of him tells of the time that Nightshade robbed a friend of his wife's second cousin, or some such. Balderdash, sir! I have yet to meet anyone who has encountered this legendary badman face to face."

Deakins took a deep breath. "You're lookin' at one now," said the old man in grim tones.

"You've seen Nightshade?" Grayson's skepticism was evident in his voice.

Deakins flushed with anger. "I've seen him," he insisted. "I've sat and looked at Nightshade, and him not any farther away from me than you are right now, mister."

"Oh? And what did he look like?"

"Well . . . I couldn't rightly say. He had a mask on, you know; more of a hood, really, so that you couldn't see nothin' except his eyes, burnin' into you and darin' you to do something different than what he told you to do. He was dressed all in black, from his hat to his boots, and he rode a horse as black as midnight. Couldn't hardly tell where the man ended and the horse started. A devil horse it was, too, snortin' and pawin' until I figgered to see steam risin' from its nose. I tell you, mister, I got home that day with my life, but to this moment, I ain't sure I understand *how*." Deakins shook his head. "Nightshade'd just as soon shoot a man as look at him. You take what happened over at Silsbee Junction—"

"I'm afraid I don't have the time," interrupted Grayson. "That's quite an interesting yarn you spin, though, Mr. Deakins. Very colorful. I daresay you could write it up and sell it to a company that publishes penny dreadfuls. But now I really must be on about my business."

"Don't believe me, do you?" challenged Deakins.

"Well, sir, I'd hate to say that, but—"

"See if you get any horses from me!" the old man suddenly blazed. "I ain't doin' business with anybody who calls me a liar!"

And with that, Deakins turned and stomped back into the barn, brushing past Jim without seeming to even notice the youngster.

Jim stayed where he was beside the door for a moment longer. Grayson was blinking and squirming a little like a fish that has just been yanked out of a stream to its great and enduring surprise. After a few seconds, he looked over at

Jim and said, "I didn't mean to insult him. I really didn't. Please, son, talk to your grandfather and convey my apologies."

"He's not my grandfather," said Jim. "I'm not sure I even work for him anymore. But I'll talk to him, Mr. Grayson. I can't promise anything, though."

"I understand." Grayson pulled a cloth from his pocket and wiped it over his face. "Some of these old-timers are quite touchy, you know."

Jim had to smile slightly as he remembered some of the outbursts that Deakins had directed toward him. "I know," he said. "Believe me, I know."

"I'm sure you do. Just tell him I'm sorry and that I really would like to do business with him, if I might."

"Sure," nodded Jim. "I guess I'd better get back inside." He gestured at the poster. "I'd leave that up, if I was you, since Deakins probably forgot to tell you to take it down. I can't swear that he won't come out here later and rip it down, though."

"I got hundreds of them," Grayson said with a shrug. "See you around town, son."

"Yeah," said Jim slowly. "See you around."

He stood and watched as Grayson climbed back into the buggy and then sent it rolling down the street. Lights were beginning to be lit in the buildings as twilight settled over the town, and Jim could tell that Grayson pulled up again in front of the Moser Hotel. The Easterner stepped down and went into the hostelry.

Jim turned, sidling back into the stable. He had not forgotten the argument he and Deakins had been engaged in when the arrival of Grayson with his tack hammer had momentarily distracted them.

The old man was bustling around the office, heating water on the stove and taking the ingredients for a stew from a bin. Jim watched him for a moment, then said, "I reckon you want me to leave now. Should I give the boots back to you, or keep them?"

"Never said I wanted you to leave," muttered Deakins without looking up from his work. "Did I?"

"Well . . . no. But you said I was worthless, that I didn't have a backbone."

"You ain't demonstrated no ways that you do," snorted the liveryman. He hesitated, then went on, still without looking at Jim, "But I kinda liked the way you spoke up to that dude. You really want to be a Pony Express rider?"

The question took Jim by surprise. He stammered and hawed for several seconds, then said, "I suppose I do."

"How are you at ridin'?"

"Not very good," answered Jim, honestly but somewhat dispiritedly.

"That Grayson fella was right about it bein' dangerous work, even if he ain't got the sense to listen to somebody who knows about Nightshade." For the first time since Jim had come back into the stable, Deakins looked up and fastened his eyes on the youngster's face. The old man screwed up his features as if calculating a difficult sum in his head, then declared, "I reckon you might last a day, maybe two, 'fore you was buzzard bait, boy."

Jim felt a quick surge of anger. "You think I couldn't do it."

"I *know* you couldn't do it. You're green, green as grass."

"What if someone taught me how to ride? Properly, I mean. What if somebody taught me how to ride so that I could avoid the Indians and the outlaws?" Suddenly, this matter was important to Jim. Somehow, it had become more than a momentary whim, a yielding to a foolish impulse. He wanted Deakins to answer his questions honestly. "Could I do it then?"

The old man shrugged. "Maybe. Who the hell knows? You'd have to do more thinkin' for yourself than you ever did back East, at least accordin' to that yarn you told me 'bout how you wound up in and out of reform school."

"I can think for myself," insisted Jim. "It's taken me months to come this far West, and I've taken care of myself all that time. I've survived; that's more than some can say."

"Maybe you got a point," allowed Deakins.

Jim went on hurriedly, "I know I didn't look like much when I came here . . . I still don't look like much, I guess . . . but I want to give this a try." He took a deep breath and plunged ahead before his nerve deserted him. "Will you teach me to ride? Will you teach me what I need to know?"

"Teach you?" echoed Deakins. "Me? What makes you think—"

Jim broke in on his protests. "You've lived out here all your life, haven't you?" The old man nodded his grizzled head. "And you've fought renegades and outlaws. You know this territory better than most men." Jim was guessing about these things, but he sensed he was right. He saved what he thought might be the most compelling reason for last. "And you've met Nightshade. If I'm going to ride through the Prophets unscathed, I'll need to know everything I can about the man. You're the only one who can teach me, Mr. Deakins."

The stablekeeper drew a deep breath and then blew it out sharply, making his drooping moustache quiver. "I reckon you're right," he said. "Durned if you ain't talked me into it, boy! I'm warnin' you, though—we ain't got much time. A week ain't hardly long enough to turn a tenderfoot like you into a Pony Express rider. But we'll give 'er a try, long as you don't go to pulin' and complainin'. You do that, and I'll kick your sorry tail right out o' here, and I won't be sorry to see you go!"

"Yes, sir!" said Jim, smiling unaccountably. For the life of him, he had no idea why he was so happy. He had just entered into a venture that was likely to fail, and even if it succeeded, he would be living a life of hardship and danger unlike any he had known before. Had he lost his mind?

Perhaps, he thought. But perhaps there were times when a man could find courage only in lunacy. . . .

FIVE

They began early the next morning.

Deakins rousted Jim from his comfortable bed of straw when the sky had barely gone gray on the eastern horizon, foretelling the coming of the sun. Jim started to let out a groan as he hoisted himself to his feet, but then he remembered Deakins' threat to call off this endeavor if he complained about the hard work. Swallowing the protest, Jim followed the old man out the rear door of the barn and into the walkway between the corrals.

"Pick you a horse," commanded Deakins.

"It's dark," said Jim. "Besides, I don't know anything about horses."

"Time you learned, ain't it, then? Here." Deakins pressed a hackamore into Jim's hands. "Get in there and get you a mount, boy. Either that, or go back to bed and forget about bein' a Pony rider."

Jim's features hardened into a sullen frown, but he took the rope bridle from Deakins and went to the gate of the corral on his left. What took him to that enclosure, rather than the one opposite, he could not have said. Not that it mattered, either, he thought. He would probably get stomped to death no matter which corral he chose.

The horses began moving nervously, blowing their breath out through flaring nostrils, as he unlatched the gate and stepped into the corral. They were not accustomed to seeing him here in their province. Jim dragged a deep draft of air into his lungs as he let the latch fall shut and then took a step toward the animals. In the gray predawn light, they appeared to be even larger and bulkier than they actually were.

Jim had heard Deakins making soft clucking sounds when he approached the animals to saddle them, so now the young man followed suit. He clucked his tongue, said, "Easy, there, easy," and moved slowly and deliberately toward the horses as they crowded back into the far side of the corral . . . all except one, that is. That one suddenly took several steps toward Jim, making the youngster freeze in his tracks. It was still too dark to make out the color of the horse's hide, but from the way it was shaped, Jim decided it had to be Rusty, the ugly roan. A whicker of challenge issued from the horse's mouth.

"Don't trust me, eh?" said Jim softly. "You were quick enough to make fun of me when I was on the other side of the fence."

Anger growing inside him, Jim advanced toward the roan. He expected the horse to step back away from him, but Rusty stood fast, as if daring him to attempt getting that hackamore on his head. Jim did not take his gaze off the horse; he sensed that to do so would be to invite disaster. But he could sense the eyes of old Deakins on him, watching intently to see how he answered the challenge.

One step followed another, each bringing Jim that much closer to the roan. Now it finally gave ground, reluctantly. Still Jim came on, until finally he was within arms' reach of the animal. The light had grown bright enough so that he could see the wildness in the horse's eyes. The young man spoke soothingly, hoping to penetrate the roan's brain and convince it that he meant no harm. With a shake of its head, as if it had indeed read his thoughts, the horse moved off another couple of steps.

Jim fought down the urge to run after it. That would ruin everything. The other horses would scatter, and he might well be trampled in the ensuing stampede. He was not a patient young man; it was difficult for him to restrain himself. At the same time, fear had grown alongside his frustration. He had no business being in this corral, a part of his mind was shouting at him. He had to turn and run, it insisted, before the danger got any worse.

With an effort of will that left him trembling slightly, Jim overcame that impulse as well, and continued advancing toward the roan. It appeared a bit puzzled now. Surely it had expected this puny young man to go away and leave it alone. That was not happening, however.

Another step brought Jim close enough to reach up and slip the hackamore over the roan's head. He performed the action quickly but somewhat awkwardly, and the roan jerked its head up, almost tearing the reins out of Jim's hands. Jim hung on, tightening his grip, not jerking but instead letting the constant pressure cause the horse to lower its head again. Jim's pulse was hammering in his ears, just from being this close to the horse. If it lashed out at him, those steel-shod hooves could crush his skull like an eggshell.

He forced those thoughts out of his mind and tried to remember how he had seen Deakins complete the act of putting a hackamore on a horse. The nosepiece still had to go on. Jim tried to slip it in place, but the roan suddenly shook its head. Again Jim almost lost his grip on the rope. Breathing fast and shallow now, he stepped even closer to the roan and let go of the hackamore with one hand long enough to catch hold of the roan's upper lip. He had seen Deakins do the same thing. He twisted on the lip, the horse's head became still, and he was able to slide the nosepiece up over the roan's jaw and into the proper position. He stepped back quickly, taking up the slack in the reins.

The roan tossed his head again, but now the action only caused the rope harness to pinch against his nose and head. When Jim said, "Come along," and started toward the gate, the roan had no choice but to follow.

"Not bad," admitted Deakins, a bit grudgingly. "You learn how to do that just from watchin' me a couple of times?"

"I have a pretty good memory," said Jim. Taking pains to conceal how nervous he still felt, he opened the corral gate and led the roan into the walkway.

"You picked a good horse. Though I reckon he picked you as much as you picked him. Wondered what you'd do when he stood there and dared you to put a halter on him."

"What now?" asked Jim.

"Snub the reins 'round that post yonder and get a saddle on 'im."

Jim tied the roan to one of the corral posts and went to fetch a saddle from the livery stable. Deakins had several on hand which were used by customers who wished to rent a mount but who did not have a saddle of their own. He returned a few minutes later, staggering slightly under the weight of the heavy saddle.

"Where's the blanket?" snapped Deakins. "I ain't goin' to have you rubbin' galls on the back of my horses."

"Sorry," muttered Jim. "I'll go back and get a blanket." He lowered the saddle to the ground.

"Don't put that down there like that! You'll ruin the skirt layin' it on the ground. Put it up on that top rail of the fence."

Jim looked at him for a moment with narrowed eyes, but he could tell the old man was completely serious. Taking a deep breath again, he lifted the saddle over his head and placed it carefully on the corral fence, balancing it so that it would not fall. Then he trudged back into the barn for a blanket to cover the roan's back.

Somehow he got the blanket and saddle onto the horse and fastened the cinches to the old man's satisfaction. This entire effort had been time consuming, and the sun was now threatening to slip up over the horizon at any moment. As he stepped back and regarded the saddled roan, Jim wished he had a good hot cup of coffee, maybe some flapjacks and bacon to go with it. A man ought to still be asleep at this ungodly hour, he thought, but if by some chance he had to be up and about, the least he could expect was a good breakfast.

"Why don't we stop for a bit and eat?" he inquired. "The horse is saddled now; it can wait for a while."

Deakins shook his head. "Nope. Take my word for it, son, you don't want what's comin' next on a full stomach." He pointed to the roan. "Well, don't just stand there. Mount up."

Under the stern gaze of the old man, there was nothing Jim could do except obey. He stepped up to the horse, caught hold of the saddlehorn, lifted his foot, and slipped it into the stirrup. He swung up, settling his weight in the saddle and finding the other stirrup. A quiver went through the body of the creature beneath him, communicating itself to him. Jim looked down at Deakins and asked, "This isn't a wild horse, is it?" He had visions of himself being bucked off, of sailing through the air and crashing to the hard-packed earth.

"He's saddle-broke," said Deakins. "That don't mean he likes it, though. Any horse can decide to be cantankerous, son. You'd best remember that."

Jim nodded. "All right. I suppose I'm ready."

Deakins untied the reins and handed them up to the youngster. "Ride up and down this lane a couple of times, so I can see how you sit in the saddle."

Jim pulled the roan's head around and used the heels of his boots to prod the animal into motion. It launched into a bone-jarring walk that had him bouncing in the saddle even more than he would have had the horse been galloping. Gritting his teeth, Jim directed the roan toward the gully at the rear of the property, then, once that goal had been reached, he swung the horse around and started back toward the barn. Deakins watched, his weathered forehead creased in a frown.

"Dammit, you look like a kid's toy, bobbin' up and down that way," complained the old man when Jim rode up. "A few miles of that, and your backbone'll be so wore down your head'll be sittin' on your hind end. You got to work *with* the horse, boy, not against it."

"Tell that to the horse," grated Jim. "I'm trying."

"Try harder. Keep ridin'. I ain't done watchin' yet."

Jim turned the horse around and started toward the gully again, this time gouging the roan's flanks harder with his heels. The anger which he had built up for Deakins flowed out of him, and he kicked the horse again, urging it to greater speed.

Instead the earth seemed to rise up underneath him, sending him into a dizzingly rapid ascent. Jim gave a yell of sheer panic as he realized the saddle was no longer beneath him. At this moment, as his arms and legs pinwheeled freely in the air, even the ever-shifting "hurricane deck" of the saddle would have seemed very stable and secure.

Then, almost before he knew what was happening, he was descending from the heights with no way to stop himself. He landed heavily; the impact forced the air from his lungs. Gasping desperately for breath and getting a mouthful of dust instead, Jim rolled over a couple of times before he finally came to a halt.

Blinking his eyes against the grit that painfully filled them, he looked up, and the first thing he beheld was the face of the roan. The horse loomed over him, and as Jim gave a hoarse cry, it leaned close to him and prodded him with its long nose. Jim forced his muscles to work and scrambled away on hands and knees.

"Told you any horse can get cantankerous," said Deakins with a chuckle. "Especially when some damn fool human starts kickin' it for no reason except he's mad at some other damn fool human. Way a horse sees things, what goes on 'tween us ain't none of its business, and it don't take kindly to bein' mixed up in the argument. Treat him decent, though, and he'll usually do what you ask."

"People can be the same way," muttered Jim as he got slowly to his feet. He brushed some of the dust off his clothes, wincing as he touched the spot on his hip where he had landed. He would have a bruise there tomorrow, and it would be sore.

Deakins was shaking his head. "Nope, there's a big difference 'tween people and horses," said the liveryman. "A horse'll meet you more'n halfway. And once there's some trust between a man and a horse, the horse'll never betray that trust. The man might, but not the horse."

"It sounds like you have a higher opinion of horses than you do of people," accused Jim.

"You said it, boy, not me. Now, you gettin' back on or not? I got to tell you, from what I've seen so far, you ain't got the makin's of a rider good enough for the Pony Express."

"We'll see about that," said Jim, his voice grim and tight. He started toward the roan, ready to mount up again. Damned if he was going to let a dumb animal make a fool of him, he thought.

The roan shied away when Jim reached for the reins and

the saddlehorn. The noise that sounded annoyingly like laughter issued from him. Jim ignored it, ignored as well the aches and pains of his body and the cramps of hunger in his belly. There were more important things, he thought, and eating and resting could wait.

It never even occurred to him that in times past, he would not have considered postponing a meal unless he had to—usually because he didn't have any food. Nor would he have stuck with something unpleasant simply because he wanted to finish it. Those thoughts did not enter his head now; his attention was centered instead on the roan.

He caught the reins first, then the saddlehorn. Pitching his voice low enough so that Deakins could not hear him, he said, "I'm sorry I kicked you, Rusty. We'll get along all right now, won't we?" What possessed him to speak to the animal as if it could understand his every word, he could not have said.

The roan stood still as Jim lifted himself onto its back. When the expected bucking did not come, Jim let out the breath he had been holding. He clucked at the horse and flapped the reins gently. His heels barely prodded its flanks.

Turning its head, the horse looked back at him, as if to say that he would have to do more than that to get any response. For the first time, Jim began to realize what a delicate balance there was in this relationship between man and beast. Like Deakins had said, it was a matter of trust.

He heeled the roan into motion again. The horse fell into the same jarring gait, but this time Jim let himself relax a little, rather than holding his back as stiff as iron. He still bounced in the saddle, but not as much.

By the time they reached the gully and turned around, Jim was ready for more speed. He leaned forward, dug in his heels, and said, "Let's go, big fella!"

The roan stopped in its tracks.

Jim kept going, sliding out of the saddle and falling forward over the horse's right shoulder. He yelled again and flung out his hands to break his fall. The impact was not as breathtaking this time, but he still wound up lying on his back in the dirt, staring up at the rosy early morning sky.

A whiskered face intruded into his line of vision. Deakins just shook his head for a long moment, then spat and walked away.

SIX

Six days had passed. Tomorrow, at the Pony Express office opened by Leland Grayson in a vacant building on Flat Rock's main street, boys and young men from all over the territory would flock to apply for the half-dozen riding jobs that were available. Grayson had put up the gaudy posters all over town, and the word had spread from the saloons and stores to the farms and ranches in the area surrounding the town, from the plains in the east to the mountains in the west. Indeed, Flat Rock and the entire vicinity was buzzing with talk about this bold new enterprise.

Six days such as Jim McReady had never known before had left him sore and bruised. When he got up in the mornings, his muscles stiff, he hobbled about like an old man. Once in the saddle, though, he rode well enough now to draw grudging praise from his mentor, old Deakins. The liveryman still insisted that Jim lacked the natural grace of a born rider, but the young man was working hard to overcome that deficiency. He could put the roan into a hard gallop, turn it sharply, and resume speed in a matter of seconds. Several times Jim and Deakins had ridden out onto the plains and the old-timer had watched critically as Jim raced the horse over the prairie, veering it smoothly around obstacles. No longer did Jim bounce crazily in the saddle so that, as Deakins put it, "A man could fire off a charge of buckshot 'tween your butt and that saddle, boy, and you'd never feel the sting!"

So caught up had they been in the basics of the instruction

that certain areas had been overlooked, and tonight, as they cleared away the plates after their supper, Jim intended to address one of em. He said to Deakins, "You never told me about Nightshade."

"What? What'd you say?"

"You never told me about Nightshade," repeated Jim. "All I know is what you told Mr. Grayson that first day, that Nightshade is some sort of outlaw and that he wears a hood and black clothes."

"Some sort of outlaw," echoed Deakins with a snort. "Hell, son, that's like sayin' the Mississippi is some sort of river or the Rockies are some sort of mountains. Sit yourself down." He waved a gnarled hand at the table.

Jim took a seat while Deakins opened a cabinet and brought out a jug and a couple of chipped cups. He carried them over to the table and set them down.

"Know what that is?" asked the old man, pointing at the jug.

"Whiskey, I imagine," replied Jim.

"Damn right. You ain't been sneakin' off to the saloons, so I know you ain't got the thirst on you like some folks. Still, it won't hurt to have a sip or two while I'm tellin' the story. Might make you more inclined to believe it." Deakins fixed Jim with an intent stare. "And you'd damn well better believe it, if you want to ever go in them mountains and come out alive again."

"I'm listening," said Jim.

Deakins snorted and then pulled the cork from the jug with his teeth, spitting it into his free hand. He tipped the jug up and poured whiskey into the glasses. "Drink up," he said.

Gingerly, Jim picked up one of the glasses and looked at the amber liquid. Unlike some of the unfortunates he'd known, trapped in poverty back East, he had never been one to seek escape in drink. He was accustomed to a beer every now and then; since coming west, he had worked as a swamper in several saloons, and it was usually easy to cadge an occasional bucket of beer from a sympathetic bartender. But he could have counted on the fingers of one hand the times he had sampled whiskey. This stuff in Deakins' jug was no doubt home brew, probably dosed with gunpowder and rattlesnake heads. But Jim took a deep breath and lifted the glass to his lips, quickly tossing down the drink.

An inferno suddenly engulfed his gullet, the fire swarming eagerly down into his body and starting an even larger conflagration in his belly. Jim gasped as the glass slipped from his fingers and clattered to the table. His other hand beat against the wood in a frenzy.

After he had swallowed his own drink and licked his lips, Deakins regarded Jim's reaction and said, "Yep, it's mighty smooth stuff, all right. You won't find any better in this part of the country."

If that was true, Jim thought in the sole corner of his brain that had not been stunned into submission by the potent liquor, then he did not intend to take another drink until he was well away from Flat Rock.

Seemingly undisturbed by Jim's continued gasping for breath, Deakins went on, "So, you want to hear about Nightshade . . . well, I'll tell you what I know, boy, but it ain't much. First off, don't nobody know where he came from. Showed up sudden-like, nigh on to twenty years ago. This country here, east of the Prophets, was just startin' to see some settlers comin' in. Flat Rock weren't no more than a wide spot in the trail. I was one of the first to open up a business, along with Harveyson and Markham. They're long gone now, of course, moved on further west. But I stayed, and I reckon you could call me Flat Rock's first citizen."

"I didn't know that," said Jim, his voice weak but serviceable.

"I expect there's a whole heap you don't know about a lot of things," said Deakins. "Anyway, there weren't no ranches hereabouts then, but there were fur trappers in the mountains and prospectors, too, lookin' for gold and silver. Ol' Digger Fitzgerald found the Jimpson Lode, and that brought even more folks. Mines opened up all through the foothills. Sodbusters drifted over from the plains, and other folks discovered what good grazin' land there is around here. The town started growin' pretty fast.

"Well, when you've got good folks flockin' into a place,

you're bound to get some bad folks, too. We'd always had our share of brawls in the saloons, maybe a shootin' or knifin' every now and then, but the road agents left us alone, pretty much. That changed when the mine owners started shippin' out ore. Seemed like ever' other shipment got held up."

"By Nightshade," guessed Jim.

"Don't go gettin' ahead of me," snapped Deakins. "I didn't say no such. Reckon there was half a dozen or more gangs operatin' in the foothills and in the mountains. They'd stop the ore wagons, raid farms and ranches, sneak into town and cause mischief sometimes. When the stagecoaches started comin' through here, they got hit, too. One month we had over a dozen folks killed in robberies of one sort or another. It was a mighty bad time, all up and down this stretch, from Benedict up north to Cavassos down south and all the way over the mountains to Moss City. Flat Rock here was right in the middle. I figured if nothin' happened, the town might just dry up and blow away."

Jim spoke up again. "That's when Nightshade showed up, right?"

"Dadblast it! There you go again, gettin' ahead of the story!" Deakins poured himself another drink and tossed it back. Wiping the back of his hand across his mouth, he scowled at Jim. "You want to hear this, or do you already know all of it?"

"I'm sorry," said Jim, holding up his hands in surrender. "I didn't mean to interrupt."

"Well, see that it don't happen again," muttered Deakins. "As I was sayin', things was lookin' mighty bad. And you're right—that's when Nightshade was first heard of. After that . . . things got even worse."

Jim wanted to ask how that could be, but he refrained, having learned his lesson from the earlier outbursts. Deakins got to his feet and paced restlessly across the office, his hands in the rear pockets of his denim overalls.

"Nightshade stopped a shipment comin' down from the Jimpson and took it over. By himself, he was, just one tall drink of water in black clothes and that black hood. Got the drop on the guards and made 'em throw down their guns.

Then he made 'em take off their boots and pants and toss 'em down in this gully where they couldn't get at 'em. 'Fore he drove off with the wagon, he told those boys to make sure everybody around here knew it was Nightshade who held 'em up. Said he was takin' over and that the other gangs weren't goin' to be allowed to operate in these parts no more. It was mighty bold talk, and he had to've known it'd get back to the other outlaws. It was like he was throwin' a challenge right in their faces."

Deakins poured himself another drink, swallowed greedily, and wiped his mouth before continuing. "Back durin' this time I'm tellin' you about, there was a little whiskey shack over at the foot of the mountains, right there on the trail that led up to the pass. Fella name of Gaspard ran it. He was some sort of Frenchman who'd come down from Canada. Only sampled his bug juice once myself, and it was fearsome, let me tell you, nothin' like this drinkin' liquor." The old man indicated the jug on the table with a callused finger. "But it was the only place a man could get a drink 'tween here and Moss City, so folks stopped there. Place didn't look like much, built of logs and rough planks, and there was barely room for the bar and half a dozen drinkers. No point in lookin' for it, if "you're ever over that way. Whole shebang burned to the ground, on this night I'm tellin' you about.

"You see, there was this ol' boy named Homer Guyette, and he fancied himself a fast gun and a desperado. Truth be told, he *was* pretty handy with a gun, and he drew a bunch around him who were all cut from the same cloth. Homer ran things 'cause he was the meanest. Killin' didn't mean nothin' to him. When Homer heard about what Nightshade had told those guards on the ore wagon, he swore he'd kill Nightshade. He was over there at Gaspard's shack with three of his boys on the night I'm talkin' about, and he'd been puttin' away that Frenchie's brew hot an' heavy. Gaspard was there, too, of course, along with a squaw he rented out to anybody who had the money and the itch. They was behind the bar, and Homer Guyette and his men were standin' in front of it.

"Now, I don't think I mentioned there was one little table

in the room, stuck in the corner beside the door. This fella slipped inside and sat down, but nobody paid him much mind 'cept Gaspard, who came out from the bar long enough to pour him a drink and take his coin. Then the Frenchie went back and listened some more to Homer, who was rantin' and ravin' about what he was goin' to do to Nightshade when he caught up with him.

"And then this voice says, sort of slow-like, 'Nightshade's already here, boys.' Homer and his gunnies jumped and turned around, and that stranger that nobody paid any attention to has got a black hood pulled over his head, so they can't see his face no more. He's sittin' there real peaceful, like he ain't got a worry in the world.

"Homer sort of squinches up his eyes and says, 'So you're the son-of-a-bitch who thinks he's goin' to run off ever'body else.'

"And Nightshade says back to him, 'Nope, I'm the son of a bitch who *is* goin' to run off ever'body else. And if you don't think so, Homer, you can give me a try right here and now.'

"Wasn't no way Homer could let that pass. He grabbed for his gun, and so did the fellas with him. Gaspard hit the floor behind the bar, then reached up to try to pull the squaw down.

"By that time, Nightshade'd come up from behind that table, knockin' it over on the way, and he had guns blazin' in both hands. His first shot hit one of Homer's men in the shoulder and knocked him around just as the fella squeezed the trigger. The bullet hit that squaw of Gaspard's in the head. Bored her nice and neat, killed her right away, so at least she didn't suffer none. Nightshade's burnin' powder right and left, and another of Homer's men goes down. The third man takes a bullet in the chest. He's out of the fight, and that just leaves Homer. He's triggered a couple of times, and he figgers he must've hit Nightshade, but Nightshade's still on his feet, not budgin'. I'm just guessin' on that part, mind you, because there ain't no way of knowin' for sure what went through Homer's mind right then. Because in the next couple of seconds, Nightshade shoots him to doll rags.

"Gaspard's layin' there under the body of that Injun

woman, which fell on him after gettin' hit by that stray bullet, but when things get quiet all of a sudden, he pushes her over and lifts himself up enough to peek over the bar. He sees Nightshade standin' there. Nightshade holsters his guns and comes over to the bar. He sees that the squaw is dead, and his voice is pure mournful as he tells Gaspard how sorry he is she got plugged. He says, 'I reckon money can't ever make up for your loss, friend, but I want you to have this anyway.' And he plunks down a sack of coins on the bar.

"Now, Gaspard ain't mournin' anything except the bulletholes he'll have to patch in the walls, so I reckon them coins would've eased his grief just fine. He dumps 'em out of the sack and goes to countin' 'em as Nightshade turns to leave. That was the only time anybody knows of that he made a mistake, mind you. He didn't check to make sure that the first fella he shot, the one he hit in the shoulder, was really dead. The ol' boy wasn't, and he got hold of his gun again and made it to his knees. He was liftin' that six-shooter toward Nightshade's back when Nightshade heard him and spun around, drawin' and firin' slick as you please. The bullet spilled the fella over, and this time, the wild shot he got off as he was dyin' hit the lamp over the bar. Well, that was the end of Gaspard's place. Burned to the ground, just like I said. Gaspard got out in time to save himself. Nightshade was gone by then, which didn't come as no surprise to nobody. Gaspard took the money Nightshade give him and pulled up stakes. Nobody knows for sure where he went, maybe back to Canada, but before he left, he told ever 'body who'd listen about how Nightshade had faced down and killed those four owlhoots—and they were all fast on the draw!"

Jim had listened raptly to the story, Deakins' words drawing him into the yarn until it was like he had actually been there in the squalid little roadhouse and seen the lightning storm of gunplay and sudden death with his own eyes. Now, as Deakins concluded the tale, Jim gave a little shake of his head and asked, "Is that why people are so afraid of Nightshade, because he killed some other outlaws in a gunfight?"

"That was just the start of it, boy," said Deakins. "Homer

Guyette wasn't the only one who figgered Nightshade was too big for his britches. There were others who tried to cut him down to size. But they wound up dead, and Nightshade's still alive. In time, he gathered up a gang to work with him some of the time, even though he still pulls some of his jobs by himself. They're a salty bunch, too, them that ride with Nightshade, but he's the saltiest jigger who ever came out of the Prophet Mountains. I wouldn't go up against him with a whole troop of cavalry, no siree."

"You said you had seen him once yourself," prodded Jim.

"That's right. I had business over in Moss City, and like a damned fool, I decided to take the stagecoach over there, 'stead of ridin' through the pass by myself. You see, son, Nightshade'll sometimes let a lone rider go through without botherin' him, unless the fella happens to be a banker or a mine owner or some such that'd make a good target for robbin'. But Nightshade's known to favor stagecoaches particular-like. Reckon that's one reason we ain't on the regular route no more. Folks from Flat Rock got so's they wouldn't ride the coaches, 'cause you never knew when Nightshade'd take it in his head to stick one up. The stage line still ran through here, though, the time I'm talkin' about."

"So Nightshade stopped the stagecoach you were on."

"That he did!" said Deakins. " 'Stand and deliver!' he said, and by gum, we did. All the passengers got out of the coach and turned over their valuables, after Nightshade'd already got the express box."

"Did he shoot anyone?" asked Jim.

"You think anybody was fool enough to try to draw on him?" Deakins shook his head. "By that time, ever'body in these parts had heard about him bracin' Guyette and more'n a dozen others. We didn't have no idea how many Nightshade had killed, but we all knew we didn't want to add to the sum. No, sir, we done as we were told, and there wasn't a shot fired. Nightshade got away slick as a whistle."

"What about the other gangs these days? You said he'd been operating in this area for a long time."

"What other gangs?" snorted Deakins. "They've all cleared out, save for Nightshade's bunch."

Jim mulled over what Deakins had told him. Finally, after several moments, he said, "It's hard to believe that one man could run roughshod over the whole territory like that for so many years."

"When that man's Nightshade, ain't nothin' too hard to believe," avowed the old stablekeeper. "Still figger you want to be a Pony Express rider, now that you know you'll be ridin' right through the heart of his country?"

The question gave Jim pause. He had already spent some sleepless nights pondering the dangers he'd have to face if he overcame the odds and did indeed become a rider for the Pony Express. The threat of savage Indians and ruthless outlaws was bad enough, from what Deakins had told him, Nightshade was much more dangerous than any ordinary bandit.

But Jim had put his mind to this task, and he did not want to give up so easily. Leland Grayson had insisted that Nightshade did not even exist, that the mysterious hooded outlaw was just a story with which to frighten youngsters at bedtime. Even though Deakins claimed to have seen Nightshade with his own eyes, the old man could be exaggerating, blowing a simple stagecoach robbery well out of proportion. It was even possible that Deakins had been telling the story for so long that he actually believed it himself.

"I'm going ahead with it," said Jim, reaching his decision. He shrugged and smiled slightly, adding, "Shoot, I probably won't get the job anyway. So there's no need for me to waste any time worrying about Nightshade."

"If you ever do run into him, son," warned Deakins grimly, "you'll change your tune. And you'll do it in one damned hurry!"

SEVEN

At last the day had dawned. Jim felt an undeniable excitement coursing through him as he arose that morning. His slumber the night before had been restless, haunted by dreams of being pursued on horseback by a huge figure in black whose features were masked by a hood. Through the eyeholes in the disguise, however, Jim could see two blazing orbs as the menacing specter closed in on him.

Every time Jim's dream rose from the depths of his sleeping mind, he awoke before it could reach its conclusion, and he was profoundly grateful for that. He sensed that if the phantasm had ever caught him, the black hood would be ripped away to reveal the hideous countenance of a demon straight from the pit of Hades.

Either that—or the features staring at him would be his own.

As Jim rose from his makeshift bunk in an empty stall, he knew that the hour was even earlier than usual. He did not want to be late arriving at the office of the Central Overlands Express, and he did not doubt for an instant that Deakins would insist on his performing his usual chores before he could leave. After all the painful hours he had spent during the last week learning how to ride, it would be utterly disheartening to find out that all the openings for Pony Express riders had been filled before he reached Grayson's office.

He lit a lantern and began fetching grain and water for the horses in the stalls, then did the same for the animals kept in the corrals out back. The eastern sky was beginning to lighten as Jim worked. The stars riding high in the heavens over the Prophets gradually faded from view. By the time Deakins emerged from the rear door of the building, yawning and scratching, Jim was finished with his tasks.

"Real go-getter this mornin', ain't you?" asked Deakins. "Reckon I know why, too . . . you don't want to be late gettin' down to the Express office."

"I think I'll start now, if it's all right with you," said Jim. "Everything is taken care of."

Deakins frowned. "What? You ain't goin' to eat breakfast?"

"Well, I'm not really hungry . . ."

"First time I ever knowed that to happen," snorted the old man. "Sure, go on, if you're of a mind to."

Jim started into the barn, moving almost at a trot, and Deakins followed more slowly. Pausing only for a moment, Jim took a handful of clean straw and wiped as much of the dust and manure from his boots as he could, then headed for the front door.

"Hold on, boy," called Deakins.

Jim stopped, impatience growing within him as he looked back over his shoulder at the grizzled liveryman. Deakins trudged toward him. "What is it?" asked Jim.

"If you're goin' to be a Pony rider, you'll need a hat. Wouldn't do to have you ridin' out in the sun all day long without one." Deakins had reached the door to the office, and now he disappeared through it, only to emerge a moment later carrying a broad-brimmed, flat-crowned brown hat. He flipped it toward Jim and went on, "Here, see how that fits."

Deftly, Jim plucked the hat from the air and turned it over in his hands. As far as he could tell, the headgear was new, never worn. He looked up at the old man and wondered when Deakins had bought it. "This is for me?" he asked.

"Tarnation, but you're slow to catch on to an idea!" exclaimed Deakins. "I don't see nobody else here. Now put the blamed thing on."

Grinning, Jim settled the hat on his head. It felt like it was the proper size, and as he studied his reflection in a chunk of broken mirror hung on the wall, that judgment was confirmed. The hat fit as well as if it had been made specially for him.

"I . . . I don't know what to say . . ."

"Might try thanks," snorted Deakins. "If that ain't too hard for you."

"Thank you," said Jim sincerely. "Thank you for everything—"

"Go on, get out o' here! You wind up bein' late, you won't have no use for that hat." Deakins waved Jim toward the street, then turned toward the office door.

The young man hesitated, then stepped through the big double doors at the front of the stable and strode down the street. Quite a few people were out and about already, and Jim's heart sank as he saw the crowd that had gathered in front of the Express office. Surely, with that many applicants, he would not be able to secure one of the few available jobs. Still, after preparing for a week, he was not in the mood to give up without at least making an effort.

Tugging at the brim of his new hat, Jim walked up to the edge of the assemblage. Not only were there a couple of dozen young men in evidence who had obviously come to apply for one of the riding jobs, but quite a few of the townspeople had congregated to watch the proceedings. As Jim stood there, shifting nervously from foot to foot, the door of the office swung open and Leland Grayson appeared, as nattily dressed as ever. He looked over the crowd with satisfaction, then called out, "If the young men who have come to apply for jobs will form a line up here on the sidewalk. . . ."

The quick shuffle of feet prevented Grayson from saying anything further. Jim had plenty of experience at pushing and shoving from his years back East, where there was a line for every job, but despite his best effort, he still wound up more than halfway to the end of the row of young men that stretched along the fronts of several buildings. Grayson went back inside, and the line of would-be Pony Express riders began to advance ever so slowly. With every second that passed, Jim felt his heart sinking. Surely at any moment, Grayson would reappear and announce to the crowd that all the jobs had been filled.

As Jim drew closer and closer to the office, however, he allowed hope to spring inside him again. Maybe there was a chance, he told himself.

He recalled other times when he had waited like this for some good news, for something promising. Never had his patience been rewarded. Without fail, he had been unsuccessful. This would probably be just another such instance, he thought, his attitude swinging wildly toward pessimism. After all, nothing had really changed . . . he was still the same hapless youth he had been back in the city. Or so he thought at this moment.

As he waited, a desultory conversation between two men who were loafing in the street caught his attention, especially when he heard one of them say the name *Nightshade.* Jim looked over at them as the second man replied, "Nope, I wouldn't want to be in those boys' boots, either. Fella would have to be a plumb fool to tempt an owlhoot like that."

"I'd be willin' to bet they change their route once they realize they're dealin' with Nightshade," said the first man. "Come on, let's get a drink."

The two townies wandered off and left a frowning Jim McReady behind them. The brief exchange had reminded him of the nightmares that had plagued him. If there really was anything to the story of Nightshade, the Pony Express riders would be risking their lives. That possibility was enough to give any man pause.

If by chance he got the job, and if Nightshade tried to rob him, what was the worst thing that could happen? Nightshade might kill him—in which case, what would the world have lost? A worthless young drifter who might never contribute anything to improve the lot of anyone. Who would miss him if he was dead? Deakins? Not very likely, thought Jim.

The line continued to move while Jim was brooding over his fate, and without really being aware of it, he soon reached the door of the Express office. His head jerked up in surprise as he heard Grayson's voice saying, "Well, don't just stand there, young man. Come on in."

Jim saw that Grayson was watching him with a faintly impatient look on his face. Stepping quickly into the office as he regained his wits, Jim approached the desk where Grayson sat. He reached up, tugged his hat off, and said, "Hello, Mr. Grayson. I don't know if you remember me or not—"

"The boy from the livery stable," cut in Grayson. "Of course I remember you, my boy. Have you had any luck in getting Mr. Deakins to reconsider his decision not to sell me any horses?"

Perhaps Grayson thought that was the only reason he was here. Jim wanted to correct that impression as quickly as he could. He said, "No, sir, I'm afraid not. Whenever I bring up the subject, Mr. Deakins just snorts and stomps off. But the reason I came here today is to sign up as a Pony Express rider."

"Oh, yes," said Grayson. "I remember now. You were interested in being one of the riders for this territory. Of course. How could I forget?" He turned around a piece of paper that he took from a large stack on the desk. Sliding it toward Jim along with a stub of pencil, Grayson continued, "Fill this out, if you please."

Jim went over to the desk, picked up the pencil, and frowned down at the paper. He could read well enough to tell that it simply requested his name, age, and place of residence. Quickly, Jim scrawled the proper responses and handed the document back to Grayson. The Easterner glanced at what Jim had written, then lifted a hand and pointed to a door behind him. "Through there," he said.

Now that he thought about it, Jim did not recall having seen seeing very many of the previous applicants coming back out of the office. They had to be going somewhere, and this seemed the most logical explanation. They had left through the rear door. But where was Grayson sending him? What was on the other side of that door?

There was only one way to find out, he realized. Ignoring the multitude of questions clamoring in his brain, he took a deep breath, stepped over to the door, and opened it.

Jim sighed in relief when he saw that he was not being summarily dismissed. Instead, the door led out into the large rear yard behind the building. The other applicants who had already come through the office were waiting there, some standing around patiently, others pacing. On the far side of the yard stood several horses, saddled and ready to ride. Holding the animals' reins was a tall, lean man with dark, placid features. His hat was shoved to the back of his head. One cheek bulged with tobacco, and he leaned over occasionally to send a stream of brown spittle arching to the ground.

Jim moved to one side of the yard and stood quietly, listening to some of the conversation going on around him. He knew none of these young men; old Deakins was the only person in Flat Rock he knew, besides Leland Grayson. But from the talk he overheard, many of the applicants were friends. Feeling somewhat left out, Jim concentrated instead on what was to come. From the looks of things, they would each be asked to ride so that their skills on horseback could be evaluated.

If that was the case, he probably would not make much of a showing compared to these others, most of whom were doubtless excellent riders. But he had come too far to back out now.

More young men emerged from the rear door of the building and took their places in the yard, and at length, Grayson himself appeared, now wearing his coat and hat. The Express company agent nodded at the man holding the horses and said, "That's the lot of them, the ones that fit the bill enough to try out. I'm ready whenever you are, Bob."

The lanky man grunted in acknowledgment, then pointed to three of the applicants in turn. "You and you and you," he said. "Mount up. Ride over there to that cedar tree. Turn around and come back. Fast as you can."

Jim stood up on his toes and peered toward the tree, a good three hundred yards away, at the crest of a small hill. The route to it was straight and free of any obstructions, and Jim could not see how such a ride would be much of a test. But under the circumstances he would do whatever the two expressmen requested of him. As the first three applicants mounted up, he studied the horses. They were fine-looking animals, and Jim could almost see the speed in the play of muscles under their smooth hides.

"This isn't a race," added Grayson as the three young men prepared to ride out. "We want you to make your best speed, but don't think that the first man back will be assured of a job. It doesn't work that way."

Then, with a wave and a nod, he sent the riders on their way. The wiry youngsters urged their mounts into a gallop. Hat brims blew back and chin straps were drawn tight by the wind as the horses raced across the open ground. The riders leaned forward in the saddle. Along with all the other applicants, Jim watched with keen interest. The riders seemed to be as one with their mounts, young centaurs testing their speed, one against the other. They started up the hill, still riding neck and neck. Reaching the cedar, they circled it and began the return journey.

Moments later, the three riders drew rein in a cloud of dust as they arrived back at the rear yard of the Express office. With anxious looks on their faces, they swung down from the saddle, but if Grayson and Bob had reached any decisions, they kept their judgments to themselves. Bob quickly pointed at three more riders, and the process was repeated.

All the other lads were excellent riders, just as Jim had feared. His hopes began to evaporate again as he watched them. Their level of competence seemed approximately equal; no more than a few yards separated any of them when they arrived back at the starting point. Grayson was not going to have an easy chore in picking his riders; only one of the candidates would be easily eliminated, and that would be him, Jim mused gloomily.

His turn came sooner than he might have wished. Taking a deep breath, he strode forward and was handed the reins of a large bay. As he took the reins from Bob, he sensed the man's eyes studying him, assessing his size and weight. Jim slipped his foot in the stirrup and stepped up into the saddle. Scarcely had he settled himself when Bob waved for him and the other two riders to begin.

Jim dug his heels into the sides of the bay and sent it leaping forward. His fingers tightened on the reins, pulling the leather lines taut. As the other riders drew slightly ahead of him, he realized that he had reined in too much to suit the bay. Its gait grew rougher, and Jim felt himself begin to bounce in the saddle, as he always did whenever he made a mistake.

Forcing back the feeling of panic that threatened to well up inside him, he loosened his grip on the reins and relaxed, settling back into the horse's chosen rhythm. The momentary lapse had allowed the other two riders to open up a gap ahead of him, however, and despite Grayson's statement that this test was not intended to be a race, Jim knew he had to catch up if he was to have any chance of being hired. He leaned forward, urging the bay on to greater speed.

On they ran, and though the wind of their passage buffeted Jim's face, the pace seemed incredibly slow to him. Finally they reached a point halfway to the tree, and Jim saw to his dismay that not only had he not cut down on the lead held by the other riders, they had actually enlarged the gap. This was fast becoming hopeless.

Jim lashed the horse's neck with the trailing reins as they started up the hill. Perhaps his horse had more strength and could negotiate the slope faster than the other mounts, he thought, grasping at any faint hope. That was not the case, however, he saw as they charged up the rise. The other horses were just as fast, and they had rounded the tree and started back down when Jim and the bay were still some thirty yards from the crest.

Tasting bitter despair in his mouth, Jim kept riding. It would have been easier to give up, to simply rein in, turn the horse, and trot back to the Express office without ever reaching the goal. He knew he would not be able to face Deakins if he did such a thing. Instead, he tried to drag every ounce of speed out of the horse.

The cedar loomed in front of him. Jim pulled the horse's head to the right to veer around the tree, and as the cedar flashed past on his left, he began hauling on the reins, pulling his mount into as tight and quick a turn as he could manage.

Suddenly the bay stumbled. Jim's eyes went wide with fear as the horse lost its balance. He tried to hold the animal up, but it was futile. Kicking his feet free of the stirrups as Deakins had warned him to do if he was ever on the back of a falling horse, Jim let himself go limp. The bay went down.

Jim sailed through the air for a second, then crashed heavily against the rocky ground on the far side of the slope. He scrambled quickly to one side as the fallen horse rolled toward him. The life would be crushed out of him, he knew, if the big bay pinned him.

As he came to his feet, the blood hammering in his head, he looked around and saw that the horse was up again, too, seemingly unhurt. Jim's hat had fallen off during the fall; he scooped it up and then stepped over to the bay. He ignored the breathless pain he had suffered from his own landing and made soothing sounds while he approached the horse. The animal was nervous, but it calmed down quickly as Jim stroked its flanks and checked it over for injuries. Seeing none, Jim gathered up the reins, grasped the horn, and swung up into the saddle again. He cast a glance down the hill and saw that the other two riders had already reached the rear yard of the office. They dismounted and joined the others in watching him as he rode down the hill.

Jim felt his features burning in embarrassment. All of them had witnessed his humiliating fall. All he wanted to do now was to put this debacle behind him as quickly as possible. He heeled the bay into a run again, and this time the gallop was smooth and even, the horse covering the ground in great, distance-consuming strides. In a matter of moments, Jim reached the yard. He dismounted and handed the reins to Bob without looking up to meet the tall man's eyes.

As he turned away, he saw the smirks on the faces of the other riders, and he knew they no longer considered him part of their competition. Grimacing from the bile of defeat, he started toward a gate at the side of the yard, intent only on getting away from here.

Bob's hand fell on his shoulder, the fingers like iron as they stopped him. "Wait up," said the man. "Nobody leaves just yet."

Jim saw no reason to stay; it was utterly beyond belief that he still had a chance of being hired. As he looked up at the stern features of the horse handler, however, he could tell that Bob would tolerate no argument. Jim jerked his head in a nod, then went over to stand alone by the fence when Bob released his shoulder.

Several other applicants were still awaiting their turn to ride. Jim ignored them as they did so. He was quite sure none of them would make a spectacle of himself as he had. He kept his eyes downcast, seeming to study the toes of his boots. In actuality, though, he was seeing the long line of failures that had marked his life; this was only the latest in a long series.

When all the applicants had ridden to the tree and back under the watchful eyes of Grayson and Bob, the Express company agent said, "If you gentlemen would be so kind as to wait here, we'll have a decision for you shortly." Along with Bob, Grayson retreated into the office and shut the door behind them.

Jim hunkered on his heels, leaning his back against the fence as he waited. The only thing for which he was thankful was that Deakins had not been present to witness his failure. It would be hard enough telling the old man what had happened. Still, things could have been worse, Jim told himself. Deakins would probably allow him to continue working at the stable. At least, that way he'd be able to eat and he'd have a place to sleep at night. Compared to some of the places he had been, his existence in Flat Rock was not too bad.

He was unsure how much time had passed when Grayson finally stepped out of the office again. "Gentlemen," said the Easterner, "thank you all for coming here today, and I regret that I cannot hire all of you. However, these are the six who were chosen: Jonas Kirk . . . Ben Simmons . . . Dave Wright . . . Matthew LeFarge . . . Sam Richardson—" With each name that Grayson called out, a whoop or a shout of exultation went up from a member of the eager audience. Grayson hesitated for a long moment, then added the sixth and final name. ". . . And James McReady."

Jim heard his name, but for a few seconds, it did not sink in. He looked up, blinking and frowning. Had Grayson really called his name? But the man was announcing the applicants who had been chosen for the jobs as Pony Express riders, so there must have been some mistake. . . .

Then Jim saw that Grayson was smiling across the yard at him, and behind him, the man called Bob was standing with a grin on his leathery features. There was no doubt they were both looking at him.

His heart took a great leap, feeling as if it was going to come right out of his chest. He did not understand this, did not understand it at all, and judging from the mutters and frowning stares that came from some of the applicants who had not been chosen, his puzzlement was no greater than theirs. After all, his riding was at times awkward, and he had even let his horse take a spill.

He was not fool enough to question his good fortune, though. He rose to his feet and strode quickly over to the building, joining the other youngsters who were shaking hands with Grayson and Bob and being congratulated by them. As he stepped up and grasped Grayson's hand, Jim could not help murmuring, "Why . . . ?"

"Why did we pick you?" asked Grayson, completing Jim's question.

"Not for your riding skill," put in Bob. "But you sit a horse pretty well part of the time, and you're a stubborn cuss, too. There'll be times out on the trail when things go wrong and it'd be a whole heap easier just to forget about your job, your duty to the company. I don't reckon you'd do that."

Not many people who had known him would have had that much confidence in him, Jim thought, and truthfully, they would have had no reason to believe in him. Bob's words filled him with pride, and his voice quivered a little as he replied, "I'll try not to let you down, sir."

The boys who had not been hired began drifting away, many of them still complaining. Grayson gestured to the six who had been picked, saying, "Come on into the office, lads. We have business to attend to."

Jim and the other five new Pony Express riders followed Grayson and Bob into the building. Grayson opened a drawer in the desk and took out several small pieces of paper. As he distributed them to the six new employees of the Central Overlands Express, he asked, "Can all of you read?" A couple of the young men shook their heads, so Grayson continued, "I'll read the pledge aloud, then. All employees of the company must sign it and adhere to its tenets. Mr. Alexander Majors insists upon it."

Jim read the words to himself as Grayson solemnly intoned them. " 'While I am in the employ of Russell, Majors, and Waddell, I agree not to use profane language, not to get drunk, not to gamble, not to treat animals cruelly, and not to do anything else that is incompatible with the conduct of a gentleman. And I agree, if I violate any of the above conditions, to accept my discharge without any pay for my services. So help me God.' " Grayson looked up from the document in his hand. "If you will sign, please, gentlemen, or make your mark, we can proceed." He held out a pencil to each one in turn.

When all of them had signed the pledges and returned them to Grayson, the Express company agent reached into his desk again and this time produced several small books bound in reddish-brown leather. He handed one to each rider, and as Jim took his copy, he saw the words *Holy Bible* on the spine. Engraved into the front cover was the legend *Presented by Russell, Majors, & Waddell, 1858.*

"Mr. Majors had these Bibles printed for his wagon-train crews, but he thought you lads should each have a copy, too," explained Grayson. "Keep it with you at all times to remind you of the pledge you signed."

Jim nodded. He did not think he would have any trouble living up to the pledge. He cursed and drank only rarely, and he had never been one to be cruel to animals.

"You will also be issued a carbine and a pair of revolvers, but you won't be getting those until the operation of the Express relay actually begins. That should be in a few weeks. Until then, Bob here will ride over the route with you so that you can be familiar with it. He'll also teach you everything you need to know about riding for the Pony Express."

"Ride fast and keep your eyes open," said Bob in a dry tone of voice. "Those are the most important things."

"Well, gentlemen, that will be all for now. Welcome to the Pony Express."

Grayson's words echoed in Jim's ears as he left the office with the other riders. He still found it difficult to believe. He had actually achieved a goal he had set for himself, for one of the few times in his life.

But, he asked himself as he headed for the livery stable to tell Deakins the news, what would that achievement bring him?

EIGHT

"Well, look at you," said Deakins. "Ain't you a sight?"

Jim stood just inside the entrance to the stable. He wore the hat and boots Deakins had given to him, but the rest of his outfit was new. Fringed buckskin pants hugged his legs and were tucked into the high tops of the boots. His shirt was dark blue and had a bib front. Around his waist was buckled a wide belt, and a pair of matching .36 caliber Navy Colts rode in the holsters. The pouch strapped onto the belt contained an extra Colt cylinder, already loaded. Tilted jauntily across one shoulder was a Sharps carbine.

"You appear to be loaded for bear, boy," went on Deakins. "Do all them Pony Riders carry so much armament?"

"This is standard equipment," replied Jim, "although there's some talk that all the weapons add too much to the weight the horses have to carry. There may be a change in the future, once the routes have been ridden long enough for the company to be sure exactly how much danger is involved."

For somebody who had not even carried the mail yet, Jim thought, he sounded awfully well versed. But he had listened attentively to everything that Grayson and Bob Lind had had to say over the past few weeks, and he had learned a great deal. The horse handler, Lind, had taken all the riders over the route between Flat Rock and Moss City. The first time they had approached the pass through the Prophet Mountains, Jim had felt a distinct shiver of apprehension. This was the place where Nightshade most often struck.

Evidently the legendary outlaw had no interest in fledgling Pony Express riders, however, because no one bothered them on their trips through the mountains as they learned the trails. Still, Jim could not look at the Prophets without thinking about the hooded man in black. Was Nightshade real? Was he only a myth? Perhaps Jim would find out before many more days had passed.

A week and a half earlier, on April 3, the Pony Express had been launched from St. Joseph, Missouri, and San Francisco, riders leaving both cities on the same day, one heading west, one traveling east. It had taken several days after that for the mail pouches to reach this remote, isolated section of the route, but reach it they had. So far, the more experienced riders had handled the chore, galloping over the road between Flat Rock and Moss City. The eastbound man and the westbound one usually met each other in the mountain pass, but from what Jim had heard, their greetings consisted only of a wave from the saddle as they galloped past one another. There was no time in the schedule for stopping and chatting.

None of the riders had been bothered by robbers, and everything was proceeding as smoothly as the triumvirate of Messrs. Russell, Majors, and Waddell could have hoped. Soon, Jim had been promised by Grayson and Lind, he would take his turn carrying the pouch.

That would be a great moment, thought Jim, and he wondered if it could equal the feeling of pride that had welled up within him as he had told Deakins about being hired for the job. The old man had said little when Jim broke the news to him; he had merely nodded, spat tobacco juice into the dust of the stable floor, and said, "Figgered as much." That simple declaration of faith had meant more to Jim than anything.

Since then, he had divided his time between the Pony Express office and the stable, still sleeping in one of the stalls at night, even though he was no longer able to do as many chores around the place as he once had. Deakins had said nothing about the arrangement, and evidently he was not displeased. Once he began drawing his salary as a Pony Rider, Jim had decided, he would pay the old man something to cover his room and board. That is, if Deakins was agreeable to letting him remain there.

"When's your first ride?" asked Deakins as Jim strolled into the barn.

"Mr. Grayson hasn't said for sure," replied the young man, "but I'm hoping it'll be tomorrow. Otherwise, I don't think they would have gone ahead and given me these guns."

"You know how to use 'em, do you?"

Jim shrugged. "Bob Lind and I practiced with them for a while this afternoon. He said I did all right. Anyway, they're not expecting any trouble. So far, everything has gone as smooth as can be." In truth, Jim thought he had been mediocre at best in handling the firearms. The Colts were heavier than he would have expected; lifting them and holding them steady put a strain on his wrists. And his shoulder was pretty sore from the recoil of the carbine. His ears had rung for an hour after the practice session.

Deakins grunted. "Grayson still after you to get me to sell him some horses?"

"The Pony Express could always use more good horses," said Jim. "But Mr. Grayson bought quite a few mounts from the ranchers around here. I think there are enough to do the job."

"Good. The fella may have enough sense to hire you, but I still don't like him. Damned Easterners always think they know ever'thing. Shouldn't've made sport of me when I was tryin' to tell him 'bout Nightshade." Deakins grimaced and pulled at his whiskers. Something was obviously bothering him, Jim realized, and he wondered what it was. Abruptly, Deakins jerked his head toward the rear of the barn and said, "Come on."

Frowning slightly, Jim followed the old-timer. Deakins led the way out the rear door and into the lane between the two corrals. He waved a hand toward the enclosure on the left. "Take your pick," he said.

Jim's puzzlement grew. "I don't understand," he said.

"Don't understand what?" snapped Deakins. "Plain English? I said take your pick, boy. You'll need a good mount, and I trust these nags more 'n any that Grayson fella might've bought."

"You're giving me a horse?" asked Jim, his surprise evident in his voice. "But why?"

Deakins put his hands on his hips and glared at him. "Goin' to make me explain it, are you? Well, it's on your own head, then, because I plan on speakin' plain. When you wandered up, boy, you weren't worth a damned thing. You were just a tramp. Leastways, that's what I thought."

"You were right," said Jim in a soft voice as he looked down at the ground.

"Nope, don't reckon I was. Oh, you were mighty close to bein' worthless—but mighty close ain't the same thing. There's somethin' inside you, boy . . . you've let life push you around for years. You floated along like a stick in a flooded stream, goin' wherever the current took you. I said you didn't have no backbone, and I was almost right. But somethin' in you changed since you come here. You showed you could be stubborn when you wanted to. You showed some gumption. Maybe you got enough to make somethin' of yourself after all, and maybe you don't. Could be that if things get too rough, you'll go back to bein' a tramp. I'm just curious enough to want to find out." Deakins drew a deep breath. "There. I've said my piece."

For a long moment, Jim stood there silently, thinking about Deakins' speech. It was more than he had ever heard the old-timer say at one time, except for the day Deakins had told him the story of Nightshade. Finally, Jim put his thoughts in order enough to say, "You want me to have a good horse so that I'll have a better chance if I run into trouble."

"That's about the size of it."

The old man's gesture touched Jim, but he restrained

himself from offering effusive thanks. That would only have annoyed and embarrassed Deakins, he knew. Instead, as he turned and looked at the horses in the corral, spotting the one he wanted, he said, "All right. I'll take Rusty."

"That jughead?" Deakins' sudden grin belied the scorn in his words. "Well, I reckon you could do worse."

Jim moved over to the corral fence and reached through the poles with one hand. Immediately Rusty came over to him, nuzzling his nose against Jim's palm. Jim patted the horse and said, "How about it, boy? You want to work for the Pony Express?"

Rusty just kept rubbing against Jim's outstretched hand, and in that moment, the young man knew he had made a wise decision. If he ever encountered trouble on his route, Rusty would devote every ounce of his speed and stamina to bearing him out of danger. The ugly roan would run himself right into the ground if need be.

"You ain't said where you got them fancy duds," commented Deakins as Jim patted the horse.

"Mr. Grayson gave me an advance on my salary," replied Jim. "My old clothes were just about worn out, so I bought these at Mr. Mitchell's trading post."

Deakins nodded. "They'll do you all right." He rubbed his whiskered jaw. "Yeah, boy, I'd say you're all ready to go. All they need to do is give you the mail and send you on your way."

Jim took a deep breath. He was ready; even Deakins could see that. Ready to start a new life.

And he hoped the moment came soon.

Jim's heart thudded almost painfully in his chest as he stood in front of the Central Overlands Express office and waited for the sound of hoofbeats. He was not alone; Leland Grayson waited on the sidewalk with him, glancing at his pocket watch from time to time, and Bob Lind was leaning against the hitch rack, elbows hooked indolently over the rail. Jim turned to look at Grayson and asked, not for the first time, "Is he late?"

Grayson snapped shut his watch and replaced it in his pocket. "Not yet. There's still ten minutes before the rider from Carson is due. Don't worry, Jim."

But Jim could not stop himself from feeling anxious. If the westbound rider was late arriving in Flat Rock, then Jim would be expected to make up for that lost time. He would have to shave minutes off the time required to cross the mountains and reach Moss City. It would not be an easy task, especially for a rider on his first run.

Rusty was at the hitch rack, saddled and ready to go. Grayson had told Jim early that morning that he would be up today and instructed him to get his horse ready. There had been no argument from Grayson when Jim told him that he wanted to use his own horse; that allowed the Express company's mounts to get some extra rest.

There were no swing stations between Flat Rock and Moss City. It was one of the shorter sections of the Pony Express trail that stretched from St. Joe to San Francisco, so the riders did not change horses along the way. However, because the path led over rugged terrain, animals of great strength and endurance were required. As far as Jim was concerned, Rusty fit that description, but there was no way of knowing for certain how well the roan would hold up to the course, not until it had been covered. That uncertainty only added to Jim's anxiety. He doubted himself enough already, he mused; he did not need to doubt Rusty too.

Suddenly, the faint pounding of hoofbeats to the east made Jim's head lift sharply. Beside him, Grayson smiled and said, "I think that's probably our man now."

In the street, Bob Lind stepped away from the hitch rail and motioned to Jim. "Best get down here and mount up," said the tall man.

Jim's stomach lurched. Now that the moment had finally arrived, his nerves were playing havoc with his belly. He tried to ignore his queasiness as he stepped up to Rusty and put a foot in the stirrup. He swung up into the saddle, then swallowed hard.

Grayson came over to him, and the Easterner reached into his coat. He withdrew a long white envelope. "This was brought up by a rider from Cavassos, along with the fee for sending it," he said. "We'll add it to the pouch."

Jim nodded as he took the envelope. Letters could be added to the mail pouch at any of the major stations along the route. The pouch itself was locked, but the station managers such as Grayson had keys that would open it. Jim's eyes studied the address on the envelope; he concentrated on the carefully printed words in order to take his mind off his nervousness.

There was nothing to indicate who had sent the letter, but it was addressed to Miss Virginia Rawlings, 112 Dubins Street, Harker City. That was the next stop following Moss City, Jim recalled from studying the maps of the route that Grayson and Lind had shown him. From the feel of the envelope, there was only one sheet of paper folded up inside it. Jim had no idea what was in the letter, and it was none of his business, of course, but he felt a special pride as he held it. Whoever this Virginia Rawlings was, whoever had written to her, they were showing their trust in him by turning the missive over to the Pony Express. He would play his part in its delivery, proving not only that he had finally become a man, but that he was a trustworthy one as well. As he looked at the letter, holding it almost reverently, the name and address burned themselves into his brain.

The hoofbeats were louder now. A few people along the sidewalks looked up curiously, but most of the town's citizens paid no attention. The crowds that had turned out to welcome the first riders to arrive in Flat Rock had quickly dwindled. The Pony Express was still in its infancy, but already the novelty of the idea had worn off. No longer did cheering throngs line the streets of Western towns to greet the Pony Riders. These young men were already simply a part of everyday life.

Not for Jim McReady, however. He watched with wide eyes as the rider appeared, far down the trail to the east. The figure drew nearer and the hoofbeats grew louder, and soon Jim could make out the haggard features of the young man who had just covered some forty miles at top speed. Already the other rider had reached down and lifted the saddlebag-like mail pouch. This transfer would be a bit slower than usual because Grayson would have to unlock the pouch and allow Jim to slip Virginia Rawlings' letter in with the other mail. The oncoming rider would not be aware of that fact, however.

The rider slowed down when he saw that Jim was not going to spur his mount into motion so that the transfer could be achieved on the run. As he reined in with one hand, he used the other to flip the pouch to Jim, who caught it awkwardly and slapped it down across the pommel of his saddle. The pouch had two compartments, each fastened with a small padlock. Grayson thrust a key into the lock on the side nearest him, and once the pouch was open, Jim required only a second to slip the letter to Virginia Rawlings in with the other mail. Then Grayson closed the lock again and stepped back hurriedly while Bob Lind slapped the horse on the rump and let out a yell. Jim tightened his fingers on the reins as Rusty leaped into motion.

Before horse and rider reached the western end of the street, the roan had settled into a steady gallop. Jim felt fairly comfortable in the saddle. Now that he was actually on his way, the brooding and worrying that had plagued him all day suddenly disappeared. The ball of sickness in his belly vanished. All he felt was a surge of excitement and anticipation. A few weeks earlier he had never even heard of the Pony Express, but now it seemed like the realization of a long-held dream for him to be galloping along the trail like this, carrying the mail and linking one coast of the continent to the other. He seemed to see the other riders stretching out in unbroken lines to the east and west, and he was a proud part of that succession. No matter what had happened in the past, his future was in his own two hands, his to do with what he would. It was a wonderful feeling.

Jim rode on, the Prophet Mountains looming ruggedly in front of him.

* * *

Rusty was still running strong and steady as Jim approached the foothills an hour and a half later. He cast a glance up at the mountains above him. Green was beginning to appear on the lower slopes as trees burst into life with the arrival of spring. Higher, though, the predominant colors were blue and purple and black, and higher still the peaks were yet mantled with white from the winter snows. Most of that snow melted during the spring and summer, but a few solitary mountaintops remained white the year 'round, according to old Deakins, who had lived in this country longer than anyone else Jim knew. The Prophets were beautiful, thought the young man, although their beauty had a bleak and forbidding quality about it. They would be a fitting home for a man like Nightshade.

Jim frowned. This was the first time he had thought about Nightshade since leaving Flat Rock. Approaching these majestically sinister mountains by himself was quite different from riding along here with a group, as he'd done when Lind was showing the riders the route. What would he do if Nightshade should appear? Turn his horse and gallop in the other direction as quickly as he could? He might escape that way, but it would put the mail behind schedule. Perhaps he could draw his gun and charge ahead, firing. That might drive Nightshade off, but it might also get him killed. There was a good chance the outlaw would coolly stand his ground and shoot Jim right out of the saddle.

Never having been very religious, Jim had no idea whether prayer worked or not. But he sent one heavenward at this moment anyway, beseeching the Lord to take him through the mountains unharmed, without encountering Nightshade or any other dangers.

Fifteen minutes later, he reached the bottom of the long, gentle slope that led up to the pass through the Prophets. Rusty took the rise with scarcely a slackening of speed, and as Jim's appreciation of the roan's smooth, fast gait grew, he felt even more grateful to Deakins for the gift of the horse.

The pass itself was in sight now, and still no sign of Nightshade. Maybe there *was* something to the power of prayer, Jim thought.

Suddenly, his breath caught in his throat and a vise seemed to clamp painfully around his chest as he saw a rider spur into view from behind a large boulder just to the right of the pass. Jim gasped as he saw the black clothes and the dark hood under a broad-brimmed black hat. Nothing of the rider himself would be visible in that outfit save for his eyes. There was no mistaking him.

Nightshade.

So this, thought Jim McReady, was how prayers were really answered.

NINE

Scarcely aware of it, Jim had reined in, bringing Rusty to a stop in the middle of the trail some twenty yards downslope from the man in black. Twenty yards was on the outer edges of accuracy for a pistol such as the one held by Nightshade. If he turned and ran now, Jim knew, there was a good chance any shots taken by the bandit would miss.

He did not move, though. He sat in his saddle like a statue carved from stone, staring in horror at the dark figure.

Slowly, Nightshade rode closer, taking his time, as if he knew that the young man on the roan would not flee before him. The outlaw's mount was a high-stepping Appaloosa, as magnificent an animal as Jim had ever seen. When the distance between them was barely ten feet, Nightshade stopped again. Now Jim could see the man's eyes, and just as in his dream, they seemed to blaze with an unholy fire.

"You're an intelligent young man," said Nightshade suddenly. "That's good. Pass over the pouch, please."

The voice took Jim by surprise. It was deep and resonant, ringing with power and authority. Unlike the coarse growl of many outlaws, these tones seemed to belong to an educated man, a man of some breeding. But despite that, there was no mistaking the menace couched in the words, or the threat of the slightly uptilted gun barrel. In a mere flicker of time, Jim knew, that barrel could come down and spurt flame and leaden death toward him.

He fumbled clumsily with the mail pouch, trying to lift it

from the pommel of the saddle. Its weight seemed to have increased a hundredfold. That was just the weight of his own guilt he was feeling, Jim thought. If he handed over the pouch as Nightshade had commanded, he would be betraying the trust of many people, among them Leland Grayson, Bob Lind, old Deakins, and even the unknown Miss Virginia Rawlings and her correspondent. What Deakins had first believed of him—that he was a worthless tramp—would be proved to be true. If he lost this pouch, he realized, he might as well just keep riding and never go back to Flat Rock, because he would not be able to face the accusing countenances of those who had placed their faith in him.

He could not let that happen.

Nightshade spurred the Appaloosa forward, impatience visible now in the way he held himself, and he held out his free hand for the pouch.

A shout ripped from Jim's throat, a cry that surprised him as much as it did Nightshade. He held tightly to the pouch and lashed out with it, catching the wrist of the outlaw's gun hand and driving it to one side. The Colt cracked and Jim yelled again in a mixture of terror and rage. Nightshade had tried to shoot him . . . had tried to *kill* him.

Jim jerked the roan's head around and gouged his spurs into Rusty's flanks, digging the rowels in with a cruelty brought on by his panic. He never would have treated the horse so roughly if his mind had been functioning normally. Rusty leaped in the air in response to the pain, sunfishing frenziedly. It was impossible for Jim to stay in the saddle.

For a second, earth and sky seemed to trade places as he tumbled through the air. Then everything straightened out and Jim crashed to the ground, landing on the hard-packed dirt of the trail. The roan scampered off, still bucking and dancing nervously. Jim rolled over, drawing great gulps of air into his lungs to replace what had been knocked out by the impact of his landing, and as he did so, his instincts screamed at him to draw one of the guns holstered at his waist. He sat up and reached for the Colt on the right side. The revolver had just cleared leather when a booted foot cracked viciously into Jim's wrist, the kick making him lose his grip on the Colt. It spun away.

Nightshade had gotten down from his horse, Jim saw now. The hooded outlaw stood over him, the barrel of his gun only inches from the young man's face. "You're not so smart after all, I see," said Nightshade.

Jim wanted to cry, but he blinked back the tears. If he was to be killed, he would not let death find him bawling like an infant. He glanced around, aware now that he had dropped the mail pouch when the horse bucked him off. He spotted it lying on the ground a few feet from him. It might as well have been a hundred miles away.

Nightshade went on, "I don't want to kill you, son, so don't try anything like that again. Now reach across your body with your right hand, take that other gun out of its holster, and toss it away."

Jim did as he was told. Any other course would lead to certain death. When Jim was disarmed, Nightshade stepped back and motioned to him with the barrel of the pistol. "Get up," said the outlaw. "I don't like talking to a man unless he's on his feet."

That was another mistake Nightshade had made, Jim thought: the bandit had taken him for a man, instead of for the craven coward he actually was. But Jim pushed himself to his feet anyway and faced the black-clad desperado. "What are you going to do to me?" he asked.

"Nothing, if you cooperate." Nightshade gestured toward the walls of the pass behind Jim. "Take a look up there."

Warily, Jim turned his head, reluctant to take his attention off Nightshade. Glancing up where the outlaw had pointed, he felt his blood turn even colder as he saw the men stationed on each side of the pass, rifles in hand. He had ridden straight into a trap, and from the first, there had been no escape.

"All I want is the pouch," said Nightshade. "You're free to go."

Jim found that hard to believe, but he realized how foolish it would be to argue with the hooded outlaw. He stood very still while Nightshade collected the mail pouch from the ground and then strode over to the Appaloosa.

"Stay away from your guns until we're gone," commanded the outlaw. "You'll be watched, so don't get any ideas about trying some trick. After we're gone, wait fifteen minutes before you leave the pass. Once that time has gone by, you can go ahead to Moss City or turn back to Flat Rock; it doesn't make any difference to me."

Jim felt he had to say something. He could not just stand here and let Nightshade ride off in triumph. He swallowed nervously, then declared, "You won't get away with this."

"You think not?" asked Nightshade as he settled into the saddle. "I've been in these mountains for many, many years, and no lawman, alone or with a posse, has come close to finding me, lad. What makes you think this time will be any different?"

"You've robbed the Pony Express this time."

To Jim's surprise, Nightshade threw back his head and laughed. "The Pony Express!" echoed the bandit. "A collection of boys who answer to pencil pushers from back East! I doubt that I have much to fear from the Pony Express!"

As much as the scornful words galled Jim, he had to admit to himself that Nightshade was probably right. There was very little law in this territory, other than what people made for themselves, and Nightshade's long reign in these mountains was adequate evidence that he was more than a match for anyone who might come after him. Jim stood, bitterness filling his mouth, as Nightshade wheeled the Appaloosa around and urged it into a gallop.

In a matter of seconds, Nightshade topped the slope at the head of the pass and disappeared over it. Jim took a deep breath and looked up again at the stone walls above him. The rifle-wielding men he had seen there earlier were gone as well, seemingly vanished into solid stone. No doubt there were footpaths up there, trails that led further into the mountains, but only Nightshade and his men would know where to find them. Anyone else would soon be lost in the maze of jagged rocks.

Jim drew a deep breath, and then a shudder went through him, making him tremble to his very core. He had come remarkably close to death. At any moment those hidden riflemen could have gunned him down. They were all excellent shots, or they would not be riding with Nightshade. He could have died without ever knowing where the shots that killed him had come from.

Instead, when he tried to escape, Nightshade must have signaled his men to hold their fire, otherwise he would be dead now. The boss outlaw had decided to handle things himself. As fast as Rusty was, Jim figured that Nightshade would have been able to run him down on the Appaloosa, had the roan not bucked him off. It was chilling to think just how tightly the trap had sprung around him, and it was only a whim on Nightshade's part that had allowed him to survive.

Jim forced his feet to move. He picked up his Colts and slid them back into their holsters after checking to make certain dirt had not fouled their barrels. Little good the weapons had done him, he thought. He looked back down the trail and saw Rusty waiting some yards off, regarding him with a rather walleyed look. Jim called to the roan, hoping that the sound of his voice would calm the horse. If Rusty took it in his head to gallop off, Jim would be facing a long walk back to Flat Rock.

That would be fitting, he thought with a humorless grunt. He had entered Flat Rock the first time on foot and in disgrace. How appropriate now to return the same way.

He approached the roan carefully and a few moments later had the reins in his hands once again. When he mounted, Rusty danced skittishly underneath him for a short time, then settled down. Jim rested his hands on the saddlehorn and leaned forward, trying to decide what to do next.

Some men might have considered trying to follow Nightshade so that they could try to recover the mail pouch. Jim did not dwell on that possibility; he knew he'd have no chance of success. He could go back to Flat Rock, but then the rider waiting for the pouch in Moss City would not know what had happened. It would be better to go ahead, Jim decided, to continue with his run and pass the news of the robbery on to the Pony Express agent in Moss City. Then he could return to Flat Rock.

Such a course of action would postpone having to face Grayson and Deakins and the others. They would learn of his failure soon enough. When he judged that fifteen minutes had passed, he nudged Rusty into motion and rode through the pass, the roan moving at a trot now, rather than a gallop. No longer was there any hurry.

When he reached the other side of the pass, he could see the landscape falling away in front of him, the trail winding down from the heights to the foothills and on to the plains beyond. His eyes may have deceived him, but he thought he caught a glimpse through the hazy distance of Moss City itself, some fifteen miles away.

Another ten miles beyond that, Jim recalled, was Harker City, the home of Virginia Rawlings. He found himself wondering about her. Was she young or old, a schoolteacher, a store clerk, a seamstress? All he knew for certain was that she was unmarried; the letter had been addressed to Miss Virginia Rawlings.

As he rode on, that letter took on added significance in his mind. He had no idea what else had been in the mail pouch, but he had seen and held the letter for Virginia Rawlings, had felt the texture of the envelope with his fingertips. More than anything else, he realized, that letter was a symbol of his failure. It might have contained something important, something that would have changed the life of the woman to whom it was addressed. Now she would never know, because Jim McReady had let a bandit steal it.

What had Nightshade hoped to find in the mail pouch, Jim wondered? Some of the envelopes might have contained money, but surely not enough to make it worthwhile to steal the pouch. It was likely that the robbery was more for show than anything else, one more way to remind everyone for twenty-five miles on either side of the Prophets that Nightshade still ruled supreme in this territory. No one was safe from him, the outlaw seemed to be saying, and no one could escape his hand should he choose to raise it against them, not even the Pony Express.

Jim reached the foothills and rode through them, then increased Rusty's pace as the trail leveled out and led across the prairie. He was going to be late arriving in Moss City, and the rider and the station manager there would surely be concerned about him.

When he cantered down the main street of the settlement a little more than half an hour later, everyone on the sidewalks turned to stare at him—or at least it seemed that way to Jim. In reality, he supposed, most of the citizens were not paying any attention to him. It was not his imagination, though, when he saw several individuals emerge from the local office of the Central Overlands Express and come running toward him.

"Are you the rider from Flat Rock?" asked the man who led the small contingent. His narrow, bearded features wore a concerned expression.

"That's right," Jim told him, reining in and bringing Rusty to a halt.

"You're late. And—My God! Where's the pouch?"

"Nightshade stopped me," said Jim. "He took the pouch."

A curse ripped from the mouth of the man, who was obviously the Moss City Pony Express agent. He drove a fist against the palm of his other hand and repeated, "Nightshade! I was hoping he wouldn't bother us, since there hasn't been any trouble from him so far."

"Are you all right, kid?" asked one of the other men, from the looks of him Bob Lind's opposite number. He was gangling and roughly dressed.

Jim nodded. "Nightshade said he didn't want to hurt me; he just wanted the mail pouch."

"And you just handed it over?" demanded the agent angrily.

Jim took a deep breath and kept a tight rein on his own temper. "I tried to stop him. All it got me was bucked off my horse. Nightshade had some of his men with him, and I'm lucky I wasn't killed."

"Reckon that's true enough," said the horse handler. "Well, son, I'm sorry Nightshade picked you for his first strike against the Pony Express. Maybe if we're lucky it'll be his last."

"It was my first ride, too," added Jim, feeling a sick ball of despair in his stomach.

"You'll be lucky if it's not your last," snapped the agent. "The company isn't going to be happy when they hear about this. Our reputation is going to depend on fast, safe delivery of the mail entrusted to us."

Jim knew that as well as any of them, and he did not appreciate the agent's attitude. Maybe the man thought he could have done better if it had been him facing Nightshade's gun. Somehow, Jim doubted that would have been the case.

Passersby had heard the mention of Nightshade's name, and a crowd was beginning to gather as the word was passed that the famed outlaw had struck again. Townspeople ran up, and demanded to know the details of the robbery, but Jim did not feel like repeating them. He slipped down from the saddle and led the roan toward a livery stable beside the Express office, intent on getting Rusty some food and water after the hard ride. To do so, he had to push past several of the citizens, and he was the recipient of more than one resentful glance, but he ignored them.

A little time and distance had done nothing to ease the anger and guilt he felt over allowing himself to become another in a long line of Nightshade's victims. There had to be something he could do to ease his burgeoning emotions.

Again he thought about Virginia Rawlings, and as he stood by and watched a wizened hostler give grain to the roan, an idea occurred to him: if Miss Rawlings was expecting the letter that had been stolen, then surely she would be greatly puzzled when it failed to arrive. Jim was the only one who knew that it had been in the stolen pouch; the Pony Express would not be able to notify her of its loss. Of course, everyone else who had mail addressed to them in that pouch was facing the same situation. Still, there was nothing Jim could do about them; but he knew the name and address of Virginia Rawlings.

He would go to her and tell her about the robbery and the loss of the letter intended for her. The decision came to him abruptly, but he sensed the rightness of it. By all rights, he should return to Flat Rock and tell Grayson what had happened; if he went on to Harker City to see Miss Rawlings instead, he might well lose his job.

He was willing to risk that, he realized, in order to set things right. Confessing his failure would not recover the stolen letter, naturally, but at the very least, he could apologize. Besides, the extra ride over to Harker City would postpone the moment when he would have to face Grayson, Deakins, and his fellow riders.

A weary smile tugged at his mouth. The decision he had reached was not completely satisfactory, but at least he would be taking action for a change.

He walked to the door of the stable as Rusty drank from a water trough. The young man glanced up at the sun, squinting as he tried to estimate how much daylight was left. There should be time to reach Harker City before nightfall, he decided. He'd never been over the road to the west of Moss City, but it ought to be simple enough to find the other settlement. He would allow Rusty a few more moments of rest, then they would get started.

Jim's belly reminded him that he had not eaten since breakfast, having been too nervous at noon because of his upcoming ride to consume any lunch. He did not want to wait long enough to get a meal here, however. There would be time enough for that after he had seen Virginia Rawlings and broken the bad news to her.

Then would come the long ride home, the journey back to disgrace.

TEN

Weariness had a firm grip on Jim's muscles by the time he reached Harker City. Although he was becoming more accustomed all the time to being in the saddle, today he had spent even more hours on horseback than usual. The ride from Flat Rock to Moss City had been tiring enough; the added distance to Harker City had pushed him to the brink of exhaustion.

The roan was tired, too. Jim could tell that by Rusty's plodding gait as the horse entered the settlement. Harker City was more substantial than either Flat Rock or Moss City. It was nearly as large, in fact, as Cavassos, on the other side of the mountains. More than a dozen streets intersected the main boulevard through the center of town, and several roads paralleled that thoroughfare. As Jim entered the town on the main trail from the east, the last remaining edge of the setting sun slipped below the horizon. The journey had taken somewhat longer than he'd estimated. His unfamiliarity with the trail had delayed him when the road split and he had taken the wrong fork for several miles before it abruptly turned due south, which he knew was the wrong direction. Retracing his route to the other branch of the trail had taken quite a bit of time.

Lanterns were being lit in most of the buildings Jim passed. Ahead of him, he saw that the central area of town contained several substantial structures of two and three stories. The houses along the road were for the most part well-kept frame structures, freshly whitewashed behind lawns that were neatly clipped and bordered by flowerbeds. In a few more weeks, as spring advanced, those beds would be full of riotous color from the blooming flowers.

A major north-south road ran through Harker City, Jim remembered from the maps he had studied, in addition to the east-west route which he had taken. No wonder the settlement had grown rapidly. Not only that, but the land around the town was already lush with grass, even this early in the season. This was good country for farmers and ranchers and merchants.

Signposts had been erected on the corners of the streets he passed, and he strained his eyes to read them in the growing darkness. So far he had not found Dubins Street, where Virginia Rawlings lived. If he had not located it by the time he reached the center of town, he would stop and ask for directions.

The sidewalks were not crowded with pedestrians, he discovered a few minutes later as he arrived at the business district. At this hour of the day, most people were probably at home having their dinner. Still, there were a few people around, and as Jim reined in, he hailed one of them.

"Excuse me, sir," said Jim. A townsman in a gray suit and soft felt hat came over to the edge of the sidewalk in response to his call. "Could you tell me where to find Dubins Street?"

"Dubins Street," repeated the man, frowning slightly, as if strangers did not ask him for directions very often and the process puzzled him. "Who are you looking for, son?"

"Miss Virginia Rawlings, sir," replied Jim politely, even though he thought it was really none of this man's business.

"Oh. I see." There was a certain coldness in the man's voice now. "I know who you mean. Go two blocks south. You'll find Dubins Street down there."

Jim nodded, wondering what had come over the man. He said, "Thanks," then rode around the corner into the nearest cross street. He followed it for two blocks, then pulled up and studied the street sign. The fading light was so dim that he could barely make out the letters, but he saw that he had found Dubins Street. It ran east and west, like the main road. Unsure how the house numbers were laid out, he knew he would have to stop and ask for help again.

One of the nearby houses, a small bungalow with quite a bit of shrubbery in front of it, had a light burning in its front window. That looked promising, Jim decided, and he rode over to the dwelling. A sturdy-looking bush provided a place for him to tie Rusty's reins, and then he walked up a narrow path to the front porch. A couple of shallow steps led to the porch itself. Jim's bootheels rang on the planks as he went to the door and rapped sharply upon it.

For several moments, there was no response, and he was about to lift his hand and knock again when he heard a swift patter of footsteps on the other side of the panel. The knob rattled, and then the door swung open. "Yes? What is it?" came a sweet, clear, woman's voice.

Jim blinked as if he had been struck a blow in the face. He was looking at a young woman—a girl, really—about his own age, who was standing in the doorway with a quizzical expression on her lovely face. Soft hair the color of a ripe wheatfield framed her features and fell beyond her shoulders. The glow from a lantern somewhere behind her struck highlights in her hair and seemed to create a golden halo around her head. She wore a blue dress with a demurely high neckline, but it was tight enough to reveal the slender curves of her lithe figure. Jim thought she was just about the prettiest girl he had ever seen.

He realized he was standing there staring when her small, noncommital smile threatened to turn into a puzzled frown. Giving a little shake of his head, he found his voice and said, "Excuse me, ma'am. I'm looking for a Miss Virginia Rawlings. Do you happen to know where she lives?"

"A Miss Virginia Rawlings," repeated the girl, and Jim wondered if everybody in this town had to say everything twice. She went on, "I wasn't aware there was more than one Virginia Rawlings here in Harker City."

"Then you do know her?"

"Indeed I do," nodded the girl. "Do you mind if I

ask what your business is with her?"

Everybody in Harker City was definitely nosy, Jim thought. He did not want to offend this fetching young woman, but he was tired and hungry and still plagued by the guilt he felt from the robbery. In a sharper tone than he had intended, he said, "I'm afraid it's personal. Now, can you tell me where to find Miss Rawlings?"

"Of course I can," she said, her own tone cool and somewhat mocking. "Fate has led you to the right house, sir. I am Virginia Rawlings."

Jim's eyes narrowed in surprise. He had been all too aware of the fact that all he knew about Virginia Rawlings was her name and address, but somehow he had never expected her to be so young and pretty. He'd have thought that she was an older woman, a spinster. He wanted to ask this girl if she was sure she was Virginia Rawlings, but he realized the ridiculousness of that idea.

"Now you have the advantage of me, sir," continued the girl. "You know who I am, but I have no earthly idea who you are."

Jim realized suddenly that he still had his hat on. He reached up quickly and removed it, clutching the brim tightly. "My name is Jim McReady," he said. "I ride for the Pony Express, over at Flat Rock."

Immediately, a smile lit up her face. "The Pony Express! Of course. I'm expecting a letter. Have you come to deliver it? I didn't think the riders did that personally." The words bubbled out of her mouth as her excitement grew.

Jim's heart plummeted. What he was most afraid of had come to pass! Virginia Rawlings had indeed been expecting the letter, and eagerly awaiting it. Now he had to tell her that it would never arrive, that it had in fact been stolen by Nightshade.

She was looking at him with anticipation now, and he struggled to find the words. "The Pony Riders don't deliver the mail personally," he finally began. "But I felt like I had to come and see you. There was some . . . trouble on today's run."

"Trouble?" said the girl, and Jim wanted to shout at her to stop repeating everything he said. This was the most annoying town . . .

He caught himself and took a deep breath, realizing that his anger and impatience was directed much more at himself than at this girl or any of the other inhabitants of Harker City. He went on, "I happen to know that the letter addressed to you was put in the mail pouch at Flat Rock."

"Well, where is it, then?"

"I . . . I don't know. The pouch was stolen from me up in the Prophets."

"Stolen?" Suddenly, the girl looked devastated. "I don't understand. How could it be stolen?"

"Nightshade stopped me," said Jim simply.

Virginia Rawlings sagged against the side of the door, and Jim took a quick step forward, thinking that she was about to faint and that he should try to catch her. The girl recovered her balance, however, and with a hand tightly gripping the doorframe for support, she said grimly, "So Nightshade stole the mail pouch?"

"That's right. Believe me, Miss Rawlings, I'm sorry—"

She turned away, a sob choking in her throat. Jim did not know what to say, so he stood there in awkward silence for long moments, unwilling to just turn and walk away after breaking what was evidently horrible news to her. That solitary sob was the only sound that escaped from her, but from time to time her shoulders would quiver, as if great tremors were shaking her inside.

Finally, she turned her face back toward him, and he could see tears shining on her cheeks. She forced her lips into a smile and said, "I'm being a . . . a terrible hostess. You must be tired after that long ride. Why don't you come in?"

Some instinct told Jim to turn and run to his horse, then gallop away as fast as the roan could carry him. But that would only do further injury to the girl's feelings, and he could not bring himself to be responsible for such. He nodded and said, "All right. That would be nice."

The words rang hollowly in his ears as she moved back to allow him to enter. Jim swallowed and stepped through the doorway, finding himself in a small, neat foyer. Virginia Rawlings shut the door and said, "Come into the parlor. I'll fix us some tea."

Jim wanted to protest that it was not necessary for her to go to so much trouble, but then he thought that perhaps such a mundane activity would take her mind off her loss, whatever it had been. He had expected her to be upset about the letter being stolen, but the depth of her reaction had taken him by surprise. It was almost as if he had told her that someone dear to her had died.

She ushered him into a parlor that, probably like all the other rooms in the bungalow, was a bit smaller than usual. It was furnished with a short sofa, an armchair, and a pair of fragile tables, each with a vase of dried flowers. On one wall was a gilt-framed portrait of a stern-featured, distinguished-looking man. The sofa and armchair were a bit threadbare, as was the rug on the floor.

But the room and all its furnishings were spotless. Clearly, Virginia Rawlings did not have a great deal of money, but she took good care of the few things she did possess.

Jim was curious who the man in the picture was, but now was not the time to ask questions, he sensed. There was a faint resemblance between Virginia Rawlings and the subject of the portrait; where they father and daughter, perhaps? He kept that thought to himself as she told him to have a seat. He chose the armchair, feeling a bit awkward about sitting there in his dusty riding clothes.

"Have you eaten?" asked Virginia.

"Uh, no, ma'am, I haven't," replied Jim, the words coming out of his mouth before he could think to lie. Surely she did not intend to prepare food for him, not as upset as she was. Her features were still pale and marked by the wet streaks of tears.

"I'll bring the tea first," she said, "then see what I can find in the pantry."

"That's really not necessary, ma'am—" began Jim in protest.

"Nonsense. You must be famished after that long ride. And please . . . stop calling me ma'am. I daresay I'm not any older than you. My friends call me Jinny."

With that, she disappeared from the parlor. Jim leaned back against the cushions of the armchair and took a deep breath. This visit had certainly not gone as he'd anticipated. He heard a few slight noises as Virginia Rawlings moved around in the kitchen, but those were the only sounds in the house.

Did she live here alone? She seemed awfully young for that. On the other hand, Jim supposed, he had been on his own for years, and he was roughly the same age. Of course, Virginia—Jinny, he reminded himself—was a girl, but perhaps these Western girls became more self-reliant at an earlier age than did the females back East. The rugged conditions of the frontier seemed to make everyone grow up a little quicker.

Jim leaned over and dropped his hat on the floor beside the chair. He had just straightened up again when Jinny reappeared, bearing a tray that contained a pot of tea and two cups. She placed the tray on one of the spindle-legged tables and poured the steaming brew, then brought one cup over to Jim.

"Thank you," he said as he took the tea from her. "This is mighty nice of you."

"Not at all. You're the one who's nice, Mr. McReady." She took her own cup of tea and sat down on the sofa. "After all, you didn't have to take the trouble to come and tell me what had happened. You could have left me wondering, and that would have been awful."

"Oh, yes, I suppose so." He still did not feel qualified to discuss the situation in depth, since he had no idea what had been in the envelope that bore her name. As he glanced up at her now, he saw that she had dried her face, and although she continued to be a bit pale, she looked as if she was over the worst of the shock.

"I have some cornbread, some fresh butter, and some beans and bacon," said Jinny. "Does that sound all right to you?"

Jim had to grin as his stomach reacted to her words. "It sounds more than all right, ma'am . . . I mean, Jinny. It sounds downright wonderful."

She smiled back at him. "I put the beans on the stove to heat. I hadn't eaten yet myself, so I'm glad you arrived when you did, Mr. McReady. Eating alone can be so . . . unpleasant."

He sipped the tea. It was hot and strong and good. He said, "If I'm going to call you Jinny, you should call me Jim."

"All right," nodded the girl. "I really appreciate what you've done, Jim."

This was insane, he thought behind his smile. He had allowed a bandit to steal something that was obviously quite important to her, yet she was thanking him for his consideration and feeding him a meal. Jinny Rawlings must be a very special girl indeed.

Since coming West, he had barely spoken to any females, let alone shared a parlor and tea with anyone as young and lovely and vibrant as Jinny. He felt as if he had wandered into a stream that seemed placid and slow-moving on top only to find that it contained strong, unpredictable currents beneath its surface.

Even back East, his dealings with women had been sporadic. There were girls who would allow a boy to sample her favors in return for money, of course, but Jim's coins had always been too limited for him to patronize these woman except on rare occasions. He knew a little about what passed between a man and a woman in bed, but his experience in parlors was nonexistent. Besides, it was evident just from looking at Jinny Rawlings that she was a lady, as different as could be from the slatterns he had known in the past.

The silence in the room as these thoughts went through his head was becoming awkward. He swallowed and said,

"I'm really sorry about what happened, Jinny. If there had been any way to prevent it . . ." He let his voice trail off as she began to shake her head.

"I've heard a great deal about Nightshade," she said. "Everyone in this territory knows about him. I . . . I'm just glad you weren't hurt, Jim."

He sensed that inside, her emotions were still in turmoil. She was keeping herself tightly under control. It had to be a strain for her, and his presence here might be making it worse, since she obviously felt she had to extend hospitality to him. It might be better if he got out of here.

But when he leaned forward in his chair, she said quickly, "You're not leaving, are you? You haven't eaten yet."

"No," said Jim, sitting back. "No, I'm not leaving." He had seen the sudden flare of panic in her eyes when she thought he was going. He had also seen how blue those eyes were, like the sky over the mountains on a summer day.

"The food should be hot by now," said Jinny as she stood up. "Come along into the dining room."

Jim followed her, carrying his cup of tea. The dining room was practically filled by a table covered with a snowy white cloth. The girl told him to have a seat, then went into the kitchen. She came back a moment later with two plates of beans, bacon, and cornbread, placed one of them in front of Jim, then took a seat on the opposite side of the table. Picking up her fork, she said, "Isn't this nice?"

"Yes, ma'am," said Jim, forgetting to call her Jinny. "Real nice."

She dropped her fork against her plate with a clatter and let out a wail like a lost soul in torment.

"Good Lord!" exclaimed Jim.

Jinny kept crying, ignoring her food as she buried her face in her hands and sobbed inconsolably. Jim looked wildly around the room, but there was no escape, no hope of assistance. He was alone with this weeping young woman, and he would have to deal with her, find some way to comfort her in her sorrow. The strain of controlling her emotions had finally proved to be too much for her, he supposed.

He got to his feet and started slowly around the table, intending to pat the girl on the back and assure her that everything would be all right, but before he could reach her she gave another soul-rending cry. Jim hesitated, grimacing, then summoned up his courage and tried again. This was almost as bad as going up against Nightshade, he thought.

Gingerly, he touched the girl's shoulder. "I'm sorry, Jinny," he said. "I'm really sorry. Is . . . is there anything I can do to help you?"

"The . . . the letter," mourned Jinny. "I never dreamed it would be lost!"

"I know I should have done more." Fresh guilt stabbed into Jim's heart with every sob that came from Jinny. "I should have stopped that blasted outlaw somehow!"

She kept crying. Jim glanced at his food, now growing cold on the plate. It seemed that all day, things had been conspiring to keep him from eating, but the appetite he'd had earlier was gone now, driven away by Jinny's misery.

"It was so important," she said, her voice muffled somewhat by her hands, which were still over her face. "S-so much was depending on me getting that letter." A fresh round of sobs wracked her as her head drooped even lower.

Jim's breath was coming faster now as Jinny's grief plunged him further into despair. Suddenly, it no longer mattered as much that he had failed Grayson and Bob Lind and Deakins; all that was important now was that he had inadvertently dealt a crushing blow to this young woman. From the looks and sounds of things, it would be a long time before she recovered from that blow.

He knew he could not stand that, could not stand the thought of knowing that he'd been responsible for such a tragedy. Without thinking about the full implications of his words, he leaned closer to her and said firmly, "I'll get it back."

The promise seemed to take a moment to penetrate Jinny's brain. Then she slowly lifted her head and regarded him with a surprised, wet-eyed stare. "What did you say?"

"I said I'd get it back," repeated Jim. "That letter, I mean." He took a deep breath. "I'll get it back from Nightshade . . . or I'll die trying."

ELEVEN

For a long moment, she regarded him in stunned silence, then found her voice and said tearfully, "No, I . . . I couldn't ask that of you."

"You didn't ask me," Jim reminded her. "It was my idea, and I'll say it again: I'm going to recover that letter for you."

She took a small white handkerchief from a pocket of her dress and dabbed at the tears in her blue eyes. "That would be so good of you, Jim. But I'm afraid it's impossible!"

"Why should it be impossible?" Now that he had made the rash promise, he felt he had no choice but to defend it. "I know who stole the mail pouch. All I have to do is find Nightshade and steal it back from him."

Jinny smiled; even with her face and eyes red from crying, Jim thought she was beautiful. "You don't know what you're saying," she insisted. "I was raised around here. Were you?"

"Well . . . no." He supposed his time in the West had lessened his Eastern accent to the point where it was not easily detected.

"I grew up on stories about Nightshade. It was about the same time I was born, you see, that people around here first began to hear of him."

Jim recalled the tale old Deakins had told him about how Nightshade had first appeared in this area. Nightshade himself had indicated when talking to Jim that he had been roaming the Prophet Mountains for a long time. Jinny was right; she undoubtedly knew more about Nightshade than he did.

But he had met the outlaw. He knew that Nightshade was only flesh and blood, like any other man. He was no ghostly apparition, no mysterious being with supernatural powers. Nightshade was a man. He could be tracked down and defeated.

Those were heady thoughts for someone like him, Jim knew, but Jinny's despair had spurred him on to utter the pledge. There was a good chance he would fail in this self-appointed quest, he thought, but at least he would die trying to help someone else. That was a worthy goal, wasn't it?

But how much better it would be if by some quirk of fate he succeeded. His whole life might be changed.

Those thoughts raced through his mind in a matter of instants. He said, "I know it'll be difficult, but I have to try, Jinny. Now that I know how much that letter means to you, I *have* to try to get it back for you."

She sniffed back a final sob and said, "That's so sweet of you, Jim. I'm just afraid that no one can help me now. And this was my father's last chance!"

Jim stiffened. "Your father?" Was she talking about the man in the painting that hung on the parlor wall? "You mean the letter has something to do with your father?"

"It's not really a letter," admitted Jinny. "It's a map."

"A map?" Whatever made the citizens of Harker City repeat everything that was said to them had to be contagious, Jim thought fleetingly, because he was certainly doing the same thing now.

Jinny nodded, her intense blue eyes meeting his gaze. "A map that shows the way to a fortune," she said. "Sit down, and I'll tell you about it."

Jim reached around the table, pulled his chair closer to hers, and sat, ready to hear the tale.

And quite a tale it was, he discovered over the next half-hour. Jinny's voice, weakening at times from the strain of telling the painful story, strengthening at others, transported him back eight years to a time when she had been eleven years old. Harker City was smaller then, but already it had become a growing, prosperous town. That prosperity was reflected in its bank, the president of which was one Samuel Rawlings—Jinny's father.

The bank not only held the savings of many of Harker City's citizens; it also regularly served as the depository of payrolls for ranches in the surrounding area, as well as for some of the mines in the Prophets. On a hot night in June of that year, the bank vault had held over a hundred thousand dollars.

That evening, a town constable had spotted someone slipping out the rear door of the bank, and when the lawman challenged him, the lurker had turned unexpectedly and opened fire with a pistol. The constable was gunned down, three shots grouped nicely in the center of his chest. The gunfire drew attention, but by the time someone arrived to see what the commotion was, the constable was dead and whoever had killed him was long gone. An investigation of the scene quickly discovered that the back door of the bank was unlocked, and a check of the vault showed that it had been cleaned out.

There was no sign that any locks had been tampered with, and the vault had been opened by someone who knew the combination. That fact pointed directly at Samuel Rawlings. So did the fact that the balls dug out of the constable's chest were .31-caliber, and everyone in Harker City knew that Sam Rawlings carried a .31-caliber Baby Dragoon and was expert in its use. The sheriff and a group of incensed citizens who were well aware that the thief had gotten away with their savings paid a visit to the house of the bank president, the same house in which Jim and Jinny now sat as she related the story.

Jim could hear the remembered horror all too plainly in her voice as she continued. She told him how she'd watched as the sheriff and the angry townspeople had come into the parlor and demanded to know where her father had been that evening. As it happened, Samuel Rawlings had just recently arrived himself, as he freely admitted. That was confirmed by the Widow Patterson, who sometimes stayed with young Jinny, especially when her father had to be away at night. Jinny's mother had died in childbirth, leaving Rawlings to raise his daughter alone.

When one of the citizens lost his temper and accused the banker of robbing his own institution, Rawlings reacted in stunned surprise. Insisting that he knew nothing about the affair, he wanted to rush down to the bank, but the sheriff stopped him. After explaining how the rear door had been opened and the vault looted, once again the lawman demanded to know where Rawlings had been.

Samuel Rawlings had merely glanced once at his daughter and then stubbornly refused to answer. An outcry arose from the mob, as they howled that Rawlings should be thrown in jail or maybe even strung up from the nearest tree if he refused to say where he had hidden the stolen money. The Widow Patterson had hustled Jinny out of the room at that point, although she could still hear the angry cries of the crowd. Terrified and sobbing, the adolescent girl had watched from the window of her room as her father was taken away.

At that moment, she had not been sure she would ever see him again.

Now, as she sat at the dining room table eight years later and told the story to Jim McReady, she drew a deep breath and said, "I found out later that Father had . . . been with a woman that evening. He refused to admit it out of respect for my sensibilities, and then later he wouldn't divulge her identity for fear of ruining her reputation. My father is a stubborn man, Jim."

"What happened?" he asked as he leaned forward in his chair, his own ordeal of earlier in the day forgotten now in light of the tragic tale Jinny was spinning. He knew her father could not have been hanged; she had spoken of him earlier as if he were still alive.

"The sheriff asked Father to produce his gun, to determine whether or not it had been fired. Father didn't have it. He had lost it several days earlier, he said, and he hadn't gotten around to replacing it yet."

That excuse sounded lame to Jim even now, but he did not comment on it. He let Jinny proceed.

"Later they came back and searched the house." She swallowed. "They found five thousand dollars hidden in my father's room. He wouldn't say how he had come by it or what it was doing there. The official theory was that he hid the rest of the loot from the bank robbery. He never told them where it was, of course, because he didn't know. He was innocent."

Even having known Jinny for such a short time, that conclusion was what Jim would have expected from her. Of course she would believe in her father's innocence; she would be incapable of anything else.

"He was put in jail anyway. There was talk before the trial of lynching him. Everyone seemed to forget that he was one of the town's leading citizens, that he had helped to found it and had helped it grow. All they could see was that their money was gone, and they had to have someone to blame for the loss."

From what Jim had heard so far, Samuel Rawlings sounded like the most likely culprit. Again he kept the thought to himself.

"The sheriff and the judge kept things from getting out of hand, though. The trial was over quickly. Father was found guilty of bank robbery and murder, and he was sentenced to . . . to life imprisonment." Jinny's voice quivered as she pronounced the words. "He's still in the penitentiary. I think the judge gave him life instead of ordering him hanged, in hopes that someday Father would reconsider and reveal where he hid the money. That's ridiculous, of course."

"But you said the letter you were expecting was really a map," said Jim. "Did you mean a map showing where that loot was hidden?"

Jinny nodded. "That's right. My uncle was sending it to me."

"Your uncle? What does your uncle have to do with any of this?"

"It's quite simple, really. He's the one who actually robbed the bank and killed that constable."

Jim blinked in astonishment, wondering what twist this tale would take next.

As Jinny explained it, her uncle, Baxter Rawlings, had formerly been an employee at the bank and knew its routines, including the days on which a considerable amount of money was likely to be in the vault. Tired of being under the thumb of his older brother, Baxter had decided to leave Harker City and strike out on his own, but a week before the robbery, he had returned to pay a short visit to his brother and niece. It was then, Jinny speculated, that he had stolen Samuel Rawlings' gun and made a wax impression of the key to the rear door of the bank.

"What about the combination to the vault?" asked Jim. "Would he have known that?"

Jinny nodded. "Father didn't change the combination when Uncle Bax left the bank. He should have, but it never occurred to him that his own brother might someday rob the place." The girl looked down at the table. "Uncle Bax had had a rough time of it. He'd opened several businesses that failed, and I suppose he thought robbing the bank was the only thing he could do other than crawl to my father and ask for his job back. The two of them had quarreled, you see, when Uncle Bax decided to leave in the first place."

The story was beginning to make sense to Jim. He said, "So you think your uncle robbed the bank and planned to let your father take the blame for it."

"I don't know about the last part of that. My father being blamed may have been a coincidence; I'm not sure Uncle Bax thought it through that far. But I'm certain he stole that money. He admitted he did."

"To whom?" asked Jim. "Did he go to the law?"

The girl shook her head. "No, he came here to see me a couple of months ago. I hadn't seen him since that visit just before the robbery. I . . . I almost didn't recognize him. He had become a gambler, and he had been drinking heavily for years. He was down on his luck, he said, but he wasn't looking for a handout."

"I should think not," said Jim sharply. "After all, didn't he have all that loot? Why would he need to gamble?"

"He had the money, all right," admitted Jinny with a slight smile. "But he couldn't bring himself to spend it. He told me he was the one who robbed the bank and that afterwards, he hid the loot. When he found out that my father had been blamed for the crime, though, his guilt wouldn't let him go back and get the money. He said he couldn't stand to touch it."

Jim stood up abruptly and began to pace back and forth. "But that's ridiculous!" he protested. "He felt so guilty about your father that he wouldn't use the stolen money, and yet he didn't come forward to admit his crime and save your father from prison!"

"You have to understand," said Jinny, looking up at him. "He was afraid. He didn't want to go to prison himself. Poor Uncle Bax didn't know what to do, so he did nothing except sink deeper and deeper into a bottle of whiskey."

Jim stopped, looked at her, and drew a deep breath. Yes, he supposed he *could* understand Baxter Rawlings. He knew what it was like to be afraid and confused, how easy it was to postpone a decision when making it would have meant only hardship and pain. And he realized he could not stand in judgment of the man. But there were still things he wanted to know.

"Why did your uncle come to you and tell you this story?"

Jinny's face became more solemn. "He . . . he was dying. He said he couldn't live with it on his conscience anymore, and he didn't want to die without people knowing the truth."

"So why didn't he tell you then where the money is hidden?"

"He wasn't sure how long he was going to live, and he didn't want his last days to be spent in jail. I . . . I had to respect his wishes. There was nothing else I could do. He promised that when he was . . . gone, he would see to it that I got the map showing where to find the money. Last week, I got a letter from a lawyer in Cavassos. Uncle Bax was dead, and the lawyer was handling his estate, although it didn't amount to much. He said that Uncle Bax had left a sealed envelope for me and that it would be sent on to me as soon as all the legal details were cleared up. I'm certain the map was in that envelope, Jim. It had to be."

If everything she'd already told him was true, thought Jim, then her conclusion concerning the map was logical enough. He said, "After your uncle was here, did you go to the law and tell them what he told you?"

"Who'd have believed me?" asked Jinny. "Without a legitimate confession from Uncle Bax, that story would sound like a wild effort on my part to free my father, wouldn't it?"

Jim had to admit that without any solid evidence to support it, the yarn was more than a little farfetched. A fortune in stolen money sitting untouched for eight years because the thief felt too guilty to spend it . . . an innocent man imprisoned for a crime he had not committed . . . a beautiful young girl's only hope of freeing her father snatched away by a mysterious masked bandit. . . . It was an incredible tale, Jim thought. But it was just incredible enough to be true.

"You were going to get the money and use it and the map drawn by your uncle as proof of your father's innocence, weren't you?" he asked.

Jinny nodded. "That's what I intended," she said. Fresh tears welled up in her eyes and spilled onto her cheeks. "But now there's no chance . . ."

"You've forgotten that I intend to recover that map for you," said Jim.

"But when Nightshade sees it, he may figure out what it leads to," protested Jinny. "At the very least, he may be curious enough to follow the map just to see what he'll find. Then he'll have the money and my father will never be free!"

"I'll just have to beat him to it," said Jim, all too aware as the words left his mouth that he had no idea how to go about such a quest. To keep his mind off that difficult question for the moment, he asked, "How did you live after your father was sent to prison? Surely you didn't stay here by yourself."

"The Widow Patterson moved in to look after me, since I was still a child. My father wouldn't explain what that five thousand dollars was doing in his room, so the court took it and gave it back to the bank, but Father had some other money saved up. It wasn't much, but it was enough for us to live on as long as we were careful. The house was ours, so I didn't have to worry about a place to live. There was talk of taking it and selling it to recover some more of the loss, but the judge wouldn't allow it as long as I was living here. I've been on my own since the widow died last year. It hasn't been easy, but I'm managing. A few of the townspeople have taken pity and helped out over the years, although most of them seem to look down on me." She shrugged. "To them, I'm just the daughter of the thief who nearly ruined the town."

For a long moment, there was silence. Jim did not know what to say to comfort her, but he was more determined than ever to find Nightshade and get that map . . . not only for her sake, he realized, although that was very important, but to redeem his own honor. He was not even going back to Flat Rock, he decided. He would buy some supplies and head into the mountains to begin his search. Deakins and Grayson would think he'd run away, but so be it. If he was successful in his mission, they would learn the truth later.

Evidently there was little that went on in the mountains that Nightshade did not know about. Perhaps the notorious bandit would come to him and make the task that much easier.

As if reading his mind, Jinny looked up and said urgently, "You can't go through with this, Jim. I appreciate the promise you made to me, but I release you from it. I don't want you risking your life for my sake."

"I'm not," Jim told her flatly. "I don't want Nightshade to think he can get away with holding up the Pony Express. I have my own reasons for wanting to catch up with him again." That was not the complete truth; her story had affected him deeply, and if he had not come here tonight, he probably would never have even entertained the idea of pursuing the outlaw. Jinny did not have to know that, though.

"But . . . but you're talking about Nightshade!"

"I know," said Jim, his tone much more calm than he really felt.

Jinny looked down at the table, and a brief look of regret crossed her face as she studied the food that had grown cold. Then her expression became more determined, and she pushed her chair back and stood up.

"Very well," she said. "If I can't talk you out of this, Jim, it seems like there's only one thing I can do."

Send me on the journey with your blessing, Jim thought, wondering suddenly what it would be like to slip his arms around this girl and kiss her. The very idea thrilled him, even though he had only just met her this evening.

Instead of coming into his embrace, however, Jinny turned and strode firmly to the door of a small closet. She opened it, reached inside, and turned around holding a carbine. Her long, slender fingers tightly clutched the breech and the wooden stock. Jim's eyes widened in surprise, and he could not stop himself from asking, "What are you going to do with *that?*"

"Why, it's simple," she said, smiling at him. "If you're going after Nightshade, I'm going with you."

TWELVE

For a moment, Jim stared at her in amazement. Then he began to shake his head. "That's impossible," he said.

"No more impossible than saying you'll track down Nightshade and take that map away from him," declared Jinny. "At any rate, who has a bigger stake in this, Jim McReady? Freeing my father from prison, not to mention restoring his good name, can't be accomplished without the stolen bank money. The only thing you want is to keep from being embarrassed in front of your friends."

Jim did not like to admit she was right, but try as he might, he could not come up with an argument against that point. Still, the idea of a girl going along with him into the mountains was ludicrous.

"It simply can't be done," he said. "I'll be living under rugged conditions—"

"I can take care of myself," she interrupted. "You won't have to spend a minute of your time worrying about me."

Jim knew better than that; if she accompanied him, he would doubtless spend *most* of his time worrying about her. "This is insane," he muttered. He turned, intending to walk to the door, get his hat from the parlor, and leave the house. He regretted missing the meal, but the food was already cold and he could always buy something to eat elsewhere in Harker City.

The unmistakable double click of the carbine's hammer being drawn back stopped him in his tracks.

Jim looked over his shoulder. Jinny had the heavy carbine trained on him, and although the barrel trembled slightly as her muscles strained to support the weight of the weapon, it looked menacing. Jim felt a jolt of fear and panic go through him, but then reason prevailed, and he said, "What good would it do to shoot me?"

Jinny sighed and let the gun sag until it was pointed toward the floor. "No good at all," she said dismally. "I just wanted to help. Nightshade hurt me when he stole that letter, just as he hurt you."

He understood the anger she felt. "I'm sorry, Jinny," he said quietly. "But even if you were up to living in the mountains, how would it look for the two of us to be traveling together like that? You have to think about your reputation."

"To Hades with my reputation!" The violent exclamation burst from her unexpectedly. "I told you the reputation I have now—the daughter of a thief. Do you think I care one whit about propriety when my father's freedom is at stake?" She stepped closer to Jim, her expression imploring him. "I've visited him from time to time in prison, and his existence there is eating him alive, Jim. He used to be a strong, vital man, but now he's pale and wasting away. He can't stand many more years behind bars. I'm his only chance!"

The depth of emotion in her plea touched him. He chewed his bottom lip and frowned in thought.

"Besides," Jinny went on, "you said yourself that you're not from around here. But I grew up in sight of the Prophets! I may not know my way around them very well, but I'd wager I know them better than you!"

He could not argue that point, either. His natural desire to protect her warred against the thought that if she came with him, he would have a great deal more time to get to know her. He was taken with her beauty and her spirited nature, and he felt an undeniable urge to become better acquainted with her. He supposed it would not hurt to let her accompany him at least part of the way . . .

"All right," said Jim, nodding. "If you're determined to go, I won't stand in your way. But you have to promise that when I say it's time for me to go on alone, you won't argue with me."

Jinny placed the carbine on the table and stepped forward impulsively to clasp his hands. As her smooth, cool fingers closed over his, she said, "I agree. You won't regret this, Jim."

"I hope not," he said dryly. "Anyway, if I didn't let you have your way, you'd probably follow along anyway."

She grinned mischieviously. "That's right."

"You do have a horse, don't you?"

"Of course I do," replied the girl. "A fine mare. She's been used to pull our wagon at times, but she's a good saddle horse, too."

"Answer just one more question for me . . . Would you have really shot me if I'd tried to walk out?"

"Not with an unloaded gun."

Jim sighed, shook his head, and returned her smile. There was nothing else he could do.

Jinny reheated the food, and they dined somewhat later than either had expected when they'd first sat down at the table. The girl talked eagerly of their plans. They would leave first thing in the morning, she decided, delaying only long enough to buy some supplies and provisions for their journey. Jim had a little money in his pocket, the remainder of the advance he had received from Leland Grayson, and Jinny also had some funds on hand. They would buy flour and sugar, some bacon, some jerky, and a sack of beans.

"Powder and shot," added Jim. "I've heard that there's game a-plenty in the Prophets, especially on the lower slopes. If we run out of food, I suppose we can live off the land."

Jinny nodded. "Are you a good shot?" she asked.

Jim shrugged. He did not want to admit that he had limited experience with guns. He thought he could pick up enough skill quickly enough to keep them in meat, if it proved necessary for him to do so.

Using his guns on a man . . . well, that was a different story.

So far he had devoted little thought to what he would do when they found Nightshade. First of all, they had to locate his stronghold, somewhere up there in those rugged heights. Once that had been accomplished, he told himself, he would figure out what to do next.

When they had both talked themselves out, Jim got to his feet. "I'd better be going," he said. "We'll both need to get some sleep if we're going to start early in the morning."

"Where are you going to sleep?" asked Jinny. "There are several hotels here in town, but we'll need your money for supplies."

She was right; he had not considered how deeply the price of a hotel room would cut into his funds. "I've been sleeping in a livery stable," he said after a moment. "Maybe I can find one here that'll take me in."

"Don't be ridiculous. You'll stay right here."

"Here?" He frowned. "In this house, with you?"

"And why not? You're a gentleman, aren't you?"

Truth be told, he had never considered the question. He had certainly never thought of himself as a gentleman, yet he had to admit that he would never do anything to hurt this astounding, sometimes frustrating, but nevertheless wonderful young woman. If that was what a gentleman was, he supposed he fit the definition.

Taking his silence for resistance, Jinny went on, "We're going to be staying together on the trail. I don't see how a night spent here under my roof could be any more damaging to my reputation . . . which I don't give a fig for, anyway."

"I suppose you're right," said Jim. "I can bunk on that sofa in the parlor just fine. I've slept in plenty of worse places. No offense meant, of course."

"None taken. I'll fetch you some bedding."

He would have gladly made do without any such fuss, but Jinny insisted on providing a pillow and some blankets. While she was doing that, he went outside and brought his horse around to the rear of the house, putting it in the small lean-to stable where Jinny's mare was kept. When Rusty was unsaddled, Jim gave the roan some grain from a pouch in his saddlebags, then pumped a bucket of water for the horse. Leaving the roan hobbled for the night, Jim went back into the house.

He helped Jinny clean up after the meal, and then she retired to her room while he went into the parlor. He took off his boots and gunbelt and blew out the lamp. As he stretched out on the sofa, she called sweetly from the bedroom, "Good night, Jim."

"Good night," he replied.

Staring up at the darkened ceiling as silence descended over the bungalow, Jim thought about everything that had happened since he arose that morning. Momentous events abounded; in fact, his whole life had changed. His first run as a Pony Express rider might well turn out to have been his last. He had faced death and was planning to do so again. And he had met a woman unlike any he had ever known.

Yes, it had been quite an unusual day, all right.

Jim's sleep was deep and surprisingly dreamless, considering everything that had happened to him. When he awoke in the morning, his muscles were sore and stiff from sleeping in a strange place, but he stood up, stretched, and rolled his shoulders until most of the achiness left him. A glance out the window of the parlor told him that dawn was not far off. Gray light was beginning to filter down over Dubins Street.

A soft footstep behind him made turn around. Virginia Rawlings had emerged from the doorway of her bedroom, and she greeted him with a smile as he faced her. "Good morning," she said.

"Mornin'," replied Jim, trying not to stare at her. She looked considerably different from how she had the last time he'd seen her.

Denim pants and a man's red-checked shirt had replaced the blue dress she had worn before. Instead of slippers, her feet were shod in boots. Her long blond hair was tucked up underneath a flat-crowned hat, and the strap was pulled tight under her defiant chin. She was as lovely as ever, Jim decided, but in a different way.

"You look like you're ready to ride," he went on.

"We wanted to get an early start," she reminded him. "I'm ready whenever you are. I've already eaten, but there's still biscuits and coffee in the kitchen."

Now that she mentioned it, he could smell the rich, dark aroma of the coffee. He asked her, "Did you sleep at all last night?"

Her smile was a bit rueful. "Maybe a little. I was too excited to sleep much. After being so badly disappointed when you said the map was lost, and then regaining some hope . . . Well, I couldn't stop thinking about it."

Maybe in all her thinking she had figured out how they should go about this task, Jim mused. Somebody needed to.

"I'll be ready to ride in a few minutes," he told her as he headed for the kitchen.

True to his word, by the time the sun was beginning to peek over the jagged tips of the mountains, the two of them were riding down Harker City's main street, the object of puzzled stares from the inhabitants who were already up and about. There were quite a few of these, as many of the stores opened early. Shopkeepers were on their way to their businesses, as were customers. Jim's face reddened as he overheard some of the comments being passed back and forth as they rode by. What Jinny had told him about not being held in high esteem by the townspeople was obviously true. They were talking about her almost as if she was a sort of soiled dove, though.

"Just ignore them," said Jinny, speaking quietly to Jim. "I told you before, I don't care what they think of me."

"You may not care, but it's not right for them to talk

about you that way," declared Jim. "I'd like to set them straight—"

"We have other enemies to fight, Jim," she gently reminded him. "Or have you forgotten about Nightshade?"

"I haven't forgotten," said Jim grimly. He doubted if he would ever forget Nightshade.

They reined to a halt in front of Harker City's largest general mercantile emporium, where they would probably be able to find everything they would need in the way of supplies for the journey. Jim swung down from the saddle and looped Rusty's reins over the hitching post, then reached over to help Jinny, only to discover that she had already dismounted and tied her mare to the rail. She gave him a smile and went eagerly up the steps to the porch of the establishment. Jim followed as she disappeared through the open double doors.

When they came out twenty minutes later, Jim was carrying two canvas bags full of supplies. He slung one of the bags over Rusty's back and tied the other to Jinny's mare. Jinny gave him a rather weak smile as they mounted up. Buying the provisions had taken all of the money they had. There was no turning back now.

They rode east, toward the Prophets. For a long while they traveled in silence, neither of them knowing what to say, now that they had embarked on this adventure. Jim's head was full of thoughts, however, most of them relating to how foolish it was for a girl and a drifting tramp to be heading into some of the most rugged territory in the West, on the trail of an outlaw who had gunned down countless men and thwarted every attempt to snare him for the better part of two decades. If either of them survived this quest, he thought, it would be a miracle, plain and simple.

Suddenly Jinny said, "Jim, are you worried?"

He wondered for an instant if she had somehow read his mind. Then, forcing a smile, he said, "Worried? Why should I be worried? This is all a lark to me."

"Then you've lost your wits," snapped Jinny. "Nightshade is a dangerous man."

"I know that," said Jim, his voice serious now. "Most people would say we're crazy to even be attempting such a thing. But what choice do we have?"

"You're right," said Jinny. "We don't have any choice."

"Of course, *you* could go back to Harker City and let me handle this chore by myself. The provisions would last twice as long that way."

"I should say not! I'm in this just as deeply as you, Jim McReady. We've been through all this before, last night."

He nodded and said, "Yes, we have. Forget it, Jinny. Anyway, I'm glad you're with me."

"You are?" She sounded somewhat surprised. "I thought that you regarded me as some sort of pest."

Jim looked over at her, meeting her deep blue eyes. "No," he said softly. "I don't think of you as a pest at all."

Jinny smiled but did not say anything, and for several minutes they rode along in silence again. The quiet now was peaceful, though, not tense, as it had been earlier. No matter what had come before, no matter what would come after, at this moment Jim was very glad to be riding along under a blue sky, between grassy fields dotted with wildflowers, with this young woman beside him.

Perhaps he really owed Nightshade a debt of gratitude, he thought, because if the legendary outlaw and his gang had not robbed him high in that mountain pass, he might never have met Virginia Rawlings.

THIRTEEN

It was late in the day when they heard the sudden thunder of hoofbeats ahead of them on the road. They had already passed through Moss City and were about halfway between that settlement and the foothills of the mountains. Jim hoped to make camp in those foothills tonight; they were moving much slower than he had over the same route the previous day, but that was to be expected. After all, Jinny was not a Pony Express rider, and he supposed he wasn't, either, not after everything that had happened.

Now, as the sound of approaching horses grew louder, he reined in and stood up in the stirrups, peering down the road. A cloud of dust was being kicked up by the passage of the oncoming riders. A more experienced hand, Jim thought, would probably have noticed the dust several minutes earlier. He was going to have to learn to keep his eyes open if he and Jinny were to have any chance of survival.

"Should we get off the road?" asked the girl, who had reined in beside him. "Or do you think this could be Nightshade and his gang?"

"Not likely," grunted Jim. "I know from the stories I've heard that they often venture out of the mountains to pull their robberies, but running into them like that, when we've just set off to find them, would be an incredible coincidence."

Jinny nodded in agreement. There was no point in leaving the road and trying to conceal themselves. The horsemen had already come into sight. There were at least twenty men in the group, and they were bearing down fast on the two young travelers.

Jim swallowed nervously. As the riders drew closer, he saw their high-crowned hats, the gunbelts fastened around their waists, the polished wooden stocks of carbines protruding from saddle sheaths. These men were well armed. Loaded for bear, Deakins would have called it. And from the taut expressions on their hard, angular faces, they were able and more than willing to use the weapons.

The riders kept coming until Jim thought nervously that they intended to trample right over him and Jinny. “But then the horsemen pulled their mounts to a stop, some ten feet from them. The man in the lead had his hand lifted in a gesture that commanded the others to halt. As the gentle breeze sweeping over the plains caught the cloud of dust and swept it away, the leader crossed his hands on his saddlehorn and leaned forward to scrutinize Jim and Jinny.

He was a big man, with brawny shoulders and a barrel chest. A thick black moustache drooped over his wide mouth. He wore leather chaps over denim pants, a white shirt, and a black leather vest. His hat was black as well. A Colt with walnut grips well polished from long use rode in his holster. He fixed dark, piercing eyes on the two young people.

This individual certainly looked menacing enough to be Nightshade unmasked, Jim thought, but he realized such could not be the case. This man was larger than the outlaw who had stolen the mail pouch. While a small man could make himself appear larger with the right outfit, it was much harder for a big man to conceal his bulk.

Abruptly, the man spoke. “What're you youngsters doin' out here on the road?” he rumbled.

“Riding,” replied Jim in a cool voice. He wanted to appear calm, even though he was not. These hard-bitten men made him feel decidedly inadequate, like the Eastern greenhorn he was.

“Hell, I can see that. Who are you, and where're you headed?”

Jim considered a moment before answering. The man did not seem like the type who would be satisfied with being told it was none of his business. And with all the men backing him up, he would be able to impose his will on anyone who crossed him. Finally, he told the truth—or part of it, at any rate.

"My name is Jim McReady. This is Miss Virginia Rawlings. We're headed for Flat Rock."

There, that was true enough. The direction in which they were proceeding *would* take them to Flat Rock, if they continued long enough.

The big man pushed his hat to the back of his head. "Goin' through the Prophets, eh?" he said. "Best be careful, boy. There's bad men in those mountains. We're huntin some of 'em ourselves. Rustlers hit my herd last night. By the way, I'm Owen Shelton . . ." he waved a hand at the other riders ". . . and these are some of my men. We've been out all day tryin' to find some sign of them thieves."

Jim relaxed slightly, and he could tell from a glance over at Jinny that she was less worried now, too. Shelton and his ranch crew meant them no harm.

"Do you think Nightshade stole your cattle?" asked Jinny. The same thought had occurred to Jim.

"Well, missy, I don't rightly know," replied Shelton. "I reckon it's possible. Don't ever recall Nightshade doin' any rustlin' before, but he's the only owlhoot that still operates in these parts. So he's probably to blame, all right. Don't matter to us who did it; when we catch up with them, we plan on stringin' 'em up. You seen anybody who might be the hombres we're lookin' for?"

Frontier justice was quick, rough, and final, thought Jim, and he was glad Owen Shelton was not after *him*. He said, "We haven't seen anyone driving cattle today, Mr. Shelton. So I'm afraid we can't help you."

Shelton shrugged his massive shoulders. "We'll find 'em," he said heavily, in a manner that allowed for no argument. "Come on, boys."

The rancher waved his riders forward, and Jim and

Jinny urged their horses to the side of the road to let the cowboys move past. When Shelton and his men were gone and the dust of their leave-taking had blown away, Jim said, "We'd better get moving again."

Jinny nodded and fell in beside him as he began riding toward the foothills. "Rustlers," mused the girl. "Mr. Shelton was right. As far as I can remember, Nightshade has never stolen cattle. Of course, when he first showed up in these parts, there weren't any cattlemen, just miners and farmers and fur trappers. The ranches have only been established in the last few years, although it's good land for raising cattle."

Jim looked over at her. "I thought you were a town girl," he commented. "How do you know so much about what goes on in the country?

She grinned. "Just because I live in town doesn't mean I can't keep my eyes and ears open. And Harker City has a newspaper, too, which prints stories about what's going on in the territory. It's not too difficult to keep up with things."

Once again, Jim thought that he was going to have to learn to be more observant. Jinny's slightly mocking words were proof of that.

They camped that night in the foothills, just as Jim had planned. He fashioned beds for them by wrapping pine boughs in blankets. In his earlier wanderings, he had heard men talk about doing this, and it proved surprisingly comfortable. The night was turning chilly as they rolled in their blankets following a meal of bacon, beans, and biscuits, and Jim hoped Jinny would be warm enough. That led him to thoughts of what it would feel like to hold her body against his, sharing their warmth, and as his body reacted, he turned away from her, reddening in shame even though the night was dark and she could have no idea what was going through his head.

Sleep was a long time coming to him that night.

In the morning, over cups of coffee and more biscuits,

Jinny looked across the small campfire at Jim and asked, "What are we going to do now?"

"Look for Nightshade," he said, even though he knew that was a very simplistic answer. "We'll ride on into the mountains and ask questions of everyone we encounter. Someone is bound to have an idea where his hideout is."

"What if we meet someone who is part of his gang?" asked Jinny. "We'll be revealing our plan if we ask too many questions."

Jim shook his head. "We *want* Nightshade to know we're looking for him. Like I said, if he comes to us, then he's done part of our job. All we'll have to do is take the map away from him and escape."

The girl looked intently at him for a long moment, then said, "You're either the bravest man I've ever seen, Jim McReady . . . or the most foolish."

He just grinned, but he wished he knew which of those two things was true.

Never had he thought of himself as brave. In fact, just the opposite was the case. He'd always considered himself a craven coward. The only things he'd ever done that might be considered courageous were really acts of impulse, such as the day he'd decided to walk to Flat Rock in worn-out shoes. Some might have thought him brave to put up a fight when Nightshade accosted him in the pass, but Jim knew better. Bravery in the face of insurmountable odds *was* foolishness.

Jim finished his coffee and told himself not to waste time pondering questions he could not answer. He saddled the horses while Jinny tidied up after the meal, and then they rode on, moving deeper into the foothills.

By midday, the trail had begun to climb into the mountains. As they rode along ridges and through high-walled canyons, Jim listened closely for the sound of hoofbeats in the distance. It was possible they would meet one of the other Pony Express riders from Flat Rock, and Jim wanted to avoid that, if possible. He did not want to have to answer a lot of questions about the robbery and why he had not returned. Instead, he planned to get off the trail whenever they encountered anyone else, staying in concealment until they could be certain of the other person's identity. If they ran into someone who was not one of the Pony Riders, then they could emerge from hiding and ask their questions about Nightshade.

So far, though, Owen Shelton and his band of cowboys were the only people Jim and Jinny had run across. Even though this trail was the easiest way to travel through the mountains, it was also part of Nightshade's stomping grounds and had been for a long time. People tended to avoid it, if possible. Jim suddenly had a vision of him and Jinny wandering endlessly through these mountains, never seeing anyone, never finding Nightshade.

"Rider coming," said Jinny.

Damn it, he had done it again! thought Jim. He had allowed his mind to wander when he should have been paying attention to what was going on around him. Now that Jinny had pointed them out, he could hear the approaching hoofbeats, too. He jerked his head toward a slope dotted with large boulders to the left of the trail. "Come on," he said. "Let's get out of sight."

Jinny followed behind him as Jim turned the roan and started across the rugged ground. Rusty picked his way carefully, and Jim felt impatience growing inside him. He wanted to nudge the horse into hurrying, but being careless in terrain like this could mean a bad fall. He could break a leg; worse still, the horse could break a leg. Jim gritted his teeth and let the roan set his own pace.

He reached a boulder large enough to conceal both of them and motioned for Jinny to follow him as he rode behind it. The sound of the horseman on the trail was close now, and Jim could tell from the rapid hoofbeats that the rider was in a hurry. He waited until the man and horse had raced past, then leaned over in the saddle to peer around the side of the huge rock. It came as no surprise to him when he recognized one of the other young men who had been hired as Pony Express riders in Flat Rock. Despite the fact that he had vanished as far as Grayson and Lind were concerned, the Pony Express would go on.

"Do you know him?" asked Jinny, seeing the expression on Jim's face.

He jerked his head in a nod. "I know him. He's one of the Pony Riders."

"You miss it already, don't you? Oh, Jim, you didn't have to give up your job for me! I told you it was foolish to make that promise about the map—"

She fell silent as he gave her a sharp look. "I gave you my word," he said. "That wasn't ever worth much in the past, but things are different now." He drew a deep draft of air into his lungs and heeled the roan into motion. The Pony Express rider was long gone. "Let's go."

They ate their noon meal in the saddle: jerky and biscuits left over from breakfast, washed down by water from their canteens. They could have stopped to eat; after all, they had no real destination as yet and were in no particular hurry. Something in Jim made him want to keep moving, however, some indefinable instinct. Jinny did not argue with him.

Later in the afternoon, they met the first traveler they had seen since the Pony Express rider passed them on his way to Moss City. This time, they overtook a Mexican who was driving a wagon pulled by a pair of burros. The back of the wagon was loaded with vegetables. The broad face of the man from south of the border was shaded by the brim of his huge sombrero, but he was smiling as he looked up at Jim and Jinny.

"Hello," said Jim. He reined his horse into a walk alongside the wagon. "Heading for Flat Rock?"

"That is right," answered the Mexican. He inclined his head toward the load of produce. "I sell my vegetables over there, since the ground is rockier on that side of the mountains. It is harder to grow a garden there, no?"

"That makes sense," agreed Jim. As he took a closer look at the Mexican, he thought he remembered seeing the man around Flat Rock before. "Aren't you afraid of being stopped by Nightshade, though?"

The man threw back his head and laughed. "Why should a *bandido* like Nightshade rob me? What would he take, eh? A head of lettuce? A basket of tomatoes? No, Nightshade would have no use for me, my young friend."

Jinny spoke up. "But what about after you've sold your vegetables and are taking the money home? He could rob you then."

"*Si*, but he would not. Not Nightshade."

The certainty of the Mexican's reply puzzled Jim. How could he know that Nightshade would not rob him? After all, money was money, and the bandit had even stolen a mail pouch, which surely would not prove to be very profitable.

Jim changed his tack slightly. He said, "I've heard that Nightshade lives somewhere in these mountains. Have you ever heard where his stronghold might be?"

"You are very interested in this outlaw, no? That is strange. Most people wish to stay as far as possible from Nightshade."

Jim put a grin on his face. "Maybe that's why I'm asking. If we know where he usually is, we'll make it a point to be somewhere else."

"I see. But I am afraid I can tell you but little. It is said among my people that there is a valley high in these mountains; a green, hidden valley, and it is there Nightshade makes his home. More than that, I cannot say."

Jim sensed that if he kept pushing the issue of Nightshade, the Mexican would shut his mouth and not say anything else at all. Instead, Jim commented, "We ran into some cattlemen yesterday who were looking for a bunch of rustlers. Have you heard anything about that?"

The Mexican tapped an earlobe. "My ears, they do not always work so well. I can hear when my wife speaks to me, or when someone wishes to buy some of my vegetables. But I hear very little about anything else."

Jim exchanged a quick look with Jinny. Questioning this tight-lipped farmer was proving to be a waste of time. Jim nodded and lifted a finger to the brim of his hat. "We'll be seeing you," he said. "Good luck in Flat Rock." Then he nudged the roan into a trot. Jinny followed suit, riding just behind him.

When the Mexican had fallen out of sight around a bend in the trail behind them, Jim said, "That fellow certainly wasn't much help. I hope not everybody we run into here in the mountains is so reluctant to talk about Nightshade."

"You can't really blame him," said Jinny. "He doesn't know who we are. For all he knows, you could be one of Nightshade's gang. Don't you see, he's afraid there'll be repercussions if he talks too freely."

Jim nodded; what the girl was saying made sense. Even though Nightshade was nowhere to be seen, his presence hung over these mountains like an all-pervasive fog. No one knew where he was, what he might overhear, where he might strike next. It was better, most folks would reason, to just keep your mouth shut and hope for the best.

That proved to be the case with the next person they encountered, a peddler whose wagon was full of pots, pans, and odds and ends. He had heard of Nightshade, he said in response to Jim's seemingly idle questions, but he claimed never to have seen the outlaw. He had very little fear of Nightshade, echoing the same theme as the Mexican. Nightshade held up stagecoaches, freight caravans, prosperous-looking riders, and the like. When he ventured out of the mountains, his targets were banks and occasionally stores. No one knew everything Nightshade had done, but as Jinny cast her mind back over what she could recall about the man, she could not remember one instance when he had robbed someone who would be considered a common man.

"Well, there's a good enough reason for that," said Jim. "He picks the targets that are most likely to have money. Nothing mysterious about it."

"Maybe not . . ." mused Jinny, but her tone showed her to be deep in thought.

For two more days they rode the mountain trails, veering

away from the main road on narrow paths that looped around the heights and through the rugged canyons. As their route twisted and turned, Jim quickly became lost, and even though Jinny had claimed to know some of the trails, she too had to admit she did not know exactly where they were. She insisted that she could find her way back to the main trail whenever she wanted to, however.

They passed through a couple of small settlements, which Jim was surprised to find in the craggy landscape. The villages were tucked into small valleys. The reactions they got from the people in the settlements when they asked about Nightshade ranged from fear to disregard. Although they heard the story of the isolated valley high in the mountains from several other people, no one seemed to know exactly where it was, or anything else that might lead them to Nightshade, either.

As they made camp on the fourth night since leaving Harker City, Jim felt a strong sense of discouragement. The longer it took them to locate Nightshade, the better the chances that the outlaw had already followed the map to the hidden loot.

They might never find Nightshade, thought Jim glumly as he stared into the flickering flames of the fire while darkness gathered around the ledge where he and Jinny had made camp. The girl was preparing some cornbread as a change from the usual biscuits, and as she glanced up at Jim, she said, "Don't do that."

"Don't do what?" he asked, jolted out of his reverie by her command.

"Stare into the fire that way. Your eyes get used to it, and then if you have to look into the darkness all of a sudden, you can't see anything. You might as well be blind for a couple of minutes."

Jim transferred his attention to her. She had removed her hat and let her long blond hair fall freely down her back, and in the soft, flickering light of the campfire, she was incredibly beautiful. "How did you know that?" he asked.

"You mean about the campfire?" Jinny shrugged. "It's

just common sense. Besides, I went camping a few times with my father before—"

Abruptly, she fell silent, and Jim cursed himself for causing her to bring up painful memories. He wanted to say he was sorry, but that might just make things worse. Instead, he pushed himself to his feet and said, "I think I'll see to the horses." The animals had been hobbled near a small patch of grass, but they would need water. A small stream bubbled out of the rocks at the back of the broad ledge, and as he strode toward it, Jim took off his hat. He would scoop up some water in it, he thought, and offer it to the horses.

As he knelt beside the stream and bent over to dip the hat into the water, there was movement in the deep shadows at the base of the rock wall. Jim spotted it out of the corner of his eye and started to stand up and turn toward it. He was only halfway there, however, when the barrel of a rifle emerged from the shadows and centered on him, the light from the fire reflecting faintly on the dull metal of the weapon. Jim froze in his awkward position, stunned by the unexpected danger.

"Jus' stand still, boy," growled a voice from the darkness, "and maybe I won't blow your damn' head off."

FOURTEEN

Jim's pulse was thundering in his head as he stood there staring into the barrel of the rifle. Part of his brain identified it as an old muzzle-loader, and at this range, the heavy lead ball, fired with a potent charge of black powder behind it, might literally blow his head off his shoulders. Of course, the rifle was only a single-shot, and if he could avoid that shot, he had both of his Colts, with a total of ten loads between them. Should he try to dive out of the way and snatch his own guns from their holsters?

A new voice came from the shadows and solved Jim's dilemma. "Here, now," it said. "Put the gun down, Newk. No point in shovin' it in the boy's face like that. We're all friends here."

There was more than one of them. He had to wait, realized Jim, to find out exactly what the situation was and how bad the odds were against him.

"What is it, Jim?" called Jinny. "What's wrong?" She came to her feet, able only to see him standing strangely at the edge of the circle of light cast by the flames.

The barrel of the muzzle-loader slowly dipped, and a huge shape bulked out of the darkness, followed by two more smaller ones. The biggest man was the one who had pointed the rifle at Jim. As he stepped into the light, Jinny could not prevent a gasp of shock from escaping.

The man wore buckskins and a cap fashioned from the hide of a raccoon, with the head of the animal still intact. The striped tail hung down on the man's left shoulder. He was so broad that at first glance he appeared short and squat, until Jim realized that he had to look up to see the man's features. The entire face, save for a prominent nose that resembled a potato, seemed to be covered by a bushy growth of black whiskers. Buried in the beard was a red slash of a mouth from which tobacco spittle drooled. The deep-set eyes above the nose were small and reddish, like those of a pig. A jagged scar marred the low forehead in a red, irregular ridge. From the looks of it, someone had once tried to slice off the top of the man's head, perhaps with a broad-bladed ax or a crosscut saw.

He was quite possibly the ugliest man Jim had ever seen, and the most threatening looking.

His companions were less sinister only by comparison, and Jim was shocked when he got a look at their faces. One of them was the red-bearded fur trapper who had come crashing through the window of the saloon in front of which Jim had been sitting, that first night when he had trudged into Flat Rock. Rusty, that was his name, just like the horse. The other man was the one who had knocked Rusty through the window, sending him tumbling into the street.

Jim backed nervously toward the fire as the buckskin-clad trio ambled further into the light. Even though the one called Newk had lowered his rifle, they still exuded a palpable aura of menace. Rusty and the third man each carried a rifle, and they had pistols tucked into their belts as well. Newk wore a long-bladed hunting knife and an Indian tomahawk.

The smallest member of the group stepped forward. "Gentry's the name," he said. "This here's Rusty, and the big fella's Rafe Newcomb, but we just call him Newk. Pleased to meet you folks."

Gentry's words were cordial enough, but the oily voice in which he delivered them put Jim on his guard. These trappers were not in the least trustworthy, and he would have to remember that at all times. He saw that Newk's eyes had narrowed into an intent stare, and it came as no surprise when Jim turned slightly and saw that the look was directed toward Jinny, who had moved behind him to shield herself from the big trapper's lustful gaze.

"What you folks doin' out here in the middle of nowhere?" continued Gentry. "Mighty lonely around these parts."

"We're just traveling through," said Jim, "headed for the other side of the mountains."

Gentry rubbed grimy fingers over his scruffy black beard. "You're off the regular trail, then," he said. "This path you're on is used mostly by trappers."

"I'm sorry if we're in your way," began Jim, but Gentry shook his head.

"You ain't causin' no trouble for us. If you'd like, we could point you back to the main road in the mornin'." He smiled, but it was more of a leer. "We're sharin' your fire tonight. That's customary in these parts." His tone did not leave any room for argument.

"Sure," said Jim. He turned to Jinny. "We've got enough food to share, don't we, darling?"

"Of course," she said quickly, understanding what he was trying to do.

Gentry, Rusty, and Newk all leaned over, trying to get a better look at the girl. "That the little woman back there, mister?" asked Gentry, who was obviously the spokesman for the group.

"Yes, this is my wife. By the way, I'm Jim McReady."

Evidently, neither Gentry nor Rusty had recognized him as the young man who had wound up lying in the main street of Flat Rock with Rusty following the altercation in the saloon.

Had he changed that much in the past weeks?

Not that it mattered, he realized. The only important thing now was surviving this encounter, and to that end, he had introduced Jinny as his wife. If they thought she was a married woman, they might be less inclined to bother her. Most of the time, a woman's virtue was safe anywhere on the frontier; even Jim, with his rudimentary knowledge of life out here, knew that much. But there were a few men who recognized no code of conduct save their own, and any woman—especially one as lovely as Jinny—might find herself in danger from them.

"Glad to meet you, McReady," said Gentry. "You, too, ma'am. Now, how about we eat?"

The three men sat down without waiting for an invitation, lowering themselves cross-legged onto the ground. Jim looked at Jinny and nodded, indicating that she was to go on with their normal routine, at least, as long as possible.

"We smelled your coffee," said Gentry, pointing to the pot that was sitting on glowing coals at the edge of the fire. "You got enough for all of us?" His tone seemed to say that if there was not enough coffee for everyone, then Jim and Jinny were the ones who would do without.

"Sure," replied Jim, "but we've only got two cups."

"That's all right." Gentry dug into a pouch slung over his shoulder and produced a battered earthen mug, and the other two trappers followed his example. "We got our own."

The first batch of cornbread was ready, and Jinny began to prepare more as Gentry, Rusty, and Newk helped themselves. They ate greedily and in silence for a few moments, then Newk asked around a mouthful of food, "Got meat?"

"Just some jerky," said Jim.

The huge man stuck out a paw that looked to be the size of a dinner plate. "That'll do."

Jim sighed and reached into the sack of provisions. He gave several pieces of jerky to Newk, figuring that the trapper would share them with his companions. Newk did no such thing, however, folding all the pieces into his mouth. Seeing the expectant looks on the faces of Gentry and Rusty, Jim took more jerky from the sack and handed it to them.

"Don't worry, Jim," said Gentry, grinning. "We ain't goin' to eat you out of house and home. Come mornin', we'll be on our way."

"That's all right. We don't mind sharing," lied Jim.

At least the food seemed to have taken their minds off Jinny's beauty. As long as they were concentrating on jerky, cornbread, and coffee, they would not be planning any mischief involving the girl. The night would be a nerve-wracking one, Jim knew, but maybe they could survive it and the trappers would move on when morning came.

When he was done with the meal, Gentry leaned back on his elbows and sighed contentedly. He said, "That was mighty good, ma'am."

"Yeah," echoed Rusty, the first word Jim had heard the red-bearded trapper utter. Newk just nodded ponderously. Jim wondered after studying the dull expression in the big man's eyes if Newk had something wrong inside his head. An injury such as the one that had left the hideous scar on his forehead could have easily addled the man's brain.

"We 'preciate the hospitality," continued Gentry. His smile became a leer again as he went on, "Ain't often we get to eat anything fixed by a woman as pretty as you."

Jim did not want Jinny's beauty to become a topic of discussion; the trappers were more likely to get ideas if that was the case. To change the subject, he said quickly, "Doesn't it bother you to live in the same mountains where Nightshade roams?"

Gentry and Rusty sent curious frowns in Jim's direction, and Newk made a horrible noise that the young man identified after several seconds as chuckling. "Nightshade's never bothered us," said Gentry. "He leaves us alone, and we leave him alone."

Something in Gentry's voice made it sound as if he might know where Nightshade's stronghold was, and Jim felt a quick surge of excitement. These trappers were hardly his idea of pleasant companions, but they might have information he and Jinny could use.

"We've been hoping he wouldn't ambush us," said Jim, "but since we didn't know exactly where he stays up here, all we could do was hope."

Gentry shook his head. "Don't reckon anybody knows exactly where Nightshade's hideout is, but it ain't anywhere around these parts. We've trapped all through here and never seen hide nor hair of him. It'd be my guess he's got a place somewhere up north, closer to Paiute country, since he's got that damn redskin ridin' with him."

"What redskin?" asked Jim. This was the first time he'd heard anything about an Indian being associated with Nightshade.

"Ko'lu," grunted Newk, and for a moment Jim thought the big man had something caught in his throat. Gentry repeated the word.

"That's the bastard's name—Ko'lu. Renegade Paiute. Rumor has it he's cut the throats of over a hundred white men. He's Nightshade's *segundo.*"

Jim was able to figure out that the man was referring to a second-in-command. This Ko'lu, then, was Nightshade's lieutenant. It came as no surprise to Jim that the outlaw would have such a murderous associate.

"Well, if Nightshade's camp is north of here, we ought to be safe enough," commented Jim. "That's good to know."

"Never know for sure when you're safe," said Gentry. "Trouble can come at you when you ain't expectin' it. Besides, Nightshade roams all up and down the Prophets and fifty miles to either side. Just because his hideout's up north don't mean he stays there all the time."

Jim nodded; what Gentry was saying made sense. But once he and Jinny were away from the trappers, Jim knew, the two of them would be heading north, toward that Paiute country Gentry had mentioned.

"Wouldn't worry if I was you," Gentry went on. "I don't reckon Nightshade'd bother the two of you. No offense, but you don't look like you're carryin' a lot of cash."

"None," said Jim. "We spent all our money on supplies."

"There you go. You don't have anything anybody'd want—'cept for Mrs. McReady there." Gentry's tongue emerged from his mouth and slid over his lips. "Any man with two good eyes would want her right off. Hell, a man with *one* good eye would, too."

Jinny reddened at the trapper's coarse speech and the blatantly suggestive expression in his eyes as he looked across the fire at her. Rusty and Newk were giving her the same sort of look, their lust reappearing now that they were no longer distracted by the meal. Jim felt his jaw tightening in anger, and he issued himself a stern warning to be careful. Perhaps the men would be satisfied just to make their crude comments and leave it at that. If he reacted too strongly, he might just make things worse and push them into actually doing something.

"No offense, ma'am," said Gentry, still eyeing the girl.

"That's all right," said Jinny, her voice soft and frightened. Jim could hear the fear in it, and he was certain the others could, too.

"Well, after a fine meal like that, I could use a smoke." The trapper removed a pouch of tobacco and a pipe from the pocket of his buckskin shirt. As he poured tobacco into the pipe and began to tamp it down, he said to Jim, "We left our pack mule up at the top of the hill. Why don't you go get her for us, McReady?"

"I don't know—" began Jim.

Gentry interrupted his protest. "Ought to take you about, oh . . ." He looked at Jinny, then continued, "Half an hour ought to do. It'll take you about half an hour to find that mule and bring her back down here, understand?"

Jim understood, all right, and from the way Jinny's face went ashen, so did she. Gentry was commanding him to leave the camp for half an hour so that he and his friends could molest Jinny. They actually thought that he would be more interested in saving his own hide than he was in protecting her from them.

And yet there had been a time, not so long ago, when such an assumption would have had some truth in it. The realization was painful to Jim, but he knew that was the way it had been. He had looked out for himself first, and the devil take the hindmost.

But not anymore. By God, not anymore, he told himself.

"I think it would be better if one of you went to get the horses," he said, surprising himself with the strength in his voice. He actually sounded calm. "You know the terrain much better than I do. I might fall and break a leg, clambering around on those rocks."

"That's all right," smiled Gentry. "Anything happened to you, we'd take mighty good care of your woman. You can count on that."

It was futile to hope for a change of mind on the part of these men, Jim realized. They were determined to force themselves on Jinny, and if he tried to stop them, they would not hesitate to kill him. They would, in fact, kill him with as few qualms as if they were stepping on an insect. He knew this without being told.

At least, they would *try* to kill him . . .

"I think the three of you had better leave," said Jim, placing his right hand on the butt of the Colt on that side. "Now."

Gentry raised his eyebrows in mock surprise. "What? You ain't bein' hospitable anymore, boy?"

Jim said, "We don't want any trouble. We just want you to leave us alone."

"And if we don't?"

Jim did not have an answer to that. Aware that his silence made him look foolish, he finally managed to say, "My wife and I will find someplace else to camp. You can have this spot."

Newk gave that awful laugh again, and Gentry said, "It ain't the campsite we're interested in, boy." He did not seem worried in the slightest that Jim's hand was on his gun.

There was no point in continuing the discussion. Jim said, "Jinny, I want you to stand up and go over to our horses. Take the supplies with you."

Now Gentry's voice took on a sharp edge as he said, "Don't you do that, little lady! You stay right where you are till we're ready for you."

"Please," she said, "don't do this. We just want to leave peacefully."

Her entreaty fell on deaf ears. The three trappers were not going to be denied. Gentry shifted slightly, his hand moving toward the rifle lying beside him.

Jim drew his pistol, sliding it quickly out of the holster. "Don't move!" he said.

For a long moment, Gentry regarded him with an angry expression on his bearded face, but then the trapper laughed. "Hell, you ain't goin' to shoot nobody, and we all know it. You ain't got the guts, boy. Just let us have your woman and let's get this over with. We ain't interested in killin' nobody; you'll both live through this if you don't do anything foolish."

"You're the one who's foolish," said Jim, letting his anger fuel him now, the words coming out in a rush because he knew that if he slowed down, his tautly stretched nerves might snap. "Jinny, get mounted up. Now!"

She rose to her feet in response to his command and started toward the horses. Jim was trying to watch all three of the trappers, but it was difficult. His mouth was as dry as sand, and his belly was queasy. He turned his head for a fraction of a second, just to see how close Jinny was to the horses.

Gentry and his companions moved in that instant. Newk lunged across the fire, massive hands reaching for Jim, while Gentry and Rusty snatched up their rifles and rolled quickly to one side. Jim gave a cry of sheer terror as the huge shape hurtled toward him, and his finger jerked the trigger of the gun. He had no idea where the bullet went, but it must not have hit Newk. A split-second later, the monstrous trapper crashed into him.

Newk did not bother striking Jim with his hands. Instead, he bore the young man to the ground with his weight and pinned him there. Jim tried to bring his gun to bear again, but his arm was trapped, the wrist and hand holding the gun extending out from under Newk's body, but not far enough so that he could bring the weapon into play. The foul scent of the trapper's filthy clothing filled Jim's nostrils, making him choke. The great weight pressing down on his chest kept him from drawing breath, and within seconds, he was gripped by a lightheaded stupor caused by lack of air. Dimly, he heard

Jinny scream, and then a man cursed fervently.

At the same time, a bootheel came down on Jim's wrist, causing the bones to grind together agonizingly. Jim's fingers splayed out, releasing the butt of the gun. The booted foot lifted from his wrist, but the pain remained.

"Catch her, God damn it!" shouted Gentry.

Jinny was escaping, thought Jim, and he prayed that she was successful. It would require a miracle for her to get away from these men, on foot, in this rugged terrain with which they were familiar but she was not.

But miracles sometimes happened, didn't they?

That thought was going through Jim's mind when something slammed against the side of his head, sending him spinning away into a darkness blacker than any night.

FIFTEEN

When that darkness went away, Jim found himself standing upright. Actually, he was being *held* upright by ropes that had been wrapped around his body to the tree trunk jammed painfully against his back. He groaned as he tried to lift his head. Pain shot through his skull and washed down through his neck and shoulders. Not only was he hurting from the blow that had rendered him unconscious, but evidently he had been tied here for quite a while, and his head had been sagging forward all during that time so that his muscles were extremely sore. He managed to pry open his eyes and looked around, squinting against the light from a newly risen sun.

He saw that he was no longer on the ledge where he and Jinny had made camp the night before. He had been moved downslope, from the looks of the vegetation around him. The tree to which he was tied stood at the edge of a clearing in a stand of pines. Beneath his feet the grass was thick and green. A small stream ran across the far side of the clearing. Jim twisted his head and tried to look behind him; from what little he could make out, the land sloped upward and was dotted with large boulders, gradually rising to the heights where he and Jinny had been traveling before their fateful encounter with the trappers.

Jim wondered where Gentry and Rusty and Newk were. Better to think about that, he decided, than to concentrate on the pounding ache in his head or the faintly coppery taste of dried blood in his mouth.

And Jinny . . . where was Jinny?

The sound of horses snuffling came to Jim's ears, and he twisted his head in the other direction, trying to locate the animals. He saw the roan and Jinny's mare, tied up at the edge of the woods, and with them was a pack mule, although it was unloaded at the moment. Several buckskin pouches were piled underneath a nearby tree. From the looks of things, Gentry and his friends intended to camp here for a while. No doubt one of them had thrown the unconscious Jim over the back of a horse the night before and brought him down here while the other two searched for Jinny.

The fact than none of them were in sight boded well, Jim told himself. Jinny was still free, and the trappers were out searching for her. That was what he wanted to believe. They had left him here because they thought he was helpless.

They were right, he admitted bitterly as he strained against his bonds. He had been tied with great skill and no regard for his comfort, meaning that he could probably try for a week to wriggle out of the ropes without coming any closer to success than he was at this moment.

Jim took a deep breath and then squinted up at the sky again. Not more than an hour had passed since dawn, he judged. Still, he had been unconscious for a long time, and the ache in his head bothered him. A blow such as he'd had suffered could cause permanent damage, as witness the big trapper called Newk. That comparison was particularly appropriate, he supposed, because undoubtedly it had been Newk who had struck him.

One of the horses whinnied nervously, and Jim looked around, trying to see what had disturbed the animal. Maybe the others were coming back. If that was the case, he prayed that Jinny would not be with them.

Now the other horse and the mule were making noises, too, and Jim saw movement in the trees on the far side of the stream. A shadow slipped out of the woods, moving stealthily and low to the ground. This was no horse and rider, Jim realized, but an animal of some kind. As he watched, it stepped out of the thick shadows underneath the pines.

His breath lodged in his throat. Standing there on the bank of the little brook was a wolf—a huge, gray wolf that solemnly regarded him with yellowish eyes. The animal's tongue lolled from its mouth; the powerful jaws were open enough to reveal some of the razor-sharp teeth in the wolf's mouth. The creature was broad at the shoulder, and Jim could see the smooth play of powerful muscles under its hide as it began to pace back and forth along the stream, swinging its head around each time it turned so that it could continue watching him.

Surely the wolf would not consider him a threat, he thought, not trussed up the way he was. But if the animal was not afraid of him, would it regard him instead as easy prey? Jim was not very familiar with the ways of such beasts. He had heard of wolfpacks attacking humans, but would a solitary wolf bother a man, even one tied to a tree? Jim could not answer that question.

Evidently the wolf was having difficulty deciding as well. Its confusion was obvious in the way it paced up and down the stream. Finally the beast stopped, stared across the clearing at Jim for a long moment, and then lifted its upper lip in a snarl as more of its teeth were bared.

Jim would have shuddered had the ropes not been so tight around his body. Fighting back would be impossible. He might be able to kick a little, since the ropes that bound him did not go down any lower than his thighs, but he would not be able to muster any strength behind the blows. He would only be futilely postponing the inevitable for a few seconds.

With an effortless bound, the wolf sprang across the creek. It came toward Jim in an easy lope, not bothering to hurry. This victim was not going anywhere. Grimacing, Jim shrank against the tree. His lips drew back from his teeth, and beads of sweat popped out on his forehead despite the early morning coolness as he watched his death padding quietly toward him.

With a shriek, something hurtled down out of the sky.

Jim uttered an involuntary exclamation of surprise as the wolf let out a startled yelp and veered sharply to the side. Eyes widening, Jim watched as the hawk which had just dived in front of the wolf wheeled in the air above the furred predator and then plummeted once more. This time the hawk's talons raked the shoulder of the wolf. It yelped again and snapped at the hawk, but the bird was too fast. With a flap of its wings, it was out of reach, soaring high into the air yet again and diving for the third time.

The wolf had had enough. It turned and bounded toward the trees, where the hawk would have a more difficult time reaching it than here in the clearing. Snarling and growling its defiance, the wolf was clearly in retreat, and the hawk gave a piercing cry that seemed almost to mock the slinking canine form.

Jim lifted his head, watching the hawk as it flew above him. Never had he witnessed such an astounding event. He was familiar with the way hawks swooped down out of the heavens to pluck mice and rabbits and other small animals from the fields, but he had never heard of a hawk attacking anything as large as a wolf. True, the hawk had made no attempt to carry off the wolf as food; the bird had been content merely to turn it away from Jim . . . as if it was defending him from otherwise certain death.

But that was impossible, wasn't it? Jim gave a little shake of his head in an attempt to clear it. If he ever told anyone about this, they would not believe him. He wasn't sure he believed it himself.

No need to worry about that, he realized bleakly. He would never have a chance to tell anyone what had happened, unless it was Gentry or Rusty or Newk, and he would not waste the breath to tell them anything except that they could go to hell as far as he was concerned.

Unless they brought Jinny with them when they returned to the camp. He might be able to tell her, and he sensed that she would believe him. She would believe anything he told her, even if it was something as improbable as realizing that he had fallen in love with her in less than a week's time.

He took as deep a breath as he could with the ropes wound tightly around him. For some reason, Fate—in the form of that hawk—had intervened to save him from death. There had to be a reason for such a thing, he told himself. He could not give up hope yet. As long as he and Jinny were alive, there was still a chance . . .

But what if Jinny was no longer alive?

That possibility hit Jim with crushing force. She could be dead, even if she had escaped from the lust-crazed trappers. In fleeing from them through the darkness, she could have tumbled into a ravine or plunged off a cliff. She could be lying somewhere among the rocks now, her body battered and broken. The bloody images in Jim's mind were almost too much for him to bear. He threw back his head and howled out his pain.

"Damn, boy, you sound 'bout like that wolf we just saw runnin' through the woods. What the hell's wrong with you?"

The voice jerked Jim's attention back to earth. He looked across the clearing and saw Gentry, Rusty, and Newk emerging from the trees. They were alone, and the feeling of relief that washed through him left him weak. At least they had not captured Jinny.

His throat did not want to work, but he struggled to form the words anyway. "Wh-what h-have you d-done with her?"

"Your wife?" asked Gentry. He leaned over and spat disgustedly. "Haven't been able to find her yet. But we will, don't you worry. Ain't no way that little lady knows these mountains better'n we do. We'll find her."

Jim prayed the trapper was wrong. With any luck, Jinny

would be able to make her way down out of the mountains and reach the plains. From there, she could strike out toward Moss City. There were plenty of roads and trails; she would find someone to help her. If he told himself these things often enough, Jim reasoned, they might come true.

The three buckskin-clad men approached him. "Been thinkin' about it," said Gentry, as the other two started to build a fire. "Don't reckon we'll have to spend a lot of time lookin' for that gal. Sound travels a long way in the mountains. I figger when she hears you screamin', she'll just naturally have to come see what happenin' to you. We'll draw her right to us, and you're goin' to be the bait, McReady."

Jim shook his head, aghast at what Gentry was proposing. "I'll never make a sound," he vowed.

Gentry just grinned. "Oh, I think you will."

Jim knew what they were planning to do when he saw them begin to heat the long blade of Newk's knife in the flames of the campfire. Gentry had left him alone for a few minutes, but now the man sauntered back over to him and said, "You know, if you want to start yellin' for that wife of yours to come on down here before we go to work on you, you're more'n welcome to go ahead. No need for you to suffer. Hell, I told you we don't intend to kill either one of you if we don't have to. But we're goin' to have that woman of yours, don't you make no mistake about that."

His jaw set in a grim line, Jim made no response to Gentry's suggestion.

After a moment, the trapper went on, "Don't really matter to me, but Newk would surely enjoy makin' you holler. He ain't right in the head, you know. A few years back, a mule kicked him and near stove in his skull. Then there was that nasty business with the ax . . . ever since then, it's purely pleasured ol' Newk to watch somebody else sufferin'. I guess that's because he's gone through so much of it himself."

The inside of Jim's belly was as cold as ice, and the frigid sensation was working its way up his backbone as well. Despair gripped him tightly. There was no way out of this predicament, and although he would hold out as long as possible, he was afraid he would eventually start screaming if Newk tortured him. Unless he was lucky enough to die first.

Newk had been squatting by the fire. Now he straightened and turned around so that Jim could see the knife in his hands. The blade was glowing almost white-hot. "Ready," grunted Newk. He took a step toward Jim. Gentry and Rusty came closer, too, not wanting to miss any of the entertainment.

A sudden clatter in the distance made all three men stop. Gentry lifted his head and looked up the slope. "Rockslide somewhere up there," he said. "Not a very big one, from the sound of it."

"Reckon that gal caused it?" asked Rusty.

Gentry shrugged. "Could be. You want to go find out?"

"We'd better. Could've been the girl, could've been a mountain goat, maybe. But it could be somebody else, too."

Jim's terror eased enough for him to wonder if they were thinking of the same person he was—Nightshade. As he'd already begun to realize, people in these mountains tended to believe that Nightshade could be anywhere in the Prophets at any time. And despite Gentry's brave words the night before about not fearing Nightshade, the possibility that the famed outlaw might be nearby seemed to make all three trappers nervous.

Finally, Gentry said, "Rusty and I will go see what we can find. Newk, you stay here with the boy. If he gives you any trouble, you can hurt him some, but don't kill him."

Newk's bearded features split in an evil smile at those words. Jim had a terrible feeling that Newk would begin to torment him as soon as the other trappers left, regardless of what he did.

Gentry and Rusty hefted their rifles and moved off into the trees. Newk watched them go, then looked down at the knife in his huge hand and frowned. "Not hot enough," he grunted. He turned back toward the fire, obviously intending to heat the blade again.

Even though he knew it was hopeless, Jim strained mightily against his bonds while Newk crouched beside the flames. The ropes did not budge more than the slightest fraction of an inch. In a matter of minutes, the massive trapper would be satisfied with the temperature of his blade and would commence the prisoner's agonizing ordeal. Already, Jim could almost feel the searing heat and smell the vile odor of his own flesh blistering and scorching.

Newk stood up again, lifting the knife and twisting it back and forth in front of his face, studying the blade, his dull brain pondering the question of whether or not it was hot enough. Finally deciding that it was, he turned toward Jim again.

"Yell all you want," said the brute as he approached Jim. "Gentry said it was all right if you hollered."

Jim's eyes grew wide. He attempted to swallow, but his throat would not work. He wanted to scream, to shriek, to plead for mercy. But mercy would not be forthcoming, as he knew all too well. He could tell that from the unholy glee in Newk's piggish eyes. The giant was not going to be denied his pleasure.

For the second time today, movement across the creek caught Jim's eye, as Jinny Rawlings stepped out of the trees.

His first thought as he stared at the girl was to shout at her to run. But that would only draw Newk's attention to her, and so far the big man had not noticed her. Jim snapped his eyes back to Newk, not wanting to give away Jinny's presence by staring at her.

Even that brief glimpse, however, had been enough to tell him that she had been through a great deal since he had last seen her. Her hair was disheveled, and her clothes were ripped and torn from the brush. She had obviously been hiding in the mountains for almost twelve hours now, too frightened to sleep, and she was exhausted.

He had seen that in her eyes.

But there had been determination in those blue orbs, too, and he was suddenly afraid that she had come here to free him. His brain screamed out a warning to her; she needed to get back in the concealment of the trees and slip on past this camp. Gentry and Rusty had gone the other way, and if she could get past Newk without him noticing her, she would have a clear path out of the foothills to the plains. She could make it to safety . . .

Only if she left him here to keep Newk occupied, however. And as Jim realized with a sinking heart, Jinny was not about to do that.

She was moving closer to them now, Jim saw when he allowed his eyes to flicker for an instant in her direction. She had stepped over the narrow stream and was walking carefully toward the two men on the other side of the clearing. If she'd had a gun, she might have been able to get close enough to Newk to fire a bullet into his head, Jim thought, but it was a futile hope. Jinny was unarmed.

She remedied that by reaching down as she passed the campfire and picking up a short length of wood. It was a piece of a thick limb that had been hacked off a fallen tree, and it would do nicely for a club, wielded by the right hands. Unfortunately, Newk's skull would probably absorb the impact of any blow and shrug it off. According to Gentry, the huge trapper had been kicked in the head by a mule and lived to tell of it. Not many men could make a similar claim.

Still, Jinny clearly intended to try to knock him out. She wrapped both hands around the makeshift club and lifted it high above her head as she approached Newk. Jim could no longer keep his gaze off her, and using only his eyes he pleaded with her to abandon this effort and escape at all costs, including his life.

Jinny came closer.

Jim never knew what alerted Newk. Perhaps Jinny made a small sound, so faint that Jim could not hear it but loud enough for Newk's ears to note it. Perhaps the brute caught her scent, like the wild animal he almost was. Whatever gave away her presence, Newk reacted with surprising speed for a man of his huge size. He whipped around, lashing out with a long arm, and knocked the chunk of wood spinning out of Jinny's hands. She cried out in surprise and fear.

His heart pounding wildly, Jim could do nothing but watch as Jinny sprang back, away from Newk. "Shouldn't have come here, girl," grunted the big man. Jim could not see his face, but he knew that Newk was grinning in anticipation.

Newk started walking slowly toward Jinny, deliberately moving the knife back and forth in front of him as if to mesmerize her. Jinny backed away from him, but she stopped when she neared the fire. Her expression reminded Jim of a frightened deer, cornered by some sort of predator. That was exactly what Newk was—an evil force of nature.

"Wait, Newk," said the girl. "I've got something for you."

She reached to the open throat of her shirt.

"No, Jinny!" cried Jim. There was no need to be silent now. "Don't do it! Run while you can!"

Newk was fast on his feet, but Jinny could outrun him, Jim believed. If she waited, though, Gentry and Rusty might show up again, and it would be stretching the odds impossibly to hope that she could slip away from all three of them again.

Jinny had unfastened the top button of her shirt, and Newk was standing still now, fascinated by what he was watching and the possibility that Jinny intended to remove the rest of her clothing. She was so beautiful, Jim thought, with the morning sun shining on her that way. Her loveliness would stop almost any man in his tracks.

"Look, Newk," she said, pulling a locket from inside her shirt. Jim had not known until this moment that she wore such a piece of jewelry. Jinny went on, "I have the sun in here."

"No, you don't," said Newk. "Can't. Sun's up there." He gestured with his knife toward the heavens.

"Just watch." And Jinny flipped open the locket.

There was a mirror inside it, Jim realized, as he saw a little of the reflected glare from the sun. Newk received the full power of the reflection, however, and he instinctively brought up his free hand to paw at his suddenly blinded eyes. With a hoarse yell, he threw himself at Jinny, slashing at her with the knife.

Jim shouted, too, an incoherent cry bolting from his lips as he saw Jinny dart aside from Newk's charge. He plunged past her, and then Jim knew what Jinny's plan had been. Newk fell headlong in the campfire.

Shrieking out his rage and pain, Newk rolled out of the flames. His clothes were on fire, and he dropped the knife as he beat at the flames with both hands. Jinny leaped in close enough to snatch up the fallen blade, then she turned and sprinted toward the tree where Jim was tied.

"Keep going!" he shouted, but he knew she would not do it, would not abandon him just to save herself. When she reached the tree, she began hacking at the ropes that held him. She had to use both hands to grip the hilt of the heavy, long-bladed knife. The strands began to part under the strokes of the razor-sharp weapon.

Newk's beard was on fire, too, Jim saw as he glanced toward the trapper. The howls issuing from Newk's mouth were loud enough to be heard for miles in these mountains; Gentry and Rusty were probably already on their way back here. A small cloud of dust rose as Newk rolled in the dirt, slapping at his face. Suddenly the last flames were extinguished, and he surged to his feet with a terrible cry of impending vengeance.

Jim felt the last strand of rope fall free around him. Luckily, he had pulled and strained against his bonds enough during his captivity so that blood had kept flowing to his extremities. He staggered a bit as he stepped away from the tree, but he was able to stay on his feet. He felt

Jinny pressing the hilt of the knife into his hand, and then she screamed again. Jim lifted his head and saw Newk charging toward him. It was probably only his imagination, he knew, but the ground seemed to shake beneath his feet, as if from a buffalo stampede.

Jim did not think, did not do anything except act instinctively. He stepped forward and swung the knife, holding it in both hands as Jinny had done. He felt the blade strike something, felt a sudden gush of hot wetness, and then Newk crashed into him. The trapper's fingers caught Jim's throat, closing on it with incredible power. Both men went down, but even as he fell, Jim was frenziedly plunging the knife in and out of Newk's body.

They landed at the foot of the tree where Jim had been tied. His head was swimming now as he gasped for breath; no air could pass the iron grip on his throat. He drove the knife one final time into Newk's side and ripped it back and forth once before his strength deserted him. His fingers slipped off the bone handle of the weapon. There was nothing else he could do.

But then a great shudder went through Newk's body, and the fingers locked around Jim's throat suddenly relaxed. Jim writhed until he tore his neck loose from Newk's grip. Gulping great drafts of air, he looked beyond the shoulder of the big man and saw Jinny leaning over them, pulling frantically at Newk's clothes. Jim got his hands against the trapper's body and shoved, and together they rolled the massive weight to the side, freeing Jim.

Jinny grasped his arm and helped him up. Now that the immediate danger was over, she was trembling in reaction, and tears rolled down her cheeks. "Look at you," she said. "Oh, God, what did he do to you?"

Jim looked down at the front of his body and saw that he was splattered with crimson from head to foot. But he knew that he had suffered no wound. He squeezed Jinny's shoulder with his free hand and said emphatically, "It's not my blood. It's Newk's."

With the blade, he pointed to the massive trapper. Not even the bushy black beard could conceal the gaping slash across Newk's throat. As soon as Jim had struck that first blow with the knife, Newk had been a dead man. It had just taken his body several moments to realize it, and all during that time, his life's blood had been pumping out on Jim, trapped beneath him.

Jinny took a deep breath, and Jim saw that she was growing slightly more calm as she realized that he was not badly hurt. His throat would be bruised and sore, but that was a trifle compared to what could have happened.

"We have to get out of here," said Jim. "The other two will be back soon. They had to hear that fight, no matter how far they got. They went to check on a rockslide."

"I know," nodded Jinny. "I caused it, hoping to lure them away."

Jim knew he owed his life to her. She had saved both of them—at least for the moment—by staying clear-headed when she had to. Now he had to do the same.

"Let's get the horses," he said.

SIXTEEN

Both the roan and Jinny's mare smelled the blood on Jim and shied away nervously when he tried to saddle them. Finally, to save time, he stepped back and relinquished the task to Jinny. While she was taking care of that, Jim went over to Newk's body and performed the unpleasant chore of stripping it of anything they could use. He took the knife and the tomahawk, a pouch full of shot, and a powder horn for the muzzle-loader which Newk had left leaning against one of the trees.

In the pile of supplies that had been unloaded from the pack mule, Jim discovered the two canvas sacks of provisions he and Jinny had brought into the mountains. Their food had been running low, so he quickly transferred what he found in the trappers' gear to the canvas sacks. He also found his hat and his gunbelt, with the two Colts still in their holsters, and eagerly put them on. The weight of the guns against his hips felt surprisingly good.

"Do we take the mule?" asked Jinny as he came over to her again.

Jim shook his head. "It would slow us down too much. We've got to put some miles between us and those trappers." He spoke bluntly. "They'll still want you, and they'll want revenge for Newk—and for us taking their supplies."

For a moment, he considered remaining behind while Jinny went on ahead. He could try to set up an ambush for Gentry and Rusty and dispose of the threat they represented right here and now. But even as the thought crossed his mind, he knew he could not go through with such a thing. He had killed Newk, true, but that was in the heat of battle, to save his own life. And to be truthful, the fact that Newk had died and not him was due in large part to luck. He could not gun down the other trappers in cold blood, and he lacked the skill to face them in an open showdown. Flight was the only course open to him and Jinny.

The roan was still skittish as Jim slung the supplies on its back, but it calmed down as he swung up into the saddle. Jinny mounted up as well, and Jim handed Newk's rifle to her. "Be careful with it," he said. "I checked it, and it's loaded. Have you ever fired a rifle before?"

"It's been a long time. I remember to point it and pull the trigger, though."

Jim grinned at her. "That's right." He picked up the reins. "Let's go."

They rode west out of the clearing, following the stream as it wound through the foothills. Jim caught an occasional glimpse of the plains stretching out to the west, and once they reached the flat land, he intended to turn north. They had a name—Ko'lu and a guess that Nightshade's stronghold was near the Paiute territory to the north. That was more than they had begun with.

When they had covered enough ground, Jim intended to stop and wash the blood from his clothes as best he could. That could wait, though, until he was sure they were safe from Gentry and Rusty.

It was difficult to believe he and Jinny had survived the ordeal, and deep inside him, there was still a part of his being that wanted to start gibbering in panic. Jim kept that impulse under tight control. They were not in the clear yet, and he had to remain as cool and calm as possible.

He suddenly wished that old Deakins was with them. The liveryman knew the mountains, and he had undoubtedly faced many dangers when he'd first come to this area so many years earlier. But Deakins was back in Flat Rock, Jim was on his own, and Jinny was depending on him—

although so far she had done more to save them than he had.

A faint cry from far above drifted down to Jim's ears, and he lifted his head to see a hawk wheeling lazily through the sky. The same hawk that had saved him from the wolf? He supposed it was possible, but if he admitted that, then he also had to consider the possibility that the hawk was following them . . . and that was too unbelievable even to contemplate.

The creek wandered out of the foothills and down onto the plain, and where it emerged onto the level terrain, Jim saw several dark, unidentifiable shapes at the edge of the stream. As he and Jinny drew closer, buzzards ascended into the air with a great screeching and flapping of wings, and Jim grimaced as he realized the shapes were dead animals of some sort. The corpses had been covered by the feasting carrion birds until they were almost totally concealed.

Jim and Jinny reined in, the stench of death coming to their nostrils. "What in the world are those?" asked the girl.

"Buffalo, I think," replied Jim. It was hard to be sure. The shaggy hides had been ripped open and much of the flesh stripped away from the bones.

"But what happened to them?"

Jim looked up toward the mountains, then lowered his gaze once again to the corpses. "Could be there was a storm in the mountains, and the creek flooded real sudden-like. The way they're lying on the bank like that, it looks like they drowned."

A shiver went through Jinny. "I don't suppose it really matters what happened to them. Let's go around."

"Good idea," agreed Jim. He did not want to get any closer to the decaying animals than they had to.

He had just turned the roan's head to the side and heeled the horse into motion again when a bullet whipped close by his head.

He had no idea why he was so certain it was a bullet; he

had never had a shot pass so near him before, and judging from the sound, it could just as easily have been a bee. But every instinct in him screamed a warning, and he drove his heels hard into the flanks of the roan. "Ride!" he shouted to Jinny as his horse lunged forward.

The girl did not waste time asking questions but instead followed Jim's example, leaning forward over her mare's neck and kicking the animal into a gallop. Jim saw dust puff up from the ground ahead of them and knew that another ball had missed them. That was the second shot, and it meant that Gentry and Rusty had both discharged their weapons. A few seconds would be required for them to reload. Jim wanted to put as much distance between them as possible in that interval.

He was vaguely conscious of hearing the echoing booms from the foothills above them. The shots had been long-range attempts, or the balls would not have reached them before the sound of the black powder exploding. Gentry and Rusty should have waited until they were closer, Jim thought. They had tipped their hand too early—or at least, so he hoped.

Despite its appearance, the roan possessed a good deal of speed, and Jim slowly drew ahead of Jinny. He had to rein in to keep from leaving her behind. She waved at him to go ahead, but he ignored her just as surely as she had paid no attention to his pleas to leave him a prisoner and save herself. The trappers were on foot, and Jim believed the horses might have already carried him and Jinny out of range of their rifles.

He pulled the roan to a stop and waited for Jinny to catch up to him. They had ridden far out onto the plain, and as he looked back toward the mountains, he thought he saw a pair of muzzle flashes. If that was the case, the shots came nowhere near them, and the distance was too great for the sounds to carry that far. Jim grinned wearily. "I don't think we'll have to worry about those two anymore," he said.

They had followed the creek during their flight, and now they splashed across it, heading north. The sun was nearing its zenith, and Jim's stomach reminded him that they had not eaten since supper the night before. As he reached behind him and delved into one of the bags for some jerky, he asked Jinny, "How did you manage to get away from them last night?"

She laughed, but there was little humor in the sound. "I ran," she said simply. "I saw that huge, horrible man leap on you, and I thought you were dead. The one called Rusty came running toward me, and I ran away from him. I managed to hide in the trees down the slope for a while, then I circled around that ledge where we had camped and started climbing. I wanted to get as high as I could, so that I could see them if they came after me."

Jim nodded. He handed a piece of jerky to her and then put one in his mouth to soften. Jinny was not finished with her story, and she continued, "When I got above the camp, I could look back down and see that they were tying you on the back of your horse. You were still alive, and I was so relieved! But I felt terribly guilty for running away in the first place."

"Don't," commanded Jim. "Don't feel guilty at all. You did the right thing."

"Later, when I thought about it, I decided maybe that was right. At least while I was still free, I could try to figure out some way to help you. I dodged those trappers all night while they searched for me." Jinny shuddered again. "God, it was awful. They almost found me several times. I was so frightened . . . it was terrifying."

"I know," Jim said softly.

She took a deep breath and went on, "This morning, I . . . I guess I turned the tables on them. I followed them back down out of the mountains and found where they were holding you prisoner. I thought maybe a rockslide would draw them away, so I started one and then circled around as quickly as I could."

It was an amazing story, thought Jim, a mixture of blind luck and incredible courage on Jinny's part. "I owe you my life," he said quietly.

Jinny just bit off a piece of the jerky and smiled at him.

It was one more reason for him to find Nightshade, recover that map, and help her win her father's freedom, Jim thought.

They rode all afternoon, gradually angling back toward the Prophets. The horses had been well rested when they left the trappers' camp that morning, so they were able to keep up a fairly fast pace. Jim was no great judge of distance, so he was unsure how many miles they had put behind them. He was confident, though, that Gentry and Rusty would never be able to catch up on foot.

Near sundown, they reached the foothills again and climbed into them a short way, looking for a place to camp. The site they chose was similar to the one where the trappers had camped the night before, at the base of a long slope dotted with trees and boulders. The ground below them was open for the most part, so that they would be able to see anyone approaching from that direction. They would have a cold camp tonight, Jim decided, preferring not to build a fire and announce their presence. Then, they would take turns staying awake through the night, just as a precaution. If the night passed peacefully and they were able to put a good day's ride behind them tomorrow, they could definitely stop worrying about Gentry and Rusty.

When they had eaten again—jerky and stale biscuits from two days before—Jim moved closer to Jinny as they sat with their backs against one of the boulders. Unsure of how to proceed, he waited for a few minutes of awkward silence, then summoned all his courage and slipped an arm around her shoulders.

"It'll get cold again tonight," said Jinny in a soft voice. Jim just nodded. It seemed nothing else needed to be said.

She dozed off, leaning against his shoulder. Jim took a deep breath and looked out across the plains. The stars were out, bright pinpoints against the field of night, and in the east a thin slice of moon rose in the darkness. In a stark way, it was all beautiful, and Jim was glad that he was seeing it with Jinny beside him.

The terror was over, he thought. Now they had to get on with what had brought them here.

He did not intend to go to sleep, and he had no idea when he actually dozed off. The question was unimportant, anyway. What mattered, he realized as he jerked his head up, blinking and peering around owlishly in the sunshine, was that he had let down his guard. Anyone could have slipped up on them while he was deep in slumber.

Jinny still slept cradled in the crook of his arm, her head pillowed on his shoulder. As Jim's eyes adjusted to the light, he realized that the sun had risen above the peaks behind the campsite. He and Jinny had slept all night and well into the morning, the strain of the last thirty-six hours finally catching up to them. Exhaustion had taken its toll.

He had the feeling that something had roused him from sleep. As he looked around, he realized suddenly that he heard sounds which were out of the ordinary for these foothills.

He heard hoofbeats.

Suddenly frantic, Jim looked out across the expanse in front of them and spotted the approaching riders. Even though they were still several hundred yards away, Jim could see the buckskins they wore and saw as well the brilliant red of one man's beard.

The trappers . . . somehow, they had gotten horses and followed him and Jinny.

"Get up!" exclaimed Jim as he shook the girl's shoulder. "We've got to hide!" Maybe there was still a chance Gentry and Rusty had not seen them yet.

"Wh—what . . . ?" muttered Jinny. She lifted her hands and knuckled sleep from her eyes. "What's wrong, Jim?"

"They're coming!"

Jinny gasped in dismay as her eyes found the approaching riders. She and Jim scrambled to their feet, and Jim caught her arm.

"Get behind the rocks!" he ordered. "Maybe they don't know we're here!"

Even as he spoke, the trappers reined in, and a moment later the blast of a rifle and the whine of a ball ricocheting off a boulder sounded together. The shot had struck close, just to their left. Jim's grip tightened on Jinny's arm. "Come on!" he cried.

They ran behind the boulder and crouched there. Jim lifted his head just enough to peer over the top of the rock, and he saw Gentry and Rusty galloping toward them at top speed. The trappers would be here in a matter of moments.

"Get up the slope!" Jim cried out as he slipped his Colts from their holsters. "Find a good place to hide and stay down. I'll hold them off."

"I can help you!" protested Jinny. "I'll get a rifle—"

"No!" Newk's muzzle-loader and Jim's carbine had been left on the horses, who had been grazing peacefully nearby until the shooting started. Now the roan and Jinny's mare had danced off some twenty feet, spooked by the gunfire. They might as well have been twenty miles away, Jim thought. He went on, "Do as I tell you! Get moving!"

Another bullet struck nearby. Jinny opened her mouth to protest again, but at an urgent look from Jim, she remained silent and began scrambling up the slope, ducking from boulder to boulder.

Jim's fingers tightened on the grips of the revolvers. Gentry and Rusty were still out of pistol range of the Colts, he saw as he ventured another look over the top of the rock, but they were drawing nearer by the second. He wished he'd had more time to practice using the guns.

A quick glance over his shoulder told him that Jinny had

climbed about sixty feet up the slope. He saw her dart into view, then disappear again behind an outcropping of stone. Suddenly he wished he had given her one of the pistols, so that if he was killed, she would be able to put up a fight herself. At the very least—and his mind tried to rebel against this thought at the same time as he realized its grim reality—if she'd had a gun, she could have saved the last shot for herself.

But it was too late now, and his inexperience had betrayed them again. He never should have tried to rise above what he was, he thought. If he had been content to remain an aimless drifter, instead of entertaining visions of respectability and even heroism, none of this would have happened.

Too late. The words echoed in his mind. Too late to do anything except fight back.

With an angry cry, he stood up and began triggering the Colts.

The heavy six-guns bucked against his palms, and the roar of their explosions assaulted his ears. Without realizing it, he was still shouting like a berserker as he pointed the revolvers toward the onrushing trappers and squeezed off shot after shot. He saw fire and smoke bloom from the barrels of their rifles and felt something pluck at the sleeve of his bloodstained shirt. A second later, what seemed to be a finger of flame drew a line across the outer part of his thigh. He staggered but kept shooting. One of the trappers went pinwheeling out of the saddle, and Jim's eyes caught a flash of red beard. Rusty was down, unmoving.

Gentry flung himself off his mount, but he ran forward as he jerked a pistol from his belt. Jim's wrists ached from fighting the recoil of the shots, but he held the guns steady as he fired yet again, at the same instant as Gentry. Jim heard the ball scream through the air beside his ear. He did not flinch, standing as steady as the mountains themselves as he squeezed off the final charge in each Colt.

The trapper went backward as if he had run into a stone

wall. The gun flew out of his hand. He landed heavily, rolling over a couple of times before he came to a stop.

Jim peered over the gunsights at the fallen form. The sudden quiet was eerie, as if he had been transported without warning to some different world where everything was hushed and still. Dragging air into his lungs, Jim stood there a moment longer, then began to tremble.

He forced down the reaction and holstered the left-hand Colt, then transferred the one in his right over to that side. Using his right hand, he pulled down the loading lever and freed the empty cylinder. It went into the pouch on his belt, and he replaced it with one of the fully loaded spares. Then, with the gun in his right hand again, he approached the bodies of the two trappers. The muscles of his legs did not want to work at first, but he willed them into motion.

Gentry was still alive; Jim saw that right away. The trapper was lying on his back, and his chest was heaving up and down as strange moaning sounds came from him. His eyes were closed and he seemed to be no threat, but Jim kept the pistol trained on him anyway until he had located the gun Gentry had dropped. It was well out of the man's reach, even if he had not been badly wounded.

Stepping past Gentry, Jim went quickly to Rusty's side. There was no question that the red-bearded trapper was dead. One of Jim's shots had caught him in the throat, another in the chest. The entire front of his shirt was drenched in blood, and his glassy eyes were staring sightlessly up at the white clouds floating in the morning sky.

Jim went back to Gentry and saw that the trapper was blinking his eyes. As Jim stood over him, Gentry gradually focused on him and rasped, "You . . . you son-of-a-bitch! You've . . . killed me!"

"You were trying to kill me," said Jim, in cold tones.

"You . . . did for . . . Newk . . . had to . . . settle the score . . ."

"Where did you get the horses?" asked Jim.

Blood trickled from the corners of Gentry's mouth as he

pulled his lips into a hideous smile. "Ran across . . . a couple of pilgrims . . . didn't mind givin' up their horses. Had to . . . kill 'em both first, though."

A shudder ran through Jim. More tragedy had befallen someone because of him, although the blame was indirect this time. Gentry closed his eyes and groaned in agony, and Jim was almost gladdened to hear it. A bloodstain on the trapper's abdomen was steadily growing. Gentry was gut-shot, and even a novice like Jim knew what that meant.

The rattle of pebbles behind him made him look around sharply. Jinny had approached, and Jim quickly said, "Stay back! You don't want to see this."

She nodded and said, "I'll get the horses."

As she moved away, Jim looked down at Gentry again and saw that the man had rolled onto his side. His hand was reaching toward the gun he had dropped when he was wounded, but the weapon was a good ten feet from him. Gentry's eyes were fixed on it, and the muscles of his face were taut with strain. Sweat streamed down off his brow.

"Keep trying," said Jim, not quite sure where the hard words came from. "You might reach it in an hour or two."

Then he turned and strode over to join Jinny. Together, they mounted up and rode away from that place.

SEVENTEEN

The sleeve of Jim's shirt was torn where a bullet had ripped through it, and there was a graze on his leg. The injury had not bled, and in fact, it looked more like a burn than a bullet wound. His leg ached a little as he rode, but it was nothing he could not tolerate.

"You were magnificent," said Jinny after they had put several miles behind them. "I never saw anything like that. The way you stood up and shot it out with those two monsters . . . Well, it was remarkable."

"No, it wasn't," said Jim, after a moment of contemplating her words of praise. "I was terrified, but I guess I was more angry than frightened. When I started shooting, I really didn't know what I was doing, and after that, it was too late. There was nothing else I could do except fire as fast as I could."

Jinny was riding close beside him. She leaned over in the saddle, and her fingers brushed his arm. "I still think it was magnificent," she said softly.

Jim smiled grimly. She could think whatever she wanted, but he knew the truth.

On the other hand, the old James Patrick McReady would never have allowed himself to be put in such a dangerous situation. He would have turned tail and run long before now. He was changing, no doubt about it.

But as he remembered his final, callous words to the dying Gentry, he wondered if he was changing for the better.

* * *

They stayed on the edge of the foothills, riding north, the rest of that day. That night, they found a place to camp and built a fire this time, enjoying a hot meal and coffee. Both of them were making an effort to put the horrible events of the last two days behind them, Jim realized, so he laughed and chatted along with Jinny as she recalled happy times from her youth, before the bank robbery that had taken her father away from her. For his part, he was glad of the excuse not to think about the men he had killed and the way he himself had almost met death.

When she asked him about his own early years, however, he turned aside the questions, insisting that there was nothing to say beyond the bare facts: he had been born in the East and had come West. His life was in front of him now, not behind him. That was the way he wanted it, and wisely, she did not press the issue.

They set up watches again, just as a precaution, and this time they were successful in keeping one of them awake at all times during the night. Both of them were a bit tired the next morning, but a certain weariness could be tolerated if it meant they would be safer. And it would not hurt if their caution became habitual, Jim knew. They were heading into country where savage Indians roamed; to become lax would be to invite disaster.

The main pass through the Prophets was far to the south, and as they rode along the edge of the mountain range the next day, Jim kept his eyes open for another passage through the peaks. The Paiutes lived mostly on the other side of the mountains, judging from what Gentry had said, and it was there they would be most likely to find another lead to Nightshade. Too much time had passed, Jim thought; it was all too likely the bandit had already found the stolen loot. And while Nightshade might not have pursued them with the greatest of determination had they taken only a map from him, the outlaw would never let them steal back the money without following them to the ends of the earth in an effort to recover it. Even not knowing too much about Nightshade, Jim realized that.

Not until late on the second day after the final battle with Gentry and Rusty did they locate another pass, this one high in the mountains where the approaches to it would be more difficult. As he and Jinny climbed toward it, following a narrow, winding trail that was often little more than a ledge with hundreds of feet of yawning space only inches to their right, Jim thought that they might have been as well off trying to scale the very heights. Such a task could not have been much more difficult than this dizzying ascension.

At last they reached the pass and rode through its narrow confines. Sheer rock walls towered above them, and Jim revised his opinion. Climbing those mountains *would* have been harder. In fact, he doubted they'd have been able to accomplish it. Thankfully, they did not have to. This route led them across the spine of the range, and less than thirty minutes later, they hit what appeared to be a well-traveled trail.

"Who do you think uses this path?" asked Jinny, as they followed it to the northeast.

Jim shrugged. "Nightshade and his gang?" he ventured. "Maybe the Paiutes themselves. It's hard to say."

This country was even more rugged than that through which they had traveled earlier. Rocky canyons led between spires and pinnacles of stone, the passages twisting and turning in a basaltic labyrinth. Jim was glad for the presence of a well-defined trail; otherwise the two of them would have been hopelessly lost in a matter of hours. He did not expect to find any villages up here, nor very many travelers. In fact, he and Jinny had not seen anyone else since the fight with the trappers. This was desolate territory indeed.

Shadows were gathering with the approach of night, and Jim began looking for a place to camp. At this elevation, there was little but stone, but a few hardy clumps of grass could be seen here and there. He and Jinny had supplies for themselves, but the horses would need something on which to graze, and they would need water. The canteens slung on the saddles were beginning to sound hollow when they were shaken.

At dusk, they found a small trickle of water wending its way from the base of a towering cliff. The tiny stream had given birth to some scrubby vegetation. As Jim reined in at the edge of the water, he said, "We'll camp here. We certainly haven't found anyplace else that looks suitable."

Jinny agreed. They dismounted, and while Jim tended to the horses, she built a fire and began preparing supper.

Both of them were quiet as they ate; they had already been through a great deal together, and their silence was now a companionable one. When they were finished, Jinny rolled in her blankets and slept first. Jim sat by the fire, remembering how she had told him not to stare into the flames. He had learned a great deal from her, he thought. Occasionally, he darted a glance at her sleeping form, and he felt a warmth in his chest. This journey had taught him a great deal indeed, some bad, some good.

Now that they were on the eastern side of the mountains, the sun peeked over the horizon earlier the next morning than they were accustomed to. That allowed them to get an earlier start on the day's riding, as well. As he put the saddle on the back of the roan—he was going to have to give the animal a new name, Jim was thinking; the other one held too many bad memories now—a strange sensation overtook him. A prickly feeling rippled up his back, and he lifted his head, the breath sticking in his throat. He let his right hand move casually toward the butt of the Colt on that side.

"Something's wrong," said Jinny.

Jim turned a little and looked at her, and he could tell from the tense manner in which she was standing that she had felt the same sensation. She looked up at the mountains around them and continued, "Someone is watching us."

That was exactly what it was, Jim thought; she had defined what was bothering them. But as his eyes searched the crags, he saw no movement, no smoke from another campfire, no sign of human habitation at all. The only thing that seemed to be moving anywhere was a hawk, idly winging along high in the heavens.

A hawk!

Jim had not told the girl how a hawk had saved him from the wolf, back at the trappers' camp. Nor had he said anything about the ridiculous idea that had crossed his mind when he saw another hawk later. Jinny would not have laughed at him, he was certain of that, but she would not have known what to make of the story, and they had both had enough to occupy their thoughts. Now, faced with the undeniable feeling of being observed, with only a bird wheeling high above them, Jim struggled with his decision. Should he explain what had happened, share his theory about the hawk somehow keeping an eye on him?

No. He drew a deep breath. It was too absurd. "I don't see anything," he said. "Let's get moving. If somebody is watching us, maybe that'll draw them out into the open."

Quickly, they finished getting ready to ride and then mounted up. Jim took the lead, clucking to the roan as he heeled it into motion. He rode along the trail, trying to look as if he had no idea they were being observed. If there were watchers, he and Jinny had to lull them into revealing themselves.

A few minutes later, though, Jim suddenly realized that the sensation had vanished. When he twisted in the saddle and looked back at Jinny, his eyebrows raised quizzically, she nodded. "It's gone, whatever it was," said the girl. "That was certainly strange."

Jim turned his gaze to the sky, seeking a small, dark, moving shape, but there was none to be seen. The hawk, if that was really what it had been, and not a lie told to him by his imagination, was gone.

"Yes," echoed Jim. "Strange."

* * *

They paused for a meal at midday, stopping and building a small fire rather than eating in the saddle. Now that their canteens were full again, Jim even deemed it safe to brew a pot of coffee.

He had not forgotten about the bizarre occurrence earlier in the day; it had stayed in his thoughts all morning. But he had no answers, and the only course of action they could follow was the one they had already taken.

Jinny brought up the subject over their bread and meat. "What do you think that was," she asked, "that unusual feeling both of us had this morning?"

Jim hesitated before replying. The silence stretched out until he began to sense that Jinny was becoming annoyed with him for not answering. Finally, he said, "I think that hawk was watching us."

"What hawk?"

"You didn't see it, flying away up in the air?"

Jinny shook her head.

"Well, it was there," declared Jim. Now that he had started, he might as well finish it, he thought. "I believe it was the same one that saved me from a wolf, back when the trappers were holding me prisoner."

She was staring at him, and he could not blame her. He had to sound like a lunatic, babbling like this about a hawk saving his life and then watching him later. He continued with the story, telling her how the wolf had come out of the woods to menace him and how the hawk had swooped down out of nowhere to turn it away. He concluded by saying, "If you don't believe me, that's all right. If I heard that yarn from somebody else, I probably wouldn't believe it either."

For a long moment, Jinny said nothing. Then, with her lovely features set in a solemn expression, she reached across to him and laid her hand on his. "I believe you," she said.

He was touched, not only by her flesh on his, but by her unquestioning faith in him. As he had told her, he himself would have found the tale farfetched, had he heard it from someone else. But in Jinny's blue eyes he saw only belief, and it gladdened him more than he expected. Her opinion had grown to mean a great deal to him.

They finished their meal in silence. Then Jinny said, "I don't pretend to understand what you've told me, Jim. But I know it happened just the way you said. The next time the hawk appears, you'll show it to me, won't you?"

"Of course," he nodded. "*If* it shows up again."

They cleansed their cooking utensils with sand, then prepared to mount up and move on. Jim bent over to scoop dirt onto the flames and extinguish them, when suddenly the eerie feeling struck him again. He stood still, raising only his head to see if the sensation had been noticed by Jinny. She was standing next to her mare, her head cocked slightly to one side, as if she was listening.

"It's back," whispered the young man.

Jinny nodded, an almost imperceptible bobbing of her head. Slowly, Jim straightened and looked up, searching in the heavens for the hawk.

There were a few lacy clouds spread across the sky, but other than that, there was nothing to be seen in the vast expanse of blue. The hawk was nowhere in sight.

Yet the feeling was unmistakably the same one that had assailed them earlier in the day. So the hawk was not responsible for it after all, and Jim cursed himself for letting his mind wander off on such a flight of fancy. By letting himself believe in such a thing, he had neglected perhaps the most obvious explanation.

They were being watched by a human being, one who was expert in seeing without being seen.

In this part of the mountain, one particular group best fit that description—the Paiute Indians they had come here seeking.

"Stay calm," said Jim. He threw sand on the fire and put

it out, as he had started to do a moment earlier. "It's either Nightshade's men, or the Paiutes. Whoever it is, they'll show themselves when they're ready."

"What do we do if it's the Indians?" asked Jinny.

"Tell them we're looking for Ko'lu. Perhaps they'll take us to him."

Jim's mind was working rapidly as he swung up into the saddle and gestured for Jinny to do likewise. The Paiutes could be dangerous, but from what he had heard, they did not kill white men on sight, like some of their more bloodthirsty brethren on the Great Plains to the East. The Paiutes might be willing to listen to reason, and if that was the case, Jim hoped to make them believe that he and Jinny were looking for Ko'lu so that they could find Nightshade. That was in fact the truth.

The sensation of being observed was still with them as they nudged their horses into motion. Jim took the lead, riding along the winding trail, his head slowly turning from side to side as his eyes searched the rugged terrain around them. Jinny followed closely behind him. Occasionally, Jim would reach down and grasp the stock of the carbine, shifting it a little in the saddle boot each time to assure himself that it could be drawn quickly. He did the same with each of the Navy Colts. Jinny was carrying the muzzle-loader balanced across the pommel of her saddle, and as Jim glanced back at her, he saw the whiteness of her knuckles as she grasped it tightly.

So far he had seen and heard no evidence of anyone following their progress: no flicker of movement behind a rock, no feathered headdress extending over the top of a boulder, no rattle of gravel as the watcher changed his position, no whinny or stamp of hooves from a concealed mount. But that did not mean the watchers were not there. He could feel their presence like a touch on his arm. They were there, all right, and it was only a matter of time until they came out into the open.

Suddenly a loud, ululating wail sounded from somewhere above and ahead of them, making Jim stiffen in the saddle and prompting a startled cry from Jinny. An answering howl came from behind them. Jim twisted, his right hand going to the butt of a Colt while his left tightened on the reins. "It's the Paiutes," he said grimly to Jinny. "It has to be."

"What do they mean to do?"

He shook his head. "I don't know. Let's keep riding, and try not to look frightened."

That last was an impossible request, as he knew all too well. Anyone looking at him would have seen the pallor that gripped his features, the wide, staring eyes, and the beads of moisture that started out on his forehead. Jinny, he was sure, looked much the same way, but he could not be sure, because he was facing forward again as he rode slowly along the trail, waiting for trouble.

He did not have long to wait.

With a sound almost like the flutter of a bird's wings, an arrow went past him on the left, angling down from somewhere above and behind them, hit the hard-packed dirt of the trail, and skidded a couple of feet before coming to a stop. As Jim reined in and Jinny started to scream, another arrow whipped past on the right. Jim drew his gun as he turned in the saddle and scanned the slope to the left of the trail.

Nothing.

The arrows had missed on purpose; somehow he knew that without being told. The Indians wanted to herd them ahead, wanted to make them rush along the trail so that they would ride right into a trap of some sort. Jim was not going to fall for it. The Indians expected them to bolt when the arrows began flying; they would ride hard, all right, just not in the direction the Paiutes desired.

"Turn around!" he called to Jinny. "Head back down the trail!"

And as she did so, Jim lifted the Colt and let off two rounds toward the mountainside where the ambushers had to be lurking. The thunderous explosions echoed back from the unyielding stone. Jim did not expect to hit anything, firing blindly that way, but he wanted the savages to know that he was armed and did not mind using his weapons.

His strategy might have been a good one. It might even have worked, had not Jinny's mare spooked at the blasts of the revolver just as she was trying to whirl the horse in a tight turn. Suddenly the mare reared back, crying out in fear and dancing nervously on its hind legs. One hoof slipped as it unwittingly drew near the edge of the trail.

Jim darted a glance in that direction. The downward slope was not a sheer precipice at this point, but it was steep enough that if the horse fell with Jinny on its back, the results would undoubtedly be tragic. Jinny would be crushed as the animal rolled over and over. As the mare struggled to catch its balance, Jim shouted, "Jinny! Get your feet out of the stirrups! Get off of there!"

He did not know if she was trying to follow his orders or if what happened next was an accident, but before his eyes, Jinny sailed out of the saddle, falling heavily at the far side of the trail while the mare finally slipped over the edge. The horse screamed in fear and pain as it tumbled down the rocky slope.

Jim threw himself to the ground and ran to Jinny's side, unmindful of the Paiute menace now. He had to make certain she was all right and had not been harmed in the fall. As he reached her, she was scrambling up onto her feet, and he grasped her arm anxiously.

"I'm fine," she told him before he could even ask the question. "We've still got to get out of here, Jim!"

He nodded and led her toward the roan. Below, the screams of the mare had ceased, and both of them knew what that meant. Hurriedly, Jim mounted and then pulled Jinny up behind him. She slipped her arms around his midsection, hanging on tightly as he kicked the roan into a gallop.

No more arrows had flown since those first two, and a

few minutes later, Jim thought perhaps they had been lucky enough to slip past the Indians. Maybe it had been only a small party composed of the two he had heard signaling each other.

Those hopes were dashed as he and Jinny rounded a bend in the trail and saw the half-dozen riders waiting for them, men in buckskins and feathers and paint, mounted bareback on small, wiry ponies. Jim tried to pull the roan into another turn, but an arrow flew past his head. He heard the pounding of hoofbeats coming along the trail from the other direction and knew he and Jinny were trapped, pinned between two groups of Indians. The Paiutes who had been behind them now started forward abruptly, waving bows and lances and whooping at the top of their lungs.

Jim had hoped for a peaceful encounter with these Indians, but obviously that was not to be. As Jinny's grip around his middle tightened to the point where breathing was beginning to be difficult, Jim cast around frantically for a means of escape. They could not go up the slope on the left side of the trail; it was much too sheer. But the right side was not as steep . . .

Jinny's mare had fallen to its death on that slope, but that was different. The mare had been panic-stricken and had lost control. Jim thought the roan had at least a chance of making it.

He had no idea what they would find at the bottom of the slope, but they could not stay here. "Hang on!" he shouted to Jinny, and then his fingers tightened on the reins. His heels dug into the roan's flanks as he turned the horse's nose toward the edge of the trail. The roan hesitated, then surged forward.

It was as if the world had dropped out from under them, Jim thought, so that there was nothing around them except the clear mountain air. But then the hooves of the roan hit the hillside with a bone-jarring impact, and it was all Jim could do to stay in the saddle. Clamping his knees to the body of the horse as tightly as he could, he prayed that Jinny would not lose her grip on him.

The roan was astounding as it bounded, slid, and leaped from side to side, picking its way down the rubble-strewn slope. Jim's heart swelled with love for and pride in the common-looking animal; inside the roan, he now knew; was the soul of a charger. Any armored knight in olden times would have been proud to ride this beast into battle. Courage and muscle worked in smooth tandem as the roan carried them down the hillside to safety.

Jim never knew what went wrong, but suddenly the roan's gait faltered even more than could be expected from this rough going. The horse lurched to one side, and Jim cried, "No! Stay up, stay up!" His entreaties were no good in the face of gravity, though, and the roan fell.

Jim threw himself from the saddle, aware briefly that he could no longer feel Jinny's arms clutched around him. He had time to shout her name once before his body smashed against the rocks.

There was no reply.

EIGHTEEN

This time, he did not pass out completely, but the grip he retained on consciousness was tenuous at best. As he rolled down the hill, bouncing from rock to rock, the pain grew until it enveloped him completely. When he finally came to a stop, he was wrapped in pain as if it was the web of a giant spider, drawn around him strand by strand until it totally enclosed him. He could still see and hear, but his senses were muffled, so that when voices intruded on his brain long moments later, the words they spoke were incomprehensible, and his eyes saw shadowy, flickering movements and nothing more. He wanted to cry out, but that would have required more strength than he possessed.

Had the roan fallen on him, crushing his organs and pulping his muscles? Jim did not think so, but it was hard to tell. And what of Jinny? When the horse fell, had she been able to catch herself, or had she tumbled all the way to the bottom of the slope as he had? Was she alive or dead?

Hands gripped him and lifted him, and this time Jim was able to scream. He screamed loud and long, or so it seemed to him. Were these the Paiutes who had hold of him? That had to be the case. No one else would be abroad in this desolation. He and Jinny had been fools to come here, he thought, fools whose heads had been full of romantic notions. Bitterly, Jim told himself that they deserved whatever happened to them.

But still he would have given a fortune to feel her hand folded in his at this very moment, and that thought galled him even more, because a fortune was what had brought them here. A stolen fortune with a legacy of suffering and death . . .

He was lifted onto a horse, thrown face down over the back of the animal. Rawhide thongs bound his wrists to his ankles. His head hung loosely from his neck. The horse stepped out in a brisk walk, and each time a hoof met the ground, Jim felt it as a white-hot poker in his vitals. Now he prayed for darkness to claim him, but it did not.

How much time was required for the journey to the Paiute village was impossible to calculate, at least for Jim's pain-wracked brain. He might have been tied over the back of the pony for a matter of minutes or a matter of days, for all he knew. But finally the jolting ride ceased, and he was taken down from the horse and dropped roughly on the ground.

Jim lay there panting for breath, his head swimming from being upside down for so long. He tried to open his eyes, but the light struck them like tiny knives piercing all the way into his skull. He moaned.

Something moved between him and the face of the sun, casting a shadow that Jim could sense. Once again he pried his eyes open, but this time he was able to keep the lids lifted. He stared up into a red, burnished face that was all hard planes and angles, topped by straight black hair adorned with a single feather. The Indian wore beaded buckskins and carried a carbine. Jim recognized it as the saddle gun he had been issued by the Pony Express back in Flat Rock. Obviously, this savage had claimed it as booty.

Jim's swollen tongue came out of his mouth and scraped along dry, cracked lips. He winced. His throat muscles were stiff and sore, but he managed to say, "Wh-what do you . . . want . . . ?"

The Indian made no reply. He turned his head, barked a command in his guttural language. More of the Paiutes closed in from both sides, and as they bent over him, Jim felt his arms grasped by fingers like iron. They lifted him to his feet, and as fresh waves of pain broke over him, he would have fallen if not for their grasp. He was marched across what he could now see was a clearing in a circle of crude wickiups. Each step brought new agony to him, but there was nothing he could do, save cooperate with the Indians. He was outnumbered and too banged up even to attempt otherwise.

Their destination was a stout pole fashioned from the trunk of a small tree. It had been shorn of its branches and driven deep into the ground, so that now it stood only about the height of a man's head. Jim was pushed against it, and his arms were grabbed and jerked around roughly so that his back was to the post. A knobby projection ground uncomfortably into one of his shoulderblades. As his wrists were pulled behind the pole, they were quickly lashed together, again with rawhide thongs. Jim's body wanted to sag forward, but the bounds would not allow it.

His hair had fallen across his eyes, and although a toss of his head would have thrown it back, even that was too much for him at the moment. Instead, he blinked and peered through the screen of hair. He saw Paiute braves striding proudly around the encampment. The women and children were less obvious, but they were there as well, peering out the entrances of the wickiups at the captive white man. Jim looked toward the group of horses which had carried his captors into the village and saw that the animals were being penned in a crude corral made of brush from further down the mountain slopes. Among the animals, Jim saw with a leap of his heart, was his roan, limping a little but apparently little the worse for the tumble down the mountainside. Given a few days' rest, the horse would probably be as good as new.

He wondered if the same could be said of him.

His legs had worked, albeit reluctantly, when he was brought over to the post. Now he wiggled his fingers and strained with the muscles of his arms and shoulders against the bonds that held him. Everything there seemed to be working all right. He took a deep breath, alert for any sudden stab of pain that would mean he was broken somewhere inside. None came. He was hurting, there was no use denying that, but the aches, the cuts and bruises, all seemed to be external. Jim was grateful for that.

Now that he had taken stock, a frantic worry began to grow within him as he looked around for Jinny and saw no sign of her. He did not know what to hope for; if the Indians had brought her to the village as a prisoner, at least he would know she was alive. Jim groaned as he realized that he was about to live through virtually the same torment of uncertainty about her as when the trappers had captured him. Had she fallen to her death on the slope? That was quite possible. Had she survived and then eluded the Paiutes, as she had Gentry and Rusty? That was less likely. It would be much more difficult to escape from the Indians in broad daylight than it had been to give the slip to the trappers in darkness.

The warrior who had ordered him bound to this stake now sauntered over to him, arrogance plain in the man's face and in every line of his body. He stopped in front of Jim and spat at the young man's feet in contempt. "Who are you, white man, to come riding so boldly into Paiute land?" demanded the brave. His English was quite fluent, though a bit guttural, and Jim found himself wondering irrelevantly who had taught the red man how to speak it.

Jim licked his lips again, and this time his voice sounded more normal as he replied, "We . . . we were looking for someone."

"Who?" The question came sharply from the Indian.

"A man named . . . Ko'lu."

For the briefest instant, Jim thought he saw something like surprise flicker through the Paiute's eyes. But the man was skilled at concealing his reactions, and his features were stony as he asked, "Why do you seek this Ko'lu?"

"We were hoping . . . he could take us to . . . to Nightshade."

Some of the other Indians had drifted closer during the

interrogation of Jim, and they began to mutter among themselves at the mention of Nightshade. The warrior who stood before Jim, arms crossed casually on his chest, turned and looked at them, and they instantly fell silent. The Indian turned back to Jim and asked, "What is your name?"

"Jim . . . Jim McReady."

"And the yellow-haired maiden with you?"

Jim felt a surge of hope that the man's question meant Jinny was still alive, but he realized a moment later that it might not mean any such thing. They had all been close enough to see her blond hair flashing in the sun. He said, "Her name is Virginia Rawlings."

"She is your woman?"

Jim's first impulse was to say yes; that was what he wanted to be the truth. But he knew that Jinny had never admitted to feeling toward him as he felt toward her. He said slowly, "I don't know."

The Indian's lip curled. "A man always knows. You are not a man but a pup, a mongrel dog fit only to beg scraps from its betters. It is fitting that another will take the yellow-hair for his wife."

His breath catching in his throat, Jim stared at the Indian for a long moment, caring not at all about the insults the man had just heaped on him. The only thing that concerned him was Jinny's safety. He said, "Then she . . . she's all right?"

At first, he did not think the Indian was going to deign to answer. But then the warrior relented and said, "The woman is being cared for. She does not seem to be badly hurt. The spirits were with you, white man, when you and the woman and the horse fell down the mountain. All of you lived." He shook his head. "A pity the spirits will not remain with you. Instead, they will desert you, leaving you to *my* mercies, which are few," he added heavily.

Jim ignored the veiled threat. Jinny was alive! That was all that mattered. They were both in deadly danger, with no foreseeable way out, but by now Jim had learned never to give up hope. As long as he was alive, he thought, he might win through to victory, either through his own efforts or by the hand of Fate . . .

Or perhaps a little bit of both.

Jim lost track of time. He was aware that he had been standing tied to the post for hours, and he had passed out from the heat of the sun beating down on him. Several times he came to, only to have his mind slide back into the welcoming darkness. Drifting in and out of consciousness this way, he was unsure if night had fallen and this was the next day, or if every minute was stretching out into an eternity. Finally, when he came to his senses and lifted his head enough to see the sun, he realized that the fiery orb had moved, that it was now in the east. This was indeed morning. Moments later, the cramping of his empty stomach confirmed the fact.

Around him, life was going on as usual in the Indian village. Now that they were accustomed to him, the women and children had become bolder. The squaws went on about their work, and the youngsters approached to within a dozen feet of the prisoner, standing there and chattering about him. He was on display, Jim realized.

Why had these Paiutes been so hostile, he wondered? The tribe had had trouble with white men before, but generally they were not regarded as being overly dangerous. These Indians, however, had been out for blood right from the start.

He had been watching for Jinny, but he was not prepared for what he saw when she finally appeared. The canvas flap covering the entrance of one of the wickiups was thrust back, and a young woman in the garb of a Paiute maiden stepped out, followed by several old squaws with faces as lined and seamed as the badlands. Jinny looked uncomfortable in the fringed, beaded, buckskin dress as she came toward Jim. Her long blond hair had been twisted into two braids, and those braids had been wound tightly around her head. She was still quite beautiful, in an exotic way, and Jim ached to reach out and touch the soft skin of her cheek as she drew near him.

Jinny was carrying an earthen bowl full of some sort of gruel, and as she stepped up to Jim, he could smell the foul odor emanating from it. Her eyes were full of pity as she whispered, "My God, Jim! Are you all right?"

He moved his head in a slight nod. "Just banged up some," he declared. "What about you? Have you been hurt?"

"Eat this," said the girl, ignoring his question. She dipped a crude wooden spoon into the vile concoction and lifted it to his lips. Jim clamped his mouth shut and would have refused to take the stuff, had she not whispered a hurried plea for him to cooperate.

"They expect you to eat it," she said. "Please, Jim."

Reluctantly he took a small sip of the gruel, and to his surprise it did not taste as bad as it looked and smelled. It was not good, by any means, but he supposed he could tolerate it. And his empty stomach was shrieking for anything to fill it.

As she spoon-fed him, she said in a voice so low that only he could hear, "I'm fine; no one has bothered me, except the squaws who took my clothes and gave me these. I'm a little sore from the fall, but not too bad."

"I saw the roan," whispered Jim, around a mouthful of the food. "He didn't look hurt too much, either."

"I know. We were all lucky."

"So the head man told me." Jim summoned up a grim smile. "I don't think he likes me too much."

Jinny lowered her eyes and her even white teeth caught her lower lip in a gesture of anxiety. Aware that he had somehow said the wrong thing, Jim quickly asked, "What is it?"

"I know the one you're talking about," replied Jinny. "I think they've decided that I'm to be his wife."

Shock gripped Jim. The Paiute leader had said something to that effect yesterday, but Jim had supposed him to be speaking in general terms. Now it appeared that Jinny's fate had already been decided.

"What are they going to do with me?" he asked.

"Well . . . you have to realize I don't understand most of what they're talking about. . . ." Jinny looked uneasy, as if she did not want to answer the question. Jim was fairly certain he knew the answer already. Finally, the girl took a deep breath and said, "They're going to kill you."

A shudder ran through her, and for a moment Jim thought she was going to drop the bowl and what was left of the gruel. He said quickly, "Buck up, Jinny! They may try, but that's not the same thing as doing it." He heard the calm strength in his words, and it surprised him as much as it evidently did her.

"But what can we do to stop them?" asked the girl. "We're helpless—"

"Right now we may be," cut in Jim. "That doesn't mean things will stay this way."

A part of him wondered if his mind had become unbalanced. That was the only explanation for the bravado he was exhibiting. Certainly this display of courage was false; after all, it was coming from a young man whose watchwords had always been caution and even cowardice. The Jim McReady who had huddled in that Eastern tenement would have died straight away before he'd have been able to stare into the face of such danger.

Perhaps that Jim McReady was already dead, thought the man tied to the stake.

The squaws approached, chattering at Jinny, and she said, "I've got to go." She turned away and started toward the wickiup from which she had emerged, but she threw one glance over her shoulder as she left, and in her eyes Jim read the proof of that which he had not known until now: She loved him, just as he loved her.

But had they made this wondrous discovery too late?

For Jinny's sake, Jim kept his head up. If he could maintain that fiction of courage, perhaps she would be able to face what was coming with greater bravery. Not until the wizened squaws had ushered her back into the wickiup did he allow a trace of despair to touch his features.

The food, despite its unsavory smell, had given him some strength. He took deep breaths of the clear mountain air, trying to keep his head clear. He had to think and think fast if they were to have any chance of escaping from this situation.

But no matter how intently he thought as he examined every aspect of the danger in which they found themselves, he could discover no way out, no means by which they might slip away from the Indians. His bonds were too tight to be budged, Jinny was obviously confined to the wickiup under the watchful eyes of the Paiute crones, and there were warriors scattered all around the village who would cheerfully slit his throat, cave in his skull with a tomahawk, or drive an arrow through his body if he did manage to get free. It was as close to hopeless as anything could be.

Jim had heard gruesome tales of tribal torture. Indians could entertain themselves for long hours with the suffering of their captives. As Jim hung on the stake, he wondered if, when the time came, it would be better for him to put up a fight, to force them to kill him rather than submitting to their hideous sport. Better a quick death than a slow one, he reasoned.

The heat of the sun increased, beating brassily down on the village. In the middle of the day, when the sun was directly overhead, the Indians withdrew into their shelters for the most part, but Jim was left to suffer through it. He grew lightheaded, and he was unsure whether he passed out or simply fell asleep.

Whichever was true, he was suddenly jolted back to awareness by a series of shrill whinnies from a very angry horse. As he lifted his head and blinked his eyes open, Jim focused his attention on the crude corral where the tribe's horses were kept. The roan was there, too, and Jim saw that one of the Paiutes had stripped off the horse's saddle and climbed onto its back, intending to ride it. The roan clearly had different ideas about the matter.

It was bucking to beat the band, sunfishing and twisting frenziedly as it attempted to throw off the unwelcome rider. Jim's eyes widened as he recognized the Indian as the leader, the warrior who intended to take Jinny as his wife. The red man was making a valiant attempt to stay mounted, but the roan was determined to unseat him. As Jim watched, the Indian suddenly lost his grip and went sailing through the air to crash against the ground. He had to roll over quickly and scramble to his feet to avoid being trampled by the slashing hooves of the furious roan.

He came up spouting what Jim supposed to be Paiute curses. Gesturing at the roan, which had withdrawn to the other side of the corral and was now regarding the Indians with a haughty stare, the warrior commanded some of his followers to close in on the horse. They did so, throwing lassos over the roan's tossing head and bringing it under reluctant control. The leader told them to bring the horse out of the corral.

Jim was able to follow those commands only because of the way the other Indians reacted to them. They led the horse out of the enclosure. Jim watched nervously as the leader followed. The Paiute snapped another command, and one of the braves ran to a wickiup and returned with the carbine that had been Jim's. The headman took the weapon and turned toward the roan, his features filled with hatred.

Suddenly, Jim realized what was about to happen, and without thinking he cried, "No!"

The Paiute glanced at him, sneered, and then lifted the carbine to his shoulder, training the muzzle on the proud head of the roan. Horrified and furious, Jim strained against his bonds to no avail. Another shout burst from his throat.

"You dirty yellow dog!"

He saw the Indian stiffen. The man understood English, Jim knew, and from the startled reaction of some of the other Paiutes, they did, too. They watched eagerly to see how their leader would respond to Jim's insult.

Slowly, the Paiute turned toward Jim and studied him. Finally, he said, "I could kill you, too, white man, as well as your ugly red horse."

"Go ahead," said Jim angrily. "It takes a lot of courage to shoot a dumb animal, so I'm sure you're brave enough to kill a helpless, unarmed man, too!"

Even as he spoke, he looked past the Paiute and saw Jinny peering out through a small opening where the hide on her wickiup had been pushed back. She looked terrified, and the fear on her face made a pang of sympathy go through Jim. But he could not stand by and watch the Indian shoot his horse without saying anything.

"So, you think I am a coward," said the Paiute after a moment.

"Well, I have noticed that you seem to pick victims who can't fight back, at least not fairly," responded Jim. He was not sure where this brazen courage was coming from, but he even managed to put a mocking smile on his face.

The Paiute's hands tightened on the carbine, and for an instant, Jim thought the man was going to whip the gun up and send a ball crashing through his head. But then the man abruptly sneered again, and he turned aside to thrust the weapon into the hands of one of his subordinates. He barked an order, then stood back with his arms folded calmly across his chest. Two Indians approached Jim, slipping keen-bladed knives from leather sheaths as they advanced, and Jim thought they were going to plunge the knives into his chest. He clamped his jaws tightly together, determined not to cry out as he died.

Instead, the Indians merely slashed the bonds that held him, and the sudden, unexpected freedom sent him falling forward onto his face.

"You mock my bravery, white man," said the Paiute headman. "Now we shall test yours."

Jim got his hands underneath him and pushed himself up onto all fours. Another few moments were required to lift himself all the way onto his feet. He staggered a bit as he caught his balance, muscles deadened by the long hours of enforced stillness now shrieking their complaint. Jim lifted a hand and wiped it across his pale features.

"Whatever you want," he managed to say as he glowered at the Paiute.

The headman suddenly stripped off his buckskin shirt, revealing a firmly muscled torso. He held out his hand, and one of the other braves placed a tomahawk in it. With a gesture, the leader commanded that a tomahawk be given to Jim as well.

From the wickiup where Jinny was being held came a cry. "No, Jim!" protested the girl. "You can't do this! You'll be killed!"

Jim hefted the tomahawk in his hand, feeling the weight of the stone head and testing the balance of the thick club to which it was bound. He lifted his head to meet Jinny's horrified gaze, and he hoped that she could read in his eyes the love he felt for her. Then he turned to the Paiute leader and said; "I'm ready, whoever you are."

"When you reach the spirit world," grated the Indian, tensing himself to strike, "you can tell them you met your death at the hands of the great warrior Ko'lu!"

NINETEEN

Jim gaped in surprise for an instant, but that was all the time Ko'lu gave him. The Paiute sprang forward, slashing at Jim's head with the tomahawk. Instinct forced Jim's muscles to work, and he darted aside, lifting his own tomahawk in an attempt to block the blow.

The weapons clashed, the impact sending a shiver up Jim's arm. He took a couple of hurried steps backward to take him out of Ko'lu's reach, but the Indian followed without a pause. Again Jim frantically dodged a blow that would have crushed his skull, had it landed.

Jim knew little about Indians, but he had always thought of them as stoic. Now he saw how false that idea was. The other Paiutes were whooping and hollering as their leader bore in on the attack, hacking and slashing savagely at the desperate young white man. Jim blocked some of the blows and ducked away from others, but his luck could not hold up forever. In fact, it came to an abrupt end when he had to jerk up his left arm to ward off a sweeping blow.

The tomahawk crashed against his arm with numbing impact. That loss of feeling lasted only an instant, however, and then pain swept through Jim, radiating from his injured arm. He cried out as the arm fell limp and useless at his side. Vaguely, he heard Jinny echoing his cry.

He leaped to the side, away from another blow aimed at his head. Even though the fight had lasted only moments so far, he was already exhausted, his reserves of strength having been drained by the long ordeal of being tied to the post. It was only a matter of time, he knew, until he moved a little too slowly. Then Ko'lu's tomahawk would smash the life out of him.

Unless he did something unexpected.

No sooner had that thought crossed Jim's mind than he was acting on it. He had no battle plan, only instinctive reactions. He dived forward, going under one of Ko'lu's blows and aiming his body at the Paiute's legs. Ko'lu grunted in surprise as Jim rolled into him, upsetting him.

Ko'lu fell across Jim's legs. For the first time the young man struck a blow of his own, aiming the tomahawk for Ko'lu's head. The Paiute was too fast and jerked out of the way, but just being on the offensive for a change felt wonderful to Jim. He scrambled up, reaching his feet just as Ko'lu was trying to get up, too. Jim rammed a boot against the Indian's chest, knocking him sprawling.

A fierce exultation went through Jim. He was up, while Ko'lu was still down. Even if he defeated the headman, he knew, the other Indians would probably kill him, but at this moment his own death would be an acceptable price to pay to feel Ko'lu's skull cracking like an eggshell under his tomahawk. Caught up in the frenzy of battle, Jim leaped toward the fallen chief, ready to deal the killing stroke.

Ko'lu rolled easily aside, the shaft of Jim's tomahawk shattering as the weapon struck the hard ground where the Paiute's head had been a split-second before. Jim shouted in disappointment and tried to recover his balance, but Ko'lu's shoulder drove into him at that moment, sending him over onto his back. His head bounced painfully on the rocky earth. Ko'lu brought a clubbed fist down hard on Jim's chest, driving the air from his lungs and leaving him curled on the ground, gasping for breath and trying to fight off the dizziness that threatened to overwhelm him. On his knees at the white man's side, Ko'lu grinned in savage triumph as he lifted his tomahawk to smash out Jim's brains.

The crack of a rifle took everyone by surprise. Jim flinched as a heavy-caliber ball bored through the Paiute's head. A foul mixture of red and gray spattered Jim's shirt as Ko'lu collapsed across him. The Indian's face was turned toward Jim, and the features were frozen in an eternal expression of utter surprise beneath the gaping hole in his forehead.

More rifles exploded as Jim tried to push himself out from under the Paiute's body. Hoofbeats filled the air like thunder. Jim scrambled to his feet as the shrill notes of a bugle sounded. Men were shouting and cursing, women were crying, and children were screaming in terror. Jim got his bearings and whirled around in time to see the wave of blue-clad riders sweeping into the Paiute village.

Dimly, his mind recognized them as the U.S. Cavalry, and he knew that he and Jinny would be safe now . . . if they could survive the chaos of the next few minutes. Indians were running all around him, some of them trying to put up a fight as they fled, others simply trying to get away. Jim waited for an opening in the tide of terrified humanity and then dodged through it, heading for the wickiup where he had last seen Jinny. He called her name as he ran.

"Jinny! Jinny!"

"Jim!"

He picked the cry out of the bedlam of gunfire and fear and pain around him and realized it came from his left. She must have run out of the wickiup, he thought as he turned in that direction, searching frantically for her. In front of him suddenly appeared one of the Paiute women, and just as suddenly she fell, blood gushing from her mouth as a musket ball drove into her back. Jim hurdled the dead woman, his mind numb now to everything except finding Jinny.

He saw more Indians falling under the fire of the soldiers. Vaguely it registered on his brain that the riders were cutting down everyone in buckskin, young and old, male and female alike. Jinny was dressed like an Indian, he remembered, and all it would take was one eager soldier, quick to fire before he saw the blond hair braided on her head . . .

Suddenly he saw her, dodging from side to side, craning her neck looking for him. She called his name and he answered, running toward her. Out of the corner of his eye, he saw one of the troopers riding through the village, slashing from left to right and back with the long saber in his hand. Indians went down screaming before the blade.

The soldier's horse loomed up, close by Jim's shoulder. He left his feet in a dive, his good arm wrapping around Jinny and bearing her to the ground. The saber cut the air where she had been. Jim rolled over, pulling Jinny with him. They scrambled out of the way as more soldiers went galloping past.

"Your hair!" cried Jim as they got to their knees. "Take your hair down!"

Understanding dawned in Jinny's confused eyes after a few seconds, and she began tearing at the braids wrapped around her head. Jim helped her as much as he could, and in a matter of moments they had her long hair loose again, the shining blond strands spread out around her face so that no one could mistake her for an Indian. They got to their feet and staggered toward the edge of the village, Jim keeping his arm tightly around her shoulders as they went.

Most of the wickiups were on fire now. The cavalry charge had passed through the village, and the soldiers were regrouping for another pass, this time to finish off any survivors. Jim found a small clump of rocks and forced Jinny down among them; they would offer some protection from stray shots. Then he stood with his hands high, calling, "Don't shoot! Don't shoot, we're white!"

The firing was sporadic as the soldiers rode through the camp this time, and one of them veered his horse toward the two young people. He was a big, burly, red-bearded bear of a man, and he wore the uniform of a captain. As he drew his horse to a halt, he grinned at Jim and Jinny and said, "Ah, what have we here? A couple o' poor white prisoners, I'm thinkin'. Are ye all right, lad?"

Jim lowered his arms and nodded. He was able to use the left arm now, he noticed, although it hurt like the dickens. "Thank you, Captain," he said. "You saved our lives."

"Ye be the lad that heathen was about to bash with his tommyhawk, ain't ya?" said the cavalryman. "Glad t' see we got here in time to stop him." He looked over his shoulder as the last of the gunfire died away. "It appears the fight's over." He swung down from his saddle and stepped over to Jim, a big hand extended. "Name's Carmichael."

"Jim McReady." He shook the man's hand, then reached down and took Jinny's arm, helping her to her feet. "And this is Miss Rawlings."

Captain Carmichael's eyes widened as he got his first good look at the girl. "Pleased to meet ya, Missy," he said, doffing his hat to reveal a thatch of coarse red hair. "How the devil did the two o' ye wind up here wi' these savages?"

"Bad luck," responded Jim with a shrug of his shoulders. "We were looking for the Paiutes, but we didn't think they'd be so eager to kill us."

"Don't surprise me that this bunch was," grunted Carmichaël. "Their chief was a renegade called Ko'lu, one of the most bloodthirsty heathens who ever put on war paint. Used to ride with that outlaw called Nightshade, he did, until not even Nightshade could stand his killin' anymore."

"You mean Nightshade put Ko'lu out of his gang?" The question came from Jinny.

"Aye," replied Carmichael. "Ko'lu got this band o' his followers and their families together. Planned to go on a rampage, he did." The captain smiled grimly. "Not now, though. Ko'lu won't ever slit another throat."

One of the other soldiers rode over to them then, and he said, "All the savages are dead, Cap'n."

"Ever' last one?" asked Carmichael, turning to his subordinate with a fierce expression on his bearded face. "Even the little 'uns?"

The trooper nodded.

"Good!" exclaimed Carmichael.

Jim felt a little ill as he looked at the burning wickiups and the scattered bodies of the Paiutes. True, Ko'lu had almost killed him, and he had never seen anything except evil in the eyes of the Indian, but surely the women and children could have been spared. Perhaps not, though; he knew little about cavalry tactics.

He wondered a bit about how an Irishman like Carmichael had attained the rank of captain. It was not unusual for these sons of Hibernia to serve as noncommissioned officers in the Army, but they rarely rose higher in the ranks, at least from what Jim had seen of military life in the few posts he had passed through in his wanderings.

Still, the question was unimportant, he decided. Of much greater concern was the fact that Ko'lu had no longer been associated with Nightshade. Obviously, the information he and Jinny had gotten from the trappers had been out of date.

Carmichael was looking at them a bit strangely now, and he asked, "Did ye say the two o' ya were *lookin'* for the Paiutes? Why in the name o' all that's holy would ye do a thing like that?"

Jim glanced at Jinny, and as he did so, his brain was quickly turning over the possible answers to the captain's question, along with some questions of his own. Did they want to involve the cavalry in their quest for Nightshade? That might not be a good idea. It was entirely possible that Jim was wanted by the law, since he had abandoned his Pony Express job and walked off with the guns and saddle which had been furnished by the Express company. It would be a fairly minor charge of theft facing him, but still he was not sure he wanted to take the chance. Carmichael might insist that he and Jinny return to Flat Rock or Harker City.

The captain was regarding them intently, waiting for an answer. Jim swallowed and said, "We're . . . we're missionaries."

"Missionaries?" echoed Carmichael in surprise. "And ye

thought ye could bring salvation to the Paiutes?" He shook his head. "Ye'd best go find yerselves some digger Injuns somewhere, lad, and leave the savages to the folks as know what to do with 'em." He poked his own chest with a blunt thumb. "Me an' me boys know all about it." He threw back his head and laughed.

Jim and Jinny exchanged another look. This man called Carmichael was certainly unlike any other Army officer they had ever encountered. The red-bearded man wiped tears of amusement from his eyes and went on, "Ye'll be travelin' with us for a while. Ye can get back to your soul-savin' when we're through with ya."

"But, Captain," protested Jim, "we can't do that. We certainly appreciate you saving our lives iike you did, but we have things to do—"

"They can wait," cut in Carmichael, and now his voice had hardened. "I ain't takin' no for an answer."

Jim took a deep breath and tried again, tightening his arm around Jinny's shoulders as he said, "I'm sorry, Captain, but we're not in the Army. We're not under your orders—"

Again Carmichael did not let him finish. "Ye are now," snapped the big officer. "We need the two of ya."

Jinny moved closer to Jim, and he was uncomfortably aware, just as she was, of the way Carmichael and the other trooper were looking at them. Surely they had not escaped the clutches of the Indians only to fall into unexpected jeopardy from their rescuers . . .

But he was growing more nervous by the second as he asked, "Why in the world would you need us?"

Carmichael grinned. "Yer gonna be the bait, lad," he said. "Just the bait I need for the trap that'll finally catch Nightshade, damn his black heart!"

By nightfall, it was obvious to Jim that whoever these men were, they were *not* the United States cavalry, despite the blue uniforms and the insignias they wore.

Carmichael had brooked no argument, and Jim and Jinny had been forced to go along with the group. Jim caught and saddled the roan, then found one of the Indian ponies that was gentle enough for Jinny to ride with a blanket thrown over its back. Surrounded by the two dozen blue-coated men, they rode away from the Paiute village and followed another twisting trail several miles through the mountains, coming at last to another camp, this one in a small bowl in the earth surrounded by towering peaks. There were a few cabins here, hastily built from the looks of them, and a pole corral for the horses. Nearby was the narrow mouth of a box canyon, closed off with a makeshift gate. As Jim looked past the barrier, he saw a large herd of cattle.

Carmichael had drifted back to ride alongside the two young people, and when he saw where Jim was looking, he grinned and said, "Spoils of war, lad, spoils of war."

"What war?" asked Jim. He had heard vague rumors the past few months about trouble developing between the northern states and the southern states, back in the East, but that seemed so far away as to be meaningless out here in the West.

"The war that never ends," replied Carmichael. "The war 'tween them that's got and them that don't. Which side are ye on?"

Jim did not know how to answer that question. He was beginning to get a glimmering of what Carmichael meant and what he and Jinny had stumbled into, but for the moment, it might be better to maintain a facade of ignorance.

"I don't know what you're talking about," he said. "We don't want trouble with anyone, do we, Jinny?"

She shook her head.

"We don't want trouble, either," said Carmichael, "but we need yer assistance, Mr. McReady, and we mean to have it. Yours, too, Missy. But talkin' about it can wait until we've all eaten."

The group rode into the camp and dismounted. The men had gone through the Paiute village, looting anything of value, and they were laughing and happy. Jim had seen quite a few bottles of whiskey being passed back and forth during the ride, and that had been the final piece of evidence he needed to prove to himself that these were not actual cavalry troopers. No group of soldiers, no matter how lax their discipline, would behave as these men did.

Yet he was fairly certain the uniforms they wore were authentic. If that was the case, how had the men gotten hold of them?

There was only one logical answer to that, and as it went through Jim's mind, he felt a cold shudder run through him.

The horses were driven into the corral once everyone was dismounted. Some of the men disappeared into the cabins. Carmichael gave orders that a meal was to be prepared. The sun was about to vanish behind the heights to the west; night would fall suddenly, and soon.

A good-sized fire was built in the clearing in front of the shacks, and most of the men sat cross-legged around it, still swigging whiskey. Others began roasting meat over the flames while a couple of men hauled a huge pot from one of the cabins and started putting together a stew.

Jim and Jinny sat over to one side, under a small tree. Tension was growing in Jim, and he wished he had his weapons back. Carmichael's men had not returned them to him, however. He'd found his hat, but Jinny's clothes had burned in the conflagration that swept through the Indian village. She was still wearing the buckskin dress.

"What . . . what are these men, Jim?" asked Jinny in a voice that was little more than a whisper. Her eyes were fastened on the drunken celebration that was developing.

Jim was equally intent on the roistering men. "I think they're outlaws," he replied quietly.

"Actually," came a booming voice from beside them, "we be pirates, but there ain't a whole hell of a lot o' difference!"

Carmichael had approached with a silence that was uncanny in such a large man. Jinny gasped in surprise, and Jim looked up at the red-bearded man looming over them. Carmichael had a bottle of whiskey in one big paw, and he took a healthy swallow from it before he squatted on his heels in front of them.

"In the old days, we sailed what used to be called the Spanish Main," said Carmichael, squinting one eye at them. "Strange, ain't it, how a bunch of rascals could start out at sea and wind up in this bone-dry, godforsaken country! But bein' a buccaneer ain't what it used to be, children. We decided to try our hands at somethin' else, see if it'd be more lucrative here on land. So far it has been."

"You rustled those cattle, didn't you?" asked Jim, nodding toward the box canyon where the herd was being held.

Carmichael chuckled. "Rustlin', is that what ye call it? Aye, then I suppose we're rustlers."

"And you ambushed a cavalry troop and took their uniforms after you killed them." It was a statement, not a question, and although Jim knew he was treading on delicate ground, he sensed that Carmichael would not kill them, no matter how much they knew about his illegal activities. Not yet, anyway.

"It was damned hard to get the bloodstains out an' patch the holes, let me tell ya, lad." Carmichael's grin broadened. "But folks tend to leave you alone when they think you're part o' the government. We been *patrollin'* these mountains for a couple o' months now. Ever since we come, we been lookin' for this here Nightshade. He's the only competition we got, ya see."

Jim was beginning to understand more and more. Jinny huddled closer against his side as the full extent of Carmichael's villainy and the danger of their situation sank in. Once again they had gone from one desperate entanglement into another.

"When we heard that Ko'lu and Nightshade had split up," continued Carmichael, "we figgered it'd be easier to get rid o' the Injuns first. Been tryin' to track 'em down, and today we got lucky. So did you two."

Jim took a deep breath. "What happens now?"

"Now, with your help, lad, we get rid o' Nightshade, and then ol' Carmichael's the king of these here mountains!" The concluding words were spoken with a fervor that bordered on the insane, Jim thought. Carmichael continued, "But there's time for that later. Come along, both o' ya. Have some food an' drink an' we'll sing ya a song or two. What d' ye say?"

Jim sensed Jinny's eyes on him as she looked up. She was waiting to see what he would do, and he knew she would follow his lead.

There was only one thing they could do, Jim thought grimly. His grin belied his thoughts as he held out his hand to Carmichael and said eagerly, "We're with you . . . Cap'n."

TWENTY

The plan was simple enough.

"Yes, sir, that's right," said Jim to the district manager of the stagecoach line. "I want to rent a coach for my wife and myself and our trunks. Three trunks." And here his voice dropped to a quiet, conspiratorial level as he leaned forward so that the other man might hear him. "The trunks are filled with gold, you know."

The district manager's eyes widened. "No, I didn't," replied the man, in the same hushed tone as Jim had employed. "*Gold*, you say?"

Jim nodded solemnly and then smiled the superior, irritating smile of a rich young man who has more wealth than sense.

They were in the town of Archer, a growing, bustling community north and east of the Prophets but close enough so the mountains were easily visible on the horizon. Nightshade and his gang had been known to venture this far from the Prophets on many occasions, especially when the potential payoff of a job was high.

Jim was wearing a brown tweed suit and a hat with a narrow, curled brim and a rounded crown. He wore town shoes on his feet. His shirt was white linen, and his dark green cravat was held in place with a diamond stickpin. In short, he looked like a dandy, an ineffectual fop.

The clothes had been provided by Carmichael, who had also given Jinny a fine gown and bonnet to wear for this masquerade. At the moment, Jinny was across the street in one of the rooms of Archer's finest hotel. In the hotel bar was a man named Hobbs, ostensibly the driver of the carriage in which Jim and Jinny had come into town. The truth of the matter was that he was keeping an eye on the young people, just in case they were not actually as cooperative as they appeared to be.

Carmichael had been quite blunt in laying out the situation. "Go along with us, and ye'll be back about yer own business 'fore ya know it, and richer to boot. Try to double-cross us, though, and Hobbs has his orders. He'll kill ya, lad, and then bring yer pretty friend back here for us to enjoy."

Naturally, Jim had promised his full cooperation.

"Nightshade's got his spies all over this territory," Carmichael had continued. "When he hears about a shipment o' gold travelin' by stagecoach, he'll be too tempted to pass it up. An' when he strikes . . . he'll find that he's waltzed right into our trap!"

This discussion had taken place several nights earlier, while the rest of Carmichael's gang had been carousing around the campfire and bellowing out a song that had undoubtedly come from what the red-bearded man referred to as the Spanish Main. For some reason, although Jim was concentrating on what Carmichael had to say, the words of the song stuck in his brain:

Sing me a song that's never been sung
And a tale that's never been told—
Of pirates bold and a fortune in gold
And life upon the Blue, oh!
And merrily on the Blue.

There was nothing merry about the situation in which he and Jinny found themselves, however. Their lives would be forfeited in an instant if Carmichael decided they were a danger to his plans. Jim, at least, would die; Jinny would be doomed to an even worse fate, he realized. The iron grip which Carmichael maintained on his men was the only thing that kept them from attacking Jinny.

So Jim had smiled and promised to do anything he could to help, and Carmichael had welcomed them into the gang. It was only temporary, of course. Jim was convinced that as soon as he and Jinny had played their parts in the outlaw's scheme, they would be dealt with harshly. Carmichael could not be trusted; and he, likewise, didn't trust them. That was the reason for Hobbs accompanying them to Archer.

In the intervening few days, they had gone over the plan until Jim's head ached from hearing the details repeated again and again. Finally Carmichael had given them the outfits they were to wear and had the carriage brought to the camp to pick them up. Jim had no idea where the clothes or the vehicle had originally come from, and he decided it would be better not to ask. For now, all they could do was play along with Carmichael and keep their eyes open for an opportunity to escape.

Now, in the district office of the stage line, Jim casually crossed his legs and leaned back in his chair, smiling that smug smile across the desk at the manager. He thought he was carrying off the masquerade successfully, but it was difficult to judge. He had never before been involved with this sort of mummery. From time to time in his travels, he had been in a town at the same time as one of the troupes of actors which occasionally toured through the West, but he had never attended a performance. The price of a ticket had always been too steep for his meager finances. Now, here he was, an actor himself, albeit an unwilling one.

The stage line manager was waiting for an answer, and Jim said, "That's right, sir, gold. I'm on my way to conclude a business arrangment with a stockman north of here. I'm purchasing his ranch, you see, and he insists on being paid in gold. It's a bit of a bother, you know, but he wouldn't be dissuaded."

God, he sounded like an ass! Carmichael had insisted, though, even going so far as to write out some of the things Jim was to say.

"You've got the gold with you?" asked the manager. He looked around nervously, as if afraid someone would overhear them, which was impossible, since Jim had insisted their meeting be conducted in absolute privacy . . . another precaution of Carmichael's to make Jim's story sound more believable . . . although everything else in the plan hinged on Nightshade finding out about the false gold shipment.

"Yes, I brought the gold up from my bank in Cavassos," replied Jim. "We've been transporting it in my carriage, but there's really not room for my wife and me to ride comfortably with those trunks in there, too. Besides, the gold weighs a great deal, of course, and it's difficult for a single pair of horses to pull it. I thought a stagecoach, with a six-horse hitch, would be much better."

"Well, we can handle it, all right," admitted the manager. "But it's sort of irregular for one fellow to hire a whole stagecoach."

Jim allowed a frown to touch his forehead. "But it can be arranged, can't it?" he asked. "I would, of course, be willing to pay a bit extra, just because of that very irregularity you mentioned."

For a long moment, the manager thought over the proposition, worrying his bottom lip between his teeth as he did so. Clearly he did not want to let this opportunity for some extra money slip past him, but he did not want to do anything that would get him in trouble with his superiors, either.

Finally, he asked, "The only passengers would be you and your wife, Mr. McReady?"

"That is correct. Oh, and our driver, of course, but he could ride on top of the coach."

The manager frowned. "I'd have to let one of our drivers handle the team, rather than turning it over to your man."

Casually, Jim waved a hand. "That's not a problem. Hobbs could serve as the guard."

"Well . . . all right." The manager sighed, as if he felt a

weight lifting from him, now that he'd had finally made a decision. "I don't see any reason why we can't arrange things however you wish." He named a price for hiring the stagecoach for a private run.

"Done!" smiled Jim, nodding in agreement. "We shall leave in the morning, but not too early."

"Would nine o'clock be all right?"

Rapidly, Jim considered. Carmichael had wanted the coach to arrive at Paxton Wells no later than noon; the former pirate figured that was the most likely spot for Nightshade's gang to attempt a holdup. From what Jim remembered of the map Carmichael had shown him, departing Archer at nine o'clock would be well nigh perfect.

He said as much, and the manager looked pleased. The man shot out of his chair as Jim leisurely stood up. Extending a hand across the desk, the man said, "It's a pleasure doing business with you, Mr. McReady."

"Same here," murmured Jim, taking the proffered hand briefly and then releasing it quickly. "I'll have a bank draft ready for you when we leave in the morning."

"That will be fine. And enjoy your stay in our fair city, Mr. McReady, short though it may be."

"Oh, I'm certain I will," said Jim. "I'm sure I'll never forget my trip to Archer."

Jinny came into his arms as soon as he entered the hotel room they had engaged. He embraced her warmly, and she laid her head against his chest. The fragrance of her hair filled his senses. He caught his breath.

"Did everything go all right?" asked the girl.

Jim nodded. "Just as Carmichael planned."

A shiver ran through Jinny's body, and Jim felt it quite plainly as she pressed against him. "He's a horrible, evil man."

"That he is," agreed Jim, but he had to smile a little. "But he doesn't hide behind a mask. We can see what he is, and maybe that'll help us deal with him."

"I was hoping—a little—that you'd go to the sheriff and

tell him everything."

Jim shook his head and said, "I couldn't do that. Hobbs was watching me through the window of the bar downstairs. If I'd gone anywhere except the stage line office, he'd have probably shot me, grabbed you, and taken off out of here."

She leaned back in his arms and looked up at him, her eyes meeting his. "Then we're going through with it?"

"I don't see what choice we have," said Jim.

Slowly, Jinny nodded. "If you think that's best," she said. He could tell she was not happy with the arrangement, however.

Of course, neither was he. He had never dreamed when they rode out of Harker City some two weeks earlier that they would endure all the dangers they had gone through, only to wind up being recruited into a gang of vicious outlaws, forced to help them in an audacious scheme to take over all the criminal activities in the territory.

Everything could still turn out for the best, he tried to tell himself. After all, he and Jinny had started out to locate Nightshade, and Carmichael's plan was designed expressly to bring the famed outlaw into the open.

The only problem was that Carmichael intended to wipe out Nightshade and all of his gang.

With an arm around her shoulders, Jim led Jinny over to the bed, and they sat on the mattress, side by side. Jim was a bit embarrassed by their surroundings, but it had been necessary to maintain the fiction of a marriage, at least to Carmichael's way of thinking. And the red-bearded desperado was calling the shots.

True, Jim and Jinny had spent quite a few nights alone together during their journey, without ever really worrying about the propriety of the situation. But camping out on the trail was different, somehow, from being in a hotel room . . . quite different, Jim decided. For one thing, there was a bed here, a large bed with a soft feather mattress. After the hardships they had endured, there was something vaguely sinful about the sheer comfort of the bed.

Since the moment in the Paiute camp when they had discovered the depth of their feelings for each other, there had been little time to discuss the matter, and besides, both of them were too uncomfortable to bring it up. Now, though, Jim felt he had to say *something.* He cleared his throat and began hesitantly. "Jinny, we . . . we don't know what's going to happen tomorrow . . ."

She laughed softly. "That's nothing new. We haven't really known what was going to happen since we left Harker City. And we certainly couldn't have predicted everything that has."

"No, we couldn't," agreed Jim a bit ruefully. "Most of the time, it's been pretty bad. Most of the time . . ."

"But not . . . all the time?"

He shook his head and smiled. "No. Not all the time. I wouldn't have missed spending the last two weeks with you."

And since she seemed to be expecting it, and he certainly felt like it, he kissed her.

The warmth of her lips surprised him, as did their sweetness. For long moments, as her arms went around his neck and his embrace tightened around her slim body, they kissed passionately, hungrily. Somehow, without Jim quite knowing what had happened, they wound up lying on the bed, luxuriating in the softness of the mattress, with its fine linen sheets, just as they were luxuriating in the closeness of each other.

It was utterly impossible, Jim had learned, to know what tomorrow would bring. But for now, for this one moment, he and Jinny were alone together, safe for the time being from all the dangers that had plagued them . . .

And for now, he thought as he broke the kiss and brushed her forehead with his lips and stroked the lush softness of her hair, that was more than enough.

They were ready to go when Hobbs knocked on the door

of the hotel room the next morning. Jim had arranged for breakfast to be sent up from the hotel kitchen, so they had already dressed and eaten when Carmichael's man got there. He had also filled in the phony bank draft Carmichael had given him to pay for the stagecoach.

Hobbs was a rangy man with coarse black hair and a drooping moustache. He inclined his head toward the stairway when Jim opened the door. "We're about ready to pull out," the outlaw said. "I had the trunks brought from the livery stable and loaded on the coach."

"All right," nodded Jim. "Did anyone bother them?"

"Nope," said Hobbs. "Nobody'd dare. Not with Nightshade around." He shifted a wad of chewing tobacco from one cheek to the other. "You think he got the word 'bout them trunks?"

Jim shrugged. "That stage agent didn't seem to be the type who could keep his mouth shut. I'd be willing to bet that he bragged to *somebody* about what the coach is going to be carrying."

"Better hope so," grunted Hobbs. "Plan ain't worth shit if Nightshade don't hear 'bout the gold." He gestured with the rifle he was carrying. "Well, let's go."

Jim stepped back and let Jinny precede him. They followed Hobbs out of the hotel and across the street to the office of the stage line. The big Concord coach was parked in front of the building, its iron-rimmed wheels and the red and yellow paint on its trim shining brightly in the morning sun. The manager stood on the sidewalk, rubbing his hands together vigorously.

"Well, good morning, good morning!" he said. "Are you and the lady ready to leave, Mr. McReady?"

Jim managed a smile, concealing his nervousness as he handed over the worthless bank draft. "What's the old saying?" he asked. "As ready as we'll ever be!"

Jinny looked lovely in her blue gown and bonnet, and as Jim took her arm and helped her up into the coach, he suddenly wished that this journey was real . . . not the part about buying a ranch and carrying around a fortune in gold, of course, but he wished that he and Jinny were boarding some sort of magical coach that would take them away from all the strife and danger which had filled their lives almost from the moment they had met. That was not possible, though, not with Hobbs watching them like a hawk. And neither of them had given up their hopes of recovering the bank loot and clearing the name of Jinny's father, either. That was, after all, what had brought them on this adventure in the first place.

As Jim settled himself on the seat next to Jinny, Hobbs shut the door and then climbed onto the driver's box next to the jehu. Jim and Jinny were in the rear seat, facing forward. A backless bench bisected the coach, allowing more passengers to ride inside when the vehicle was crowded. There was room for their feet by the bench, and in the floor on the other side was one of the supposedly gold-laden trunks. Another trunk rode in the front seat, and the third was in the canvas-covered boot on the rear of the coach.

The driver, a middle-aged man with a grizzled beard, leaned over from the box and called, "You folks ready in there?"

"Whenever you are, my good man," replied Jim.

With a shout and a crack of his whip, the driver urged the six-horse hitch into motion. The team surged against their harnesses and the coach rolled down the street. Inside, the start made Jim and Jinny sway back and forth, and he put an arm around her to steady her. She turned a brave smile toward him and said, "It's going to be all right, isn't it?"

"Yes," nodded Jim. "I'm sure it will."

But he was not sure at all, and that uncertainty lay heavily inside his belly like a ball of lead.

Jim had never ridden a stagecoach before, but he had seen plenty of them in his wanderings and had always considered them a rather luxurious method of travel. Now he learned that such was not the case. The body of the coach swayed back and forth on the leather thoroughbraces that supported it, causing a vague feeling of nausea. The frequent bumps and ruts in the road only increased the sensation. Although the windows had canvas curtains over them, dust still swirled in around the coverings, and Jinny had to hold her handkerchief over her mouth and nose to keep from inhaling too much of the gritty stuff. Jim sneezed freqently and rubbed at his watering eyes. A few days' worth of this would be pure hell, and he was glad they had only several hours to look forward to.

At least he hoped such would prove to be the case. Carmichael and his men would be waiting at the stagecoach station at Paxton Wells. If Nightshade struck there, as they all hoped, this ordeal would be over, one way or another, by afternoon.

Jim did not exactly how Carmichael planned to spring the trap. "Don't worry about that, lad," the former pirate-turned-owlhoot had told him. "Just play yer part an' leave ever'thin' else to us."

That was what he intended to do. When the shooting started—if it did—he was going to grab Jinny and find a hole for them to crawl into until the fighting was over.

The coach stopped at a swing station at mid morning, pausing just long enough to change teams. Jim and Jinny took advantage of the opportunity to stretch their legs. They traded sympathetic glances, then climbed reluctantly back into the four-wheeled torture chamber.

Paxton Wells was the next stop, and Jim was more than ready to get there. The minutes and the miles slowly rolled by as the sun climbed in the sky. Finally, the coach began to slow again, and Jim pulled aside the canvas over one of the windows. As he peered out, he saw the low, rambling flat-roofed building up ahead on the right. Behind it were corrals and a barn, and across the road from the station building was a clump of trees, an unusual sight in this dusty country. That would be where the wells were located, he thought.

He looked for the horses of Carmichael's gang, thinking they would be tied up outside, but there were no animals at the long hitching rail. The only horses visible were in the corral out back. Jim frowned. Maybe something had happened to delay Carmichael.

That was not the case, Jim saw as the coach rocked to a stop. A burly figure loomed up in the doorway of the building, and then a red-bearded man stepped out into the sunlight. Carmichael wore a once-white apron tied around his waist and his neck, and he looked faintly ludicrous in it. With a big smile on his bearded face, he lifted a hand in greeting. "Good day to ya," he called to the driver. "How ya doing'?"

"Who are you, mister?" asked the driver. "What happened to old Eli?" Jim could hear the puzzlement and confusion in the man's voice.

"Eli took sick and had to leave," replied Carmichael. "Me an' my lads are runnin' the station until he can get back. There's food ready inside for the noon meal, and we'll get to work changin' that team for ya."

The driver seemed to accept that explanation. He said, "All right, sounds good to me." He leaped down from the box, accompanied by Hobbs, who opened the door of the coach for Jim and Jinny.

Jim stepped out first, then reached up to assist the girl. When both of them were on the ground, he placed a hand on Jinny's arm and then turned toward Carmichael, pretending not to know the outlaw. He nodded pleasantly and said, "Hello."

"Good day to ya, sir. And to you, ma'am. If ye'll go on inside—"

Carmichael did not get to finish his statement. The sound of hoofbeats made everyone look up suddenly. A group of riders were approaching down the road from the north, and even at this distance, Jim could see that the man in the lead was dressed in black, his features masked by a hood.

"Good Lord!" yelled the driver. "That's Nightshade!"

The horsemen swept up to the station so quickly there was no time for anyone to move. Guns appeared in their hands, and the five people who were caught between the stagecoach and the building stood there frozen like statutes. Jim darted a glance at Carmichael and saw that the outlaw did not appear overly concerned. Neither did Hobbs. The stage driver was pale and obviously anxious, but he did not make a move. Jim merely stood there next to Jinny, his hand tightly gripping her arm. He could hear her quick breaths and knew she was as tense as he was.

Nightshade was riding the same magnificent Appaloosa. He sat easily in his saddle, a revolver held casually in his right hand. "Hello, folks," he said, his deep voice slightly muffled by the hood. The piercing eyes fastened on Jim as he continued, "I hear you're carrying a bit of gold. I want—"

His voice broke off abruptly, and Jim heard a faint, startled intake of breath. In that split-second of time, several thoughts raced through Jim's brain.

Nightshade had recognized him, Jim realized, recalling that the last time he had seen this young man, Jim had been a Pony Express rider, and there had hardly been time since then for him to amass a fortune in gold. The outlaw had to know something was wrong here.

In the same instant, Jim figured out why Carmichael was not worried. The thick adobe walls of the stage station had numerous rifle slits cut into them. The place had been built for defense, and at this moment it was no doubt full of Carmichael's men, ready to fire through the slits and cut down Nightshade's riders.

And as soon as Nightshade figured out what he had ridden into, he would know that Jim had been part of it, had been the lure that had brought him to ruin. A man like Nightshade would make sure Jim paid for that, regardless of the outcome of the battle.

So he did the only thing he could to change things, not

thinking it through, just acting on instinct and trusting to luck. He shouted, "Watch out, Nightshade, it's a trap!" and dived toward the stagecoach, taking Jinny with him.

And then all hell broke loose.

TWENTY-ONE

Jim landed underneath the stagecoach, clutching Jinny tightly beside him. They could not stay here; the team might bolt, putting them in danger of being crushed by the iron-rimmed wheels. Jim rolled, keeping his grip on Jinny, and they emerged on the far side of the coach as gunfire erupted around them.

"Run for the trees!" shouted Jim, giving Jinny a shove toward the grove. The trees would offer some protection. He ran at her heels, casting a glance back over his shoulder at the normally peaceful scene which had turned into a bloody battleground. A pall of powdersmoke overhung the area in front of the station, but Jim could still see the orange flashes of muzzle fire coming from the rifle slits in the walls. Nightshade's men had wheeled their horses around and were returning fire as best they could. Some of them had already fallen, but Jim spotted Nightshade himself, darting here and there on the Appaloosa, guns in both hands now, the weapons spouting flame and death.

The two young people reached the trees. The trunks were slender, but they offered better cover than nothing. Jim and Jinny crouched to watch the carnage, their eyes widening in horror.

As Jim had feared, the stagecoach team tried to bolt, but before they had gone ten feet, a stray bullet hit one of the horses in the head, killing the animal instantly. It fell, piling up the others and bringing the coach to a lurching halt.

Carmichael darted behind it, using it for shelter as he fired a pistol at Nightshade's men. Hobbs tried to reach the coach along with Carmichael, but a shot from one of the opposing gang stopped him, the impact of the ball flinging him backward with his arms outstretched. He fell loosely to the ground, unmistakably dead.

Jim could not bring himself to feel any sympathy for the man. True, Carmichael and the rest of the gang had rescued him and Jinny from the Paiutes, and they had not been mistreated during their stay at the outlaw camp, but Jim was all too aware of what a fine line they had been treading. Sooner or later, he knew, he and Jinny would have both been killed.

As they still would be if Carmichael won the battle. The red-bearded giant would not take Jim's betrayal lightly. The young man had sealed their fate when he shouted that warning to Nightshade. Now he and Jinny would live or die with the hooded outlaw.

The odds were against Nightshade. Somehow, he had remained unscathed so far, despite all the lead flying around him. But he had lost several men, and the enemy was solidly entrenched inside the building. Nightshade and his men could turn and flee, but that would expose their backs to Carmichael's excellent riflemen. By the time they could get out of range, Carmichael's men could shoot most of them out of their saddles.

But then, the foresight that had kept Nightshade alive all these years came into play. Jim spotted a man galloping out of the brush toward the rear of the station. Obviously, Nightshade must have positioned him there earlier, just in case of a trap such as the one which had been sprung. The rider carried something in his hand, and Jim felt a surge of excitement when he recognized it as a small wooden cask, such as black powder was stored in. The rider disappeared from Jim's sight for a moment, then came back into view as he rounded the corner of the building. His arm drew back and then came forward as he flung the cask through the window on the side wall of the station building. Jim saw a sputtering fuse trailing from it.

Someone inside the building let out a shriek of pure terror.

The next instant, there was a roar like thunder as that end of the station blew apart. The explosion shattered the wall and sent debris flying high in the air. As the echoes died away, Jim heard more screams coming from inside the place, which was now on fire. He drew Jinny against him, and she buried her face against his chest.

That bold stroke turned the tide. Carmichael's men—the ones who had not been killed in the black powder blast—came running from the flaming building only to be met with leaden death from the guns of Nightshade's riders. Carmichael himself, sensing imminent defeat, sprinted out from behind the stagecoach and ran toward the trees . . . the very trees behind which Jim and Jinny were crouching.

"Get down!" said Jim, urging Jinny lower, hoping Carmichael would not spot them. But that was not to be. The former pirate stopped in his tracks, some ten feet from the edge of the grove, as he saw the young man who had double-crossed him. And in the mind of a man like Carmichael, there was only one reward for such treachery.

He lifted his pistol as his bearded features contorted in hate and rage.

Jim had no weapon, no way of fighting back. All he could do was try to shield Jinny with his body. This was the end, then, he thought as he hovered over her. He was not surprised. Ever since he had left Harker City with her, disaster had dogged their every step. Fate had finally caught up with them.

Carmichael screamed and staggered forward as a pistol ball drove into his back and then burst from his chest. His gun slipped from his fingers, and he fell on his face, dead before he hit the ground.

Stunned, Jim looked past the red-bearded corpse and saw Nightshade sitting on the Appaloosa, one arm still extended, smoke curling from the barrel of the revolver in his hand.

That was the final shot. An uncanny silence dropped over the scene of battle. Jim helped Jinny to her feet as Nightshade holstered both his guns and heeled the horse into a slow walk toward the two young people. He brought the Appaloosa to a halt and faced them as they stood nervously at the edge of the trees marking the natural springs known as Paxton Wells. With a decidedly casual air for a man who had just come through a deadly and harrowing experience, Nightshade hooked one leg around his saddlehorn and leaned forward. Somehow, Jim knew he was smiling wearily.

"Well, my young friend," said the fabled outlaw in the resonant voice that Jim remembered so well, "I think you have a little explaining to do."

"It was all Carmichael's idea," began Jim. "We were forced into helping him—"

He stopped as he realized that Nightshade was no longer paying any attention to him. Instead, the hooded man's gaze had swung over to Jinny, and now he was regarding her intently. In fact, the power of Nightshade's stare made a cold chill go through Jim, and he felt Jinny shiver beside him at the same time.

After a moment, Nightshade spoke. "You can tell me about it later," he said. "Right now, you're coming with us." His tone made it clear that there would be no discussion of the matter. He started to swing his horse around, then paused and looked over his shoulder. "By the way, I don't suppose there's really any gold in that stagecoach?"

"Bricks," choked out Jim. "Carmichael's men filled the trunks with bricks."

"I thought as much. Come along."

And having no choice in the matter, they went.

Nightshade had lost eight men in the fighting, and several more had suffered wounds. Jim was aware of the hard looks he and Jinny received from the other members of the gang. To them, he and Jinny were part of Carmichael's gang and should have been treated accordingly. All the others were dead.

The driver of the stagecoach had survived somehow, although he had taken a ball through the muscles of his left arm. One of Nightshade's men bound it up for him while others unhitched all but two horses from the coach.

"You'll be able to make it back to Archer," Nightshade told the man. "Be sure everyone knows what happened here. I was ambushed by a man without honor—" the outlaw cast a disdainful glance at Carmichael's sprawled body, "—and that dishonorable man is now dead, along with his followers."

"Yes, sir," agreed the driver, nodding his head. "I'll tell 'em, all right."

And the legend of Nightshade would grow that much more, Jim thought.

He found the roan in the corral behind the burned-out rubble which was all that was left of the stage station, along with the other mounts that had belonged to Carmichael's gang. As Jim was patting the horse's ugly head and enjoying the reunion, one of Nightshade's men emerged from the barn and reported that the bodies of the regular stationkeeper and his hostlers were in there. All of them had been shot through the head. Jim's mouth was a grim line as he thought about Carmichael's villainy. The man had truly deserved to die.

One of the extra mounts was claimed for Jinny. The bodies of Nightshade's slain comrades were lashed to their saddles, and the hooded outlaw gave the order to move out. Jim and Jinny rode beside Nightshade after he curtly motioned for them to join him. The others trailed behind.

"I'd heard of Carmichael," said Nightshade without preamble as they rode toward the Prophets. "I knew he was probably looking for a showdown with me, and I was sure of it when I received word that Ko'lu and all of his people had been killed." His voice hardened as he continued, "Ko'lu and I no longer agreed on most things. He was a violent man, too violent when he didn't need to be. But the women and children could have been spared."

"Carmichael didn't believe in sparing anyone," said Jim. "I'm sure he would have killed Jinny and me when he was done with us."

"Jinny . . ." murmured Nightshade, looking over at the girl. "A pretty name. Is it short for Virginia?"

"Yes, it is," she said. "My father always called me Jinny."

Nightshade nodded, as if he had expected the answer. He turned his attention back to Jim and said, "So the two of you were prisoners, forced into helping Carmichael?"

"That's right." Quickly, Jim told him how they had been captured by the Paiutes, then freed in the attack on the camp by Carmichael's gang.

Nightshade listened in silence. Then, when Jim had concluded the story, he asked, "Why were you looking for Ko'lu?"

Jim took a deep breath and told the truth. "We were told he rode with you. You're the one we were really looking for, Nightshade."

It was impossible to determine the man's reaction, of course, since his features were hooded, but Jim thought he detected some surprise on Nightshade's part. After a moment, the outlaw said, "You're going to have to explain that, but not now. We're going to be riding hard so that we can get back home before nightfall. Can you keep up?"

Jim glanced over at Jinny, who nodded. After everything they'd been through, they were not going to be denied their chance to tell their story to Nightshade. "We can keep up," said Jim firmly.

"All right." Nightshade's arm lifted and then moved forward in a wave of command. His booming tones rolled out. "Ride for the mountains!"

They rode.

Jim would never forget that journey across the plains, through the foothills, and then into the mountain fastnesses. When Nightshade's Appaloosa stretched its legs, the ground seemed to disappear under it. The horse might as well have been flying like one of the hawks Jim spotted high above them. Another chill went through him when he saw the fierce birds. There was a connection between Nightshade and the hawks, he suddenly realized.

The roan kept up fairly well, and Jim found himself wondering which horse would win in a flat-out race between it and the Appaloosa. Jinny's horse was game, but it lacked the speed of the other two steeds. Jim held back so as not to leave her behind. The other outlaws trailed back, keeping up as best they could, although some of the stragglers were probably a full mile behind the leaders.

The sun dropped toward the horizon, turning the sky into a dazzling display of pink, gold, orange, and vermilion. If there were trails through the foothills and the mountains, Jim could not see them in the gathering darkness. By the time the sun disappeared behind the highest peaks, the group was deep in the rugged terrain of the Prophets.

Suddenly, Nightshade rounded a bend after a steep ascent and reined in. Jim, following several yards behind him, saw sunlight hit the masked face of the bandit. He and Jinny drew even with Nightshade, following his example and bringing their mounts to a stop. Jinny gasped in awe at the scene before them, and Jim found himself staring in wonder and disbelief.

The faint trail under the hooves of their horses led down into a mile-wide gash on the side of the mountain. A hundred yards to their right, a stream bubbled out of the rocks, and it was undoubtedly this flow that had carved out the valley over eons of time. The water fell in a bright cascade, sparkling in the last of the sunlight before dusk closed in. After its precipitous beginning, the valley leveled off somewhat. The stream ran down the middle of the canyon, and the fields on either side of it were verdant with the new growth of spring. Although this point where Nightshade and his two young companions sat was above the treeline, the floor of the valley itself was not, and it was thick with vegetation. Grass was growing, trees were putting on new coats of green, flowers were blooming. It was a little spot of paradise here in this rugged, stony wilderness, Jim thought. That was the only way to describe it.

"Welcome to Nightshade Valley," said the outlaw.

After a moment, the words penetrated Jim's brain. He tore his eyes away from the spectacular vista before him and looked over instead at the hooded bandit. "Named after you, I suppose," he said.

Nightshade gave him a sharp look, and his voice was taut with anger as he replied, "This place was known as Nightshade Valley long before I came here, youngster. I took *my* name from it, not the other way around, because after I arrived, I was no longer the same man who stumbled into the valley half-dead. The people who lived here cared for me, gave me back my life—" Breaking off his speech, Nightshade gave a shake of his head. "Time enough for that tale later. Come on."

He sent the Appaloosa picking its way carefully down the trail. Jim and Jinny followed, with the rest of the gang bringing up the rear. It was a nerve-racking descent; shadows were closing in quickly, and the trail would not have been easy to follow in broad daylight. But the Appaloosa seemed to know the way, so Jim sent the roan along the same path. Not long after they had started down into the valley, he heard a faint sound above them, as of something cutting through the air, and looked up to see several of the hawks swooping toward the riders. Nightshade lifted an arm and waved to them, and the birds circled away, vanishing into the growing darkness. Moments later, when he looked down into the valley, Jim saw a fire suddenly blaze into life. The flames climbed high, illuminating a great circle.

"Is that fire for us?" asked Jim.

"There will be a feast tonight," replied Nightshade, not really answering the question.

"It's like they knew we were coming," said Jinny in a hushed voice.

Nightshade looked back at her and nodded. "They did. The hawks told them." Then he faced forward again and rode on with no further word of explanation.

Jim and Jinny looked at one another, and Jim shrugged. When dealing with Nightshade, he sensed, there were always going to be questions that could not be answered.

They reached the floor of the valley a little later, and the faint trail turned into a road that followed the course of the stream. As they rode, they passed small cottages built of stone. Here dwelt the workers who tended the valley's farms, explained Nightshade. There were also cattle grazing in some of the fields.

"We're self-sufficient, for the most part," said Nightshade. "We can raise almost everything we need right here in the valley. In fact, many of the farmers have never been outside these mountains. Some of them have never even left the valley itself. They're a very peaceful people, as you might expect."

"And yet you recruit your bandits and killers from them," said Jim.

Nightshade shook his head. "Not so. My riders all come from the outside. And you're wrong in yet another way: my men are not killers."

"They disposed of Carmichael's gang handily enough."

"Most men will kill when forced to, in order to save their lives or the lives of someone they love," said Nightshade. "What about those trappers?"

Jim looked over at him, stunned. How had Nightshade known about the trappers? But then he remembered how it was said Nightshade knew everything that went on in these mountains. The hawks told him, Jim supposed, and the idea no longer seemed so strange to him.

Lights burned in the houses they passed. At some of

them, men, women, and children stepped out to greet Nightshade. In the glow from their lanterns, Jim could see that the people were swarthy, like Mexicans or Indians, and yet there was something about them that was different, as if they were a race that existed nowhere else except this valley. Jim supposed he could accept that notion, too, if he was willing to believe that Nightshade somehow talked to the hawks and could hear their replies.

They drew near the bonfire, which was being tended by more of the workers, and beyond it Jim could now see a huge house, a low, rambling structure of stone with a tiled roof. There was a haphazard look about it, as if it had been constructed in bits and pieces, with little thought being given to how each piece would fit in with the others. Somehow, though, the whole was pleasing to the eye. They rode past the crackling blaze and drew up in front of a gate in the low stone wall that enclosed the house. In the courtyard beyond, visible through the wrought-iron gate, Jim saw a large fountain.

Nightshade dismounted and motioned for the others to do likewise. "Your horses will be taken care of," he said. "Please, come into my home."

Jim and Jinny swung down from their saddles and handed their reins to one of the other riders. The rest of the men were circling around the big house toward some smaller buildings in the rear. Jim also spotted a large shape bulking in the darkness; it was probably a barn.

Nightshade opened the gate and ushered them into the courtyard. As Jim stepped onto the flagstone path that led around the fountain and up to the door of the house, he felt an air of antiquity about the place. The house was old, very old, and he found himself wondering just who had built it. The answer to that question was probably lost in the mists of time, he realized.

Slipping his hand into Jinny's, he followed Nightshade into the house.

The outlaw led them into a well-appointed room furnished with long, heavy sofas and overstuffed armchairs. The floors were covered with several large rugs that had been woven by Indians, to judge from the designs on them. One side of the room was dominated by a huge fireplace with a massive stone mantel over it. Another wall was hung with weapons of all sorts, ranging from a sword that might have been carried by one of the conquistadors to modern repeating rifles. There were also tapestries with a vaguely medieval look about them, depicting landscapes that were unfamiliar to Jim. In the pictures, hilltop castles with tall battlements overlooked river valleys dotted with quaint cottages unlike any Jim had ever seen. The room had a feeling of strangeness to it, but Nightshade seemed to fit right in.

A short woman, her face was lined and seamed with uncounted years, came into the room to greet them. Nightshade said to her, "We will have food and drink," and she nodded, then went back through the door by which she'd entered. A moment later she reappeared carrying a fine silver tray which bore a bottle and three glasses. She placed the tray on a side table against the wall, then retreated again.

"Dinner will be served shortly," said Nightshade as he poured the wine. For wine it was, Jim discovered when he sipped the beverage a moment later, after Nightshade handed him one of the glasses.

Nightshade had hung his hat and coat on a hook beside the doorway, but he still wore the hood, although he had raised it some so that he could drink. He sat in one of the armchairs and motioned for Jim and Jinny to take seats on the sofa facing him. "We have much to talk about," he said. When the two young people were settled, he went on, "Now, tell me why you were searching for me when you got into so much trouble."

Jim looked at Jinny, who delicately sipped from her own glass of wine. Her features had taken on more color, and Jim hoped the wine had had a fortifying effect on her. He himself was feeling a little dizzy, but he did not know if it was from the drink or the bizarre surroundings in which he found himself.

Taking a deep breath, Jim began, "It all started when you stole the mail pouch from me. There was an envelope in it addressed to Miss Rawlings here."

"Miss Virginia Rawlings," said Nightshade. "I remember the name. There was a map in the envelope, wasn't there?"

Jim felt a surge of discouragement, and when he glanced at Jinny, he saw that she shared the feeling. They had been hoping to get the map back without Nightshade knowing what he had. That might be impossible now, however.

Jim plunged ahead. "We were planning to . . . steal the map back from you," he said. Putting the notion into words like that, it now seemed like an utterly foolish idea. Now that they had met Nightshade, both he and Jinny realized it would have been impossible to do such a thing.

The bandit chuckled, but there was little true humor in the sound. "Go ahead," commanded Nightshade. "Let's hear the rest of it. Why is that map so important to you? Does it lead to buried treasure?"

"As a matter of fact, it does," said Jim.

"And finding it is the only way to clear my father's name and get him out of prison," added Jinny, hastily blurting out the words.

Nightshade leaned forward, his body tensing. "Then your father is Sam Rawlings," he said.

Jinny gasped in surprise. "How did you know that?" she exclaimed. Jim was equally stunned.

For a long moment, Nightshade did not answer. Then he said, "I make it my business to know what goes on in this territory. I heard about the bank robbery in Harker City and knew Sam Rawlings had gone to prison for it. I was . . . surprised. Rawlings always seemed like a good man to me."

"He is!" said Jinny. "He was innocent of that robbery. My Uncle Baxter was really the thief!"

Nightshade settled back in his chair. Jim had a feeling he

was frowning in contemplation. The outlaw mused, "That sounds more reasonable. Bax Rawlings was not really a bad man, but he could be a weak one at times."

"You knew my uncle Bax?" asked Jinny.

Nightshade nodded. "As I said, I keep up with what's going on around these mountains. But tell me how you know Bax Rawlings was really guilty."

"He admitted it to me in a letter," explained Jinny. Quickly, she told Nightshade the same story she had told Jim a couple of weeks earlier, about how her uncle's guilt had kept him from spending the stolen money all these years and how the map was supposed to lead her to the loot after Baxter Rawlings was dead and beyond any further punishment.

Nightshade set his glass of wine aside and lifted a hand to his head. Jim could tell he was upset, and for the first time, he sensed that the outlaw's tight control was in danger of cracking. After a long moment, Nightshade drew a deep, ragged breath and said, "My God." Then after a moment, he repeated, "My God." He stood up and paced from one side of the room to the other, then came back to face them.

"You've told me a story," he said. "Now I have one to tell you."

TWENTY-TWO

"Once there were three brothers," began Nightshade. "Three orphans. They came West to begin a new life after the deaths of their parents. They were all strong young men, willing to work, and they intended to make something of themselves. But the oldest brother was . . . impatient. He didn't want to struggle for years and years. He wanted success right away. So he determined the simplest way to get what he wanted. He took it from others.

"The oldest brother became an outlaw . . . a petty thief, actually, willing to do almost anything so long as it wasn't honest labor. That was for fools, he thought. So he went on about his wild ways, sneaking and stealing, until Fate finally caught up with him. He broke into a store, but the shopkeeper found him there. There was gunfire, and the brother who was a thief was badly wounded. He barely escaped. He pulled himself onto his horse and raced off, disappearing into the mountains. The shopkeeper knew his shot had gone home, though, and there was no doubt that the robber had slunk away to die.

"The story got around, of course; stories always do. The thief's brothers found out what he had done, and they were so shamed by it that they moved on, seeking a new place to live where their brother's villainy would not throw them into disgrace. One of the brothers was so affected by what had happened that he swore he would remain honest the rest of his life, no matter what temptations to do otherwise might arise. The other brother made the same claim—but he didn't mean it. Deep down, I suppose, he admired the thief. The only thing the oldest brother had done wrong, in this man's mind, was to get caught. I know these things . . . now."

Nightshade paused, taking a deep breath before he could bring himself to go on. Jim and Jinny sat transfixed, caught up in the outlaw's tale. A vague possibility had begun to suggest itself to Jim, but it was too farfetched, too amazing, to take seriously. And yet . . . life was sometimes amazing, was it not? Truth could be more unexpected than any fiction.

"Unknown to anyone, the oldest brother—the thief—did not die from his wounds. He rode into the mountains until he passed out and fell from his horse. When he came to, he was alone, the horse gone. Lacking the strength to walk, he began to crawl. Something drew him onward, and he followed a trail high into the mountains. Where he got the willpower to keep going, no one can say. But finally he reached the crest of the trail, and he saw that he was above a strangely beautiful valley. That sight was the last thing he saw before he passed out again."

"Oh . . ." whispered Jinny. "Oh, my God . . ."

"The people who lived in the valley found him there and took him into their homes. They nursed him back to health, and when he recovered, he found that he had changed. He had a purpose in life now. He had seen the evil that lawbreakers do . . . he had been a living embodiment of that evil. And he was determined to put a stop to it. To accomplish that end . . . he became a myth, because myths have the greatest power of all."

"You . . . you're talking about yourself," said Jim hoarsely.

Nightshade nodded. His voice was exceedingly weary as he continued, "Good men and bad alike fear me, so much so that no other outlaws dare to venture into this area. For years, no one broke the law except Nightshade. Carmichael was the first one to challenge me since the early days of my sojourn here."

"But *you* broke the law!" protested Jim. "How can you say you were doing away with evil?"

"The common man was always safe from me!" declared the outlaw. "I stole only from those who could afford it, and no one—*no one!*—was ever hurt in one of my robberies. As for the money, it was given to those who needed it, the poor and the churches."

Jim recalled the Mexican peasant he and Jinny had encountered early in their journey. The man had had no fear of Nightshade, and now Jim could understand why.

"You see what I did, don't you?" asked Nightshade. "You know why. Perhaps I was evil, yes, but my evil prevented a greater evil."

Jinny's voice shook as she asked, "What . . . what about the thief's brothers?"

"On the surface, both of them became respectable, successful men. One of them married and had a family. The other—eventually—became a thief, too."

Jinny stood up and took a step toward him, lifting a hand and reaching out tentatively, as if she wanted to touch him but did not dare. Nightshade trembled, and as Jim watched from his chair, unable to move, he knew he was seeing something no one had seen for years. The invincible Nightshade was proving himself to be only a man after all, a man subject to all the emotions of his fellows. Nightshade extended his right hand and grasped Jinny's fingers. With his left, he reached up, grasped the hood that covered his face, and pulled it free with a jerk.

His hair was thick and dark and slightly curly, the black only lightly touched with gray. The features that had been concealed by the mask were strong and handsome, but with a stern cast to them. Even suspecting what the removal of the hood would reveal, Jim gasped as he saw the resemblance between this man and the one in the picture he had seen in Jinny's house, back in Harker City.

"Uncle?" whispered Jinny. "Uncle John? Father always

said you had . . . died . . . as a young man."

"And so I did. John Rawlings is dead, child. Only Nightshade remains."

And then the outlaw drew his niece into his arms and warmly embraced her.

The reunion lasted for several moments. Nightshade patted Jinny on the back and stroked her hair. Then, finally, he released her and stepped over to Jim, who was sitting with his mouth open, trying to cope with the strange twists in the trail down which Destiny had taken them. Nightshade held out his hand, and Jim stood up and took it.

"Thank you," said Nightshade. "Thank you for trying to help my niece and my brother. From what I've heard, you've saved Jinny's life more than once."

"And she's saved mine," responded Jim. He summoned up his courage. "We're in love, Jinny and I."

Nightshade smiled as he released his grip on Jinny's hand. "I'm glad to hear it. You seem like a fine young man, Jim McReady."

Jim returned the smile and asked, "What happens now? Surely under the circumstances, you'll help us clear Jinny's father."

The features of the outlaw tightened into a grim expression. "I wish I could. I wanted to help Sam when I heard about the robbery. I thought surely there had been some mistake. But when he didn't try to defend himself—" Nightshade shook his head. "I decided I had been wrong about him. I hated to see him go to prison, but I decided that I couldn't try to break him out if he was actually guilty. Now I know he was just covering up for Bax. The fool . . . the wonderful fool. Bax wasn't worth it, but of course, Sam would never have believed that."

"Then you'll give us the map," said Jinny. "Once we've returned that stolen bank money, I'm sure the territorial governor will give Father a pardon."

Nightshade looked at her, his face sad and solemn now as he said, "The map isn't here."

Jinny looked as if she had been slapped, and in a way, Jim supposed she had. As she struggled to find words, Jim spoke up. "Not here? What do you mean, not here?" he demanded.

"I went through the mail pouch," said Nightshade. "There was nothing of value, or so I thought. I gave it to two of my men and told them to take it back to the Pony Express on the sly, so that the mail could be delivered to its rightful owners. They were to take the pouch to the Pony Express office in Moss City and leave it there in the night, so that it would be discovered the next day."

Jim suppressed a groan. If he had stuck with his job, he'd have heard about this development within a couple of days of the robbery. Everything that had happened could have been avoided.

"You mean the letter is waiting for me back home?" asked Jinny, looking as stricken as Jim.

Nightshade shook his head. "I don't think so. The two men I sent on that errand never came back. I thought they had simply gotten tired of riding with me, but now I can see how they might have noticed that map and decided to see what it led to. If that's the case, then they would have recovered the money. And I *don't* think they would have turned it in to the proper authorities. I said my men weren't killers, but they're not lambs, either."

"This is incredible!" exclaimed Jim. "If those men got the money, we'll never get it back!"

"And my father will never get out of prison," added Jinny in a hushed voice. She was pale, and her eyes were moist with tears that threatened to well out and roll down her cheeks.

"No!" said Nightshade, the sharpness of his voice making both of the young people jump slightly. "Sam Rawlings has languished in that prison for eight years, for a crime he didn't commit. Proof or no, I won't let that continue!"

"But what can we do?" asked Jim miserably.

Nightshade raised a hand and clenched it into a fist, and

Jim saw the fury and the power blazing in the outlaw's eyes.
"What can we do? We can set him free!"

The gray walls of the great prison at Shawton were high and thick, too thick for any force to breach. Guard towers stood at each corner of the compound, and the blue-coated men who kept vigil within them were armed with the finest high-powered rifles money could buy. The land around the prison had been cleared of trees and brush for a mile around in all directions, so that no one could approach unobserved. The only feature marring the flat barrenness of the land was the creek which ran behind the prison, three-quarters of a mile from the walls. The stream had slashed a deep gully in the hard ground. There were only two gates into the prison yard. The large one in front, constructed of heavy logs, weighed so much that several men were required to push it open. A smaller door of thick planks reinforced with iron bands opened on one of the side walls.. Both were kept padlocked with heavy chains most of the time, and on those rare occasions when a gate was opened, extra guards kept their rifles trained on it at all times, until it was closed and locked again.

Out of the hazy distance, a wagon rolled toward the prison. It was a small, covered vehicle drawn by two horses. The animals plodded along, in no hurry in this heat.

On the seat of the wagon were two men, both dressed in dark brown priests' cassocks. Their features were shaded by cowls, but it was still obvious that one of the priests was quite young, while the other was considerably older.

"I sure hope this works," said Jim McReady as he swayed slightly on the wagon seat next to Nightshade.

"It has to," replied the outlaw with a chuckle. "Otherwise we'll both be dead."

Two weeks had passed since that fateful evening when Jim and Jinny had first come to Nightshade Valley. Since that time they had returned to Harker City, along with

Nightshade and a few of his most trusted men, just to be certain that the map was not being held for Jinny at the local Pony Express office. When they discovered that it was not but that the stolen pouch had indeed been returned with the rest of its contents intact, their worst fears were confirmed: Nightshade's men had taken the map.

Wearing range clothes, Nightshade was able to move about without anyone suspecting that he was the famous outlaw. His face had not been seen, except by his loyal helpers in the valley, for more than twenty years. No one after all this time was going to associate him with John Rawlings, the robber who had been shot and who had disappeared into the Prophets.

All his time since that visit to Harker City had been spent preparing for this day. Nightshade's contacts had furnished him with as much information as they could about the prison, including the layout of the place. They had also learned that priests visited the prison once a month to minister to the spiritual needs of prisoners, even though most of the convicts had long since turned their backs on God.

At this moment, the real priests were tied up and stashed in a gully some five miles back down the road, attended by a couple of Nightshade's men who would release them at the proper time. Both of the clerics had been so angry that they sputtered when they were waylaid and stripped of their outfits. "You'll burn in hell for this!" one of them had threatened, but Nightshade had only laughed.

"I doubt that offending the dignity of a priest qualifies as a mortal sin," he'd said, "especially when it serves a greater purpose."

Jim was not so sure. He felt vaguely blasphemous when he donned the priest's robe, but this was the only way to get into the prison. He had to take the chance . . . for Jinny's sake.

They had grown even closer in the past weeks, and Jim had been tempted to ask her to marry him. But in the back of his mind was a nagging doubt: was he good enough to ask her such a question? Had he truly left behind the man he once was, the cowardly drifter who'd wanted only the easy way out of any dilemma? Even after all that had happened, he was not sure of the answer, and until he was, he could not ask Jinny to share the rest of his life.

The wheels of the wagon creaked as it drew nearer and nearer the prison. Jim could see the walls clearly now, and they seemed sinister, menacing, even in the bright light of day. He took his eyes off them and looked at the horses instead. His roan was on the left, Nightshade's Appaloosa on the right. The distinctive spots of the Appaloosa had been concealed with the artful application of some mud, making the animal look like a rather ugly pinto. It was impossible to hide the fine lines of the horse, though, and Jim hoped none of the prison guards thought it odd that such a horse would be pulling a priest's wagon.

"Remember, keep a cool head, Jim," said Nightshade as he drove the wagon up to the massive gate. "Everything is going to be all right."

Jim wished he could believe that. But as he slipped a hand under the robe and let his fingertips brush the butt of the Colt concealed there, he had a difficult time sharing Nightshade's confidence.

Nightshade brought the wagon to a halt and tipped his head back to look up at the guard station built on top of the wall next to the gate. One of the blue-uniformed men leaned over the railing and called, "Howdy, padre! Right on time, as usual."

Nightshade merely nodded and did not reply.

A moment later, they heard the clank and clatter of the chains being taken off inside the prison. With a tortured groan of hinges, the gate began to swing open. When the gap was wide enough, Nightshade drove through it. Jim glanced around nervously, all too aware of the guards lined up on top of the wall, their rifles held at the ready. Once inside the compound, Nightshade drove toward the low building that housed the warden's office.

This would be their first real test. The guards could not see them well enough under the cowls to realize they were not the usual priests, but they would have to come face to face with the warden. As the wagon drew up in front of the door, the man himself emerged from the building and greeted them.

"Hello, padres," called the warden cheerfully. "We were expecting you." As Nightshade and Jim climbed down from the wagon and turned toward him, a frown appeared on the man's face. He said, "Wait a moment. Where are Father Vincent and Father Joseph?"

"They've been called by our superiors to another task," said Nightshade with a smile. "I am Father John, and this is Father James. We'll be taking care of this month's visit."

The warden continued frowning for a moment, obviously pondering what Nightshade had told him. Then, he smiled again and shrugged, accepting the story. After all, he must have reasoned, if one could not believe a priest, who could one believe?

At least, Jim hoped fervently, that would prove to be the case.

"Who would you like to see first?" asked the warden. "We have several men in the infirmary . . ."

"We've been requested to speak to a man named Samuel Rawlings," replied Nightshade. "His daughter came to the mission and asked us to pray with him. She's very worried about him."

The warden nodded. "Rawlings . . . of course. He hasn't been in very good health, but he's not in the infirmary at the moment. Come along, Fathers; I'll take you to him."

Accompanied by two guards, the warden led them into the prison itself, and as soon as Jim stepped within its walls and breathed the dank, stale air, he felt a surge of panic. He wanted back out in the sunlight so badly that he had to bite his lip to keep from crying out. He kept his head downcast as he walked, so that his features would be better concealed by the hood. Anyone looking at his face would see immediately how he felt, or at least, so he feared.

He tried to remember the twists and turns they took in the corridors that led between long rows of barred cells, but within a matter of moments he was hopelessly lost. He hoped Nightshade would remember the way out, or else they were doomed. The outlaw still seemed calm and confident, and Jim told himself to adopt the same attitude.

The group came to a stop in an alcove that contained only one cell, a cell with a single bunk in it. A man was stretched out on the thin mattress, and at the sound of footsteps coming to a halt outside the cell, he turned his head to see who was there. Jim almost gasped at what he saw.

Samuel Rawlings bore little resemblance to the man he had once been. He looked even less like his brother Nightshade. Rawlings' hair was white and thinning, and his face was gaunt. His eyes, large and haunted, seemed only mildly curious about the world around him. Most of his thoughts were turned inward, Jim realized, and he felt a pang of sorrow for what had been done to this once-fine man.

Nightshade had to be even more affected, Jim thought, but if so, none of the shock and sadness was apparent in the outlaw's voice as he said quietly, "Samuel Rawlings?"

"Yes?" rasped the prisoner in a strained, little-used voice.

"We've come to talk to you, Samuel."

"I didn't ask for a priest." Rawlings' tone was dull and uninterested.

"Your daughter requested that we visit with you and pray for you," continued Nightshade. "Will you allow us to do that?"

For the first time, Rawlings lifted his head from the bunk. "Jinny?" he said. "Jinny sent you?"

"That is right, brother," said Nightshade in the same pious voice, and even under the strain he was feeling, it was all Jim could do not to laugh rather hysterically at that moment.

Rawlings swung his legs off the bunk and sat up. "All

right," he said as he stood stiffly. "I'll talk to you, but it won't do any good."

"Now, brother, there's always hope," intoned Nightshade as the warden motioned for one of the guards to unlock the cell door.

Jim knew what Nightshade was going to do next; they had gone over the plan several times. But still he was stunned by the suddenness of the outlaw's actions. As the guard swung open the cell door, Nightshade reached out with one hand and grasped the bars. He jerked the door out of the guard's grip and shoved it at the man, crashing the bars against the guard's head. The man collapsed. At the same time, Nightshade's other hand swooped beneath his cassock and brought a Colt into view.

Jim was moving, too. He twisted toward the other guard and brought his right fist around in a sweeping blow that slammed into the man's jaw. As the guard staggered back, Jim snatched away his rifle and whipped the stock around, slapping the flat of it against the side of the guard's head. The uniformed man went down in a heap.

Nightshade was covering the stunned warden. "Do as I say and you won't be hurt," he snapped, and any hint of the soft, reverent priest's voice was gone now. Instead, Nightshade's tone crackled with command and more than a little menace.

The warden stood as if frozen in his tracks, his mouth opening and closing in shock, but after a moment he managed to choke out, "Who . . . who the devil—"

"An appropriate choice of words," grinned the outlaw. "I'm Nightshade."

The warden's eyes widened even more.

Rawlings had shrunk back against the far wall of the cell, and now he stammered, "I—I don't know who you are, but I want you to leave me alone! I swear I didn't have anything to do with this, Warden—"

"Be quiet, Sam," said Nightshade, his voice gentle but firm. "We've come to take you out of here. I'd have been here eight years ago if I'd know what Bax had done."

Gaping in astonishment, Rawlings' already washed-out features became even more pallid. "John?" came from his mouth in a hoarse whisper.

"Come along," said Nightshade. "Nobody's going to hurt you anymore." To the warden, he added, "You're going to walk us out of here, sir. If you cooperate, you'll live. Otherwise . . ." He left the rest of the threat unsaid.

Jim's pulse was hammering in his temples as he watched the warden. All the official had to do was shout and more guards would come running. There would be shooting. Nightshade had made it clear to Jim that in case of trouble, they were to shoot only to wound, if possible. The guards were only doing their jobs, the outlaw had pointed out, and he would not have their deaths on his conscience.

The guards, however, would be under no such constraints, and they would shoot to kill.

"If it makes any difference," Nightshade added to the warden, "I swear to you that Samuel Rawlings is innocent of the crime which brought him here."

"I don't know why the word of an outlaw should matter to me," said the warden heavily, "but I don't want any bloodshed." He gave a weary sigh. "I'll do as you say."

Nightshade nodded curtly, and Jim felt a surge of relief. They still had a long way to go before they were safely out of here, but at least they had passed the first step.

Jim bent and grasped the guard he had knocked out. Holding the man under the arms, Jim dragged him into the cell. This guard was more slender than the other one, so his uniform would come closer to suiting their purpose. Jim began to strip the blue coat and trousers off the unconscious man.

Five minutes later, Samuel Rawlings was wearing the uniform of the guard, rather than his usual gray prison garb. When he tugged the guard's cap down on his head and lifted the rifle, it was hard to tell he was really a prisoner. Nightshade closed the cell door, locking in both guards. Then he turned to the warden and said, "All right. We'll walk out slowly and calmly, and when we reach the yard, you'll go over to the side gate and unlock it. Do you understand?"

"Of course." The warden's face was flushed with anger, but he was keeping a tight rein on his temper. With the reputation Nightshade possessed, he had to believe that the outlaw would not hesitate to gun him down.

"The three of us are going back to the wagon," continued Nightshade. "Don't think that once you're away from us you can safely raise the alarm. I'll be holding my gun all the way, and that prison yard isn't big enough for you to run out of range. I'll put a bullet in your head at the first outcry."

"You don't frighten me," blustered the warden, but the look in his eyes put the lie to the words.

"I'm not trying to frighten you," said Nightshade coolly. "I'm just making certain you understand the facts of the situation." He gestured with his pistol toward the corridor. "Let's go."

Jim could almost see the wheels of the warden's brain revolving as he tried to think of a way to foil this escape. As the four men began walking along the corridor, their footsteps echoing hollowly from the stone walls, the warden said, "You can't get away with this, you know."

"We'll see," was all that Nightshade replied.

The warden's step had more spring in it now, and Jim knew that the idea which Nightshade had subtly planted had taken root. The warden expected them to try to escape in the wagon; he would be thinking that the simplest way to deal with this might be to wait until they were outside the walls and then send the guards after them. The wagon would not be able to outdistance his men, who would be mounted on good horses.

Jim hoped that was what the man was thinking.

Just before they reached the door leading to the yard, Nightshade said, "Buck up, Sam. The light may hurt your eyes, but you can't let them see that it does."

Rawlings nodded shakily. He was the weakest link in the plan, Jim thought. If he lost his nerve and gave away the play too early, they might all be captured or killed.

They stepped through the door, and while Rawlings squinted a little against the unaccustomed glare of the sunlight, he did not flinch. With a firm step that must have cost him quite an effort, he strode toward the wagon, alongside Jim and Nightshade. The warden veered toward the side gate, in accordance with Nightshade's low-voiced command.

Jim's nerves were stretched almost to the breaking point as he watched the official trudge toward the gate. The man was not in any hurry. Jim glanced up at the guards on the wall. None of the blue-coated sentries seemed to be paying attention to them, not with a man they considered one of their own walking next to them. The warden was almost to the gate now, and he had taken a large ring of keys from his pocket.

Sliding his hand underneath the priest's robe, Jim gripped the handle of the razor-sharp knife that was sheathed at his waist. The next job was his to perform, as soon as the time was right.

The warden had reached the gate and thrust a key into the padlock that secured it. As the lock clicked open and the warden opened the gate, one of the guards leaned over on the wall and called down, "What are you doing, sir?" More guards turned their heads to look, realizing suddenly that an unprecedented event was taking place.

"Now, Jim!" ordered Nightshade in a crisp voice.

Jim slid the knife from its sheath and stepped forward. Four slashes with the blade, almost quicker than the eye could follow, freed the horses from the harness binding them to the wagon. Jim leaped onto the roan's back at the same moment Nightshade was vaulting onto the Appaloosa. The robes hindered their movements a little, but not enough to slow them down appreciably.

Nightshade held out a hand to his brother. "Come on, Sam!"

Rawlings dropped the rifle and grasped Nightshade's hand as the warden suddenly darted aside from the gate and bawled, "Stop them! Stop them, dammit! They're not priests!"

Jim already had the roan moving. He kicked it into a gallop as Rawlings settled onto the back of the Appaloosa behind Nightshade. The big stallion thundered across the prison yard behind the roan. Jim gripped his mount's mane with one hand while he replaced the knife with the other and then drew a concealed pistol. He heard the crack of a six-gun as Nightshade opened fire to drive the guards back away from this side of the wall.

They had a few seconds' grace as the stunned guards tried to figure out what was going on. Despite the shouted warning from the warden, it was difficult for a man to throw his rifle to his shoulder and open fire on a priest without even thinking about it. And by the time it sank in that these men were not priests at all, the roan and the Appaloosa had covered most of the distance to the gate.

Jim snapped a shot in the general direction of the warden, sending the official scurrying for cover. Then the gate loomed up in front of him, only about halfway open. That was enough of a gap, though. The roan squeezed through it without slackening speed, and a couple of seconds later, the Appaloosa with its double burden followed.

The sound of the warden's furious shouts came faintly to Jim's ears over the thunder of hoofbeats, and he knew that the man would be exhorting the guards to go after them. Some of the sentries would probably take some potshots at them from the top of the wall, but with the cloud of dust that was being kicked up by their passage, accurate shooting was going to be well nigh impossible.

Jim leaned forward over the roan's neck, coaxing all the speed he could from the animal. He had practiced riding bareback for over a week, and so far he had experienced no trouble staying on the roan. A glance over his shoulder told him that Nightshade and Rawlings were all right; the Appaloosa, even though it was carrying double weight, was running free and easy, its magnificent muscles playing smoothly under the dappled hide. It had almost drawn even with the roan.

While Jim was looking back, he saw men on horseback come boiling out of the prison, taking up the chase. Now would come the real challenge. If he and his companions could overcome the final obstacle, freedom would be within their grasp.

They had been angling to the left ever since galloping out of the prison, and now the gully that had been cut by the creek was visible in front of them. It was some ten feet deep, perhaps double that in width. The walls of its banks were fairly sheer; that much Jim and Nightshade had determined in a nocturnal reconnaissance of the place several nights earlier. There was no good place to take a horse down into the wash for at least two miles in either direction.

That was all for the best, Nightshade had said. And then, with a devil-may-care smile on his face, he had explained to Jim what they were going to do . . .

Now the gully seemed to be racing toward them, just as they were galloping toward it. Another look back told Jim that the pursuers were only a couple of hundred yards behind them. The guards had responded quickly, and given enough time, they would be able to ride down the fugitives, especially considering the fact that one of the horses was carrying two men. Even the Appaloosa could not bear that burden forever without slowing some.

The guards had to be feeling a surge of triumph. A long chase would not be necessary. The fleeing men had boxed themselves in by riding toward the gully, which to the minds of the guards was an impassable barrier. In a matter of moments, the attempted jailbreak would be over.

Jim urged the roan on, a grim smile tugging at his lips.

They would not be caught, he knew. They would escape . . . or they would die.

One more look at Nightshade. Their eyes met, and the outlaw nodded. Never would he have a better friend than this man, Jim knew, and suddenly all the risks seemed worthwhile. Jim saw the truth now.

A man who ran from danger, from uncertainty, from chance, was running from life itself.

The chasm yawned before them, and Jim put the roan into a jump. They sailed into the air. Jim gave a shout of triumph before they were even halfway across the gully. They would win. He knew it better than he'd ever known anything in his life.

The front hooves of the roan bit into the dirt on the far side of the creek, bit and dug in and pulled them both to safety. Out of the corner of his eye, Jim saw the Appaloosa landing cleanly beside him. No other horse in the world, he was convinced, not even the roan, could have made that leap with a double burden on its back. But the Appaloosa had, and now they put the gully behind them, racing on toward the distant blue mountains. Jim looked over his shoulder one last time and saw the guards pulling to a frantic halt on the other side of the gully, yelling in frustration and letting off a few futile shots. None of them was foolish enough to attempt to jump the creek, and by the time they rode downstream to a place where they could cross, the fugitives would be long gone. It was done, Jim thought. They were free.

And when they reached the mountains, Jinny would be there waiting for them. . . .

TWENTY-THREE

The first race of the season had the grandstands packed with spectators. The betting was quite heavy, and there was an air of gaiety around the race course. For today, the looming threat of war seemed far away. In the months to come, brother might be fighting against brother, but on this glorious day, people were more concerned about which horses were going to finish in the money.

In a box near the finish line, two men named Lomax and Drago waited for the races to begin. Both were well dressed and smoked long cigars. As they lounged in their chairs, there was a certain rawboned ease about them that said they were originally from out West. They smoked leisurely and were generally quite pleased with themselves.

Neither of them noticed the two men who sat down behind them until one of the newcomers dug the muzzle of a pistol into Lomax's back and said pleasantly, "Hello, Harry. Didn't expect to see me again, did you?"

Lomax stiffened, afraid even to look back over his shoulder. A glance was not necessary; he knew that deep voice. For months he had heard it in his dreams, dreams which had frequently turned into nightmares. Only in recent weeks had he begun to put all that behind him.

Or so he had thought. Now the fear was back, and sweat popped out in little beads on Lomax's forehead.

The second man leaned forward in his seat. He, too, had a pistol, and he prodded it against Drago's back. "Don't try anything," he warned. "I'd be happy to put a bullet through your spine if you do."

This man was smiling, just like his companion, and the coats that they had slung over their arms concealed the weapons. To a casual onlooker, it would seem as if a friendly conversation was going on among these four men. That was about as far from the truth as any assumption could get.

"I hope you still have most of that money you 'found,' Harry," said the man called Nightshade. "Otherwise we're going to be very upset, aren't we, Jim?"

James Patrick McReady nodded. "Very upset," he echoed.

"Look," said Drago suddenly, "you can't blame us! We didn't know where the money came from! We still don't!"

"I'm not mad at you, boys," Nightshade told them. "If I thought you'd known what you were doing, I'd have already pulled this trigger. No, we've spent months tracking you down because we need that money more than you do. No offense, lads."

Lomax swallowed. He turned his head and saw the intent expression in Nightshade's eyes. That look made the blood in his veins feel even colder. "We . . . we've been gambling for the past couple of months," he said. "We used the money as a stake." His voice took on a desperate edge. "We've almost doubled it, man. You're not going to take all of it away from us, are you?"

Nightshade laughed.

"Doubled it, you say? Well, I want to be fair about this. You give us what you originally found, and you can keep the rest of it. How does that sound to you?"

Both Lomax and Drago jerked their heads in nods of agreement. They could not hope for anything more generous than Nightshade's offer, and they knew it.

Nightshade and Jim stood up, the guns still well hidden under their coats. "Come along," said the outlaw. "You can come back to the races tomorrow."

Lomax and Drago had no choice but to cooperate. They

stood up and left the grandstand, walking down a ramp that led under the seats with Nightshade and Jim right behind them. There were carriages for hire along the street outside the racecourses, and Nightshade summoned one of them with an uplifted hand. The four men got in, Nightshade and Jim taking the rear seat, Lomax and Drago the front. Both of the former members of Nightshade's gang still looked quite nervous, and Drago began, "Honest, Nightshade, we didn't mean to run out on you—"

The outlaw made a curt gesture to silence him. "We didn't come for explanations, Phil, just the money."

Like the other two, Jim and Nightshade were dressed in Eastern clothes so that they would blend in with the crowds. Jim felt distinctly uncomfortable in the clothes, just as he had experienced a moment of near panic at his first sight of the city. This was not the city in which he had gotten into so much trouble, what seemed like several lifetimes earlier, but after months in the clean openness of the West, he felt a distinct unease at returning to any close, cramped, filthy warren of streets and buildings. He and Nightshade had been here only a day, but already he longed for the mountains and the plains and the clear, arching vault of blue sky overhead.

They could not leave without the money, though. That was the only reason they had made this journey.

Back in the beautiful, isolated valley in the Prophet Mountains, Jinny and her father were waiting. Weeks of rest and recovery in the valley had turned Samuel Rawlings into a new man; he was much stronger, and happy for the first time in years.

"I don't care about clearing my name, not for my sake," he had told Jim and Nightshade before they left. "I could stay right here with John for the rest of my days and be quite content. I don't mind being a fugitive; the law won't ever find me here."

"I think you can count on that," agreed Nightshade.

"But it's Jinny I'm thinking of, and you, Jim," Rawlings

went on. "I want the two of you to be able to go back and make a life for yourselves wherever you want, without the specter of that old bank robbery hanging over you. Your happiness is all that matters now."

As far as Jim was concerned, he'd have been willing to stay in the valley, too, but he could not ask such a thing of Jinny. She deserved better; his *wife* deserved better. For they had already been married in Nightshade's house by an old padre brought up from one of the mountain villages to perform the ceremony. Nightshade had been supporting the good works of the padre's mission for years, and there was no danger in revealing the location of the valley to him.

So Jim had kissed Jinny good-bye and shaken hands with Samuel Rawlings, and now he was sitting in a carriage next to Nightshade, across from the two men who had absconded with the hidden bank loot. He and Jinny were going to take that money back to Harker City, once it had been recovered, along with the letter from Baxter Rawlings admitting his guilt, and see if that would be enough to obtain a pardon for Jinny's father. If it was, so much the better; if not, Samuel Rawlings would spend the rest of his days in Nightshade Valley and still die a happy man.

The carriage pulled up in front of a hotel. The hostelry was one of the fanciest in town, and Nightshade and Jim already knew from watching Lomax and Drago that the men had taken a suite here. No one in the lobby paid them any mind as they strode over to the stairs. They looked like four respectable gentlemen, rather than an outlaw, two former members of his gang, and a drifter who once rode for the Pony Express.

Such was the fear felt by Lomax and Drago that Jim and Nightshade had been able to slip their guns back into the holsters concealed beneath their coats. The men were still perspiring a bit as they climbed the stairs, and Lomax let out a long, shaky breath when they finally reached their suite and closed the door behind them.

"Get the money, Phil," he commanded sharply.

Drago hurried over to a cabinet and opened it. Underneath a pile of dirty clothes on the floor of the cabinet was a carpetbag. He brought it out and carried it over to Lomax.

Lomax took the bag and turned toward Nightshade. "It's all here, even the extra," he said. He took a step toward Nightshade as if intending to hand the bag to him.

Instead, he shoved it forward as hard as he could, slamming it into Nightshade's chest. The outlaw staggered back and Lomax lunged after him, hitting him again with the carpetbag while digging under his coat with the other hand for a weapon.

"I won't give it up, any of it!" Lomax shouted.

Jim reacted more slowly than he'd have hoped, but he still got his hand on the butt of his gun before Drago hit him. The blow staggered him, and his fingers slipped away from the pistol. Drago tackled him around the middle, driving him backward with the strength of desperation. The back of Jim's knees struck an armchair, and both men tumbled over the furniture, hurtling to the floor.

Lomax jerked a knife from under his coat and slashed at Nightshade with it. Nightshade dodged back and let the blade go past him, then stepped forward and caught Lomax's arm while the man was off balance. Gripping the wrist and elbow, Nightshade pushed on one while pulling on the other, and there was a sudden sharp cracking sound in the room. Lomax opened his mouth to scream, but instead his breath puffed out in a whoosh as Nightshade stepped closer and planted a fist in his belly. A short hook to the jaw, and Lomax went down, his broken arm bent at an ugly angle.

Across the room, Jim struggled with Drago, and his mind went flashing back unbidden to other fights he'd had in a city like this one. Those clashes had been in dingy, rundown tenements, rather than expensive hotels, but somehow the feeling was the same. Jim's enemy was not just a man; Phil Drago represented the city that had crushed Jim until there was almost nothing left of him. Jim was battling now against all the cities, battling for the young men who had been beaten down until there was no escape. He slammed a blow into Drago's face, then another and another and another . . .

Until Nightshade caught his arm and said quietly, "That's enough, son. No need to kill him."

Jim caught his breath and let Nightshade help him up. Drago stayed on the floor, moaning through a broken nose. His face was a mass of bruises and cuts. Jim's hands ached, and he knew they would be swollen in the morning. He didn't care.

"Let's go," said Nightshade. "That commotion will draw plenty of attention. These two will be all right." He opened the carpetbag, dumped some of the contents on the bed, and closed it. Jim stared for a second at the bundles of paper money, then tore his eyes away from them. Money could not buy the things he desired most in life. He already had Jinny and freedom.

There was shouting in the hallway. Jim and Nightshade went out a window onto a small ledge. They hung from it and dropped into an alley behind the hotel, then walked over to a cross street and strolled out of the vicinity, just two men out for a walk, one of them carrying a carpetbag.

Within an hour they were on a train, heading west.

TWENTY-FOUR

Deakins rolled over on his bunk in the stable office, unsure what had disturbed his slumber. He sat up, blinking bleary old eyes and rubbing his grizzled jaw. After a moment, he stood up and thrust aside the curtain over the small, grimy window. Faint light penetrated, telling him that dawn was near.

He stepped into his pants and his boots, then pulled his suspenders up over his shoulders. Might as well put on some coffee, he thought. He had awakened a bit earlier than usual, but not early enough so that it made sense to go back to sleep. The town would be stirring soon, and that meant he would have to be open for business.

The old man took kindling from the box and started a fire in the stove. When he had the coffee brewing in the battered iron pot, he went to the door, moving slowly. He was getting too old for this job, he thought, and it was nearly impossible to find a good helper these days. He had not had a decent assistant for almost a year, since that young fellow who'd wanted to ride for the Pony Express had disappeared. Deakins paused at the door, frowning. He had not thought about Jim McReady for a long time. What had made the young man pop back into his thoughts this morning?

Deakins opened the office door and stepped out into the stable. He froze in surprise as he saw that the big double doors were already open. A man sat in the entrance on a big, handsome Appaloosa stallion. He wore dark clothes, and a hood concealed his features under a wide-brimmed black hat. The fading shadows of night made him seem even more sinister.

Nightshade . . .

Deakins stared at him, unsure what to do. He could try to duck back into the office and get hold of his shotgun, he supposed, but Nightshade would probably bore him before he had taken a full step. Or he could stand there gawking like an idiot, he thought bitterly. That seemed to be what he was best equipped to do.

"Don't worry, old-timer." The deep, ringing voice came from the dark figure. "I'm not here to hurt you. I've brought something for you."

Deakins had to swallow several times before he could manage to croak out, "Somethin' . . . somethin' for *me?*"

"That's right." Nightshade came forward a few steps on the magnificent horse. He leaned over in the saddle, holding out something to Deakins. The liveryman reached up and took the thing without thinking, and only after he had it in his hands did he realize he was holding a pair of boots.

A pair of old, worn boots that seemed remarkably familiar .

"A young friend of mine asked me to bring those to you," said Nightshade. "He said you weren't really expecting them back, but he wanted to return them anyway, with his thanks."

Deakins' breath caught in his throat. He forced the words out. "This friend of your'n . . . is he ever comin' back this way?"

"I don't know," replied Nightshade. "He might, someday."

"Well, tell him thanks. Thanks for thinkin' of me."

Nightshade lifted a finger to the brim of his hat. "I'll do that. *Vaya con Dios, amigo.*"

And with that, he turned and rode out of the stable.

Deakins frowned again. Something was strange about the boots. They weighed too much. He thrust his gnarled old hand down inside one of them and brought out a small sack that clinked meaningfully as he lifted it. His pulse hammering in his head, Deakins dropped the boots and poured the contents of the sack into his open palm, staring in amazement at the gold coins.

Then he dashed to the door, crying, "Wait, mister!" He had no idea what he wanted to say to Nightshade, but a gesture like this required some sort of response.

It was too late. The sun was up now, peeking over the eastern horizon, the golden rays touching the peaks of the mountains to the west.

Nightshade had vanished into the morning mists.